A CURSE OF HONOR

DELANEY NICOLE

Copyright © 2024 by Delaney Nicole

Published by Carnation Library LLC

Cover design by Rachel McEwan Designs

All rights reserved.

No part of this book may be reproduced in any form or by any electronic or mechanical means, including information storage and retrieval systems, without written permission from the author, except for the use of brief quotations in a book review.

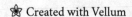 Created with Vellum

For the girls that put everyone elses happiness above their own. My fellow archer girls. Your time is coming.

CHAPTER 1

 00 BCE

THE SOUND of swords and shields clashing fill my ears in the open arena. Sweat drips from my body. My breathing has turned to pants. One wrong step and everything ceases.

I pull from my being all of my remaining strength to slice my sword through the humid air toward my adversary. The muscles in my lips pull for the shortest second, knowing it's the perfect kill shot.

"You're improving. You kept your balance centered and used your breathing to drive the sword." Athena nods, panting hard.

"It could've been better," I say breathlessly. My hair started sticking to my neck and forehead a while ago. I desperately try to calm my breathing by bracing my hands on top of my head. The dust from the sand mixes with the air, making it slightly harder to calm the need for oxygen in my lungs. I am not ready to be done. "Let's go again."

A huff leaves Athena. "Elena, you must rest. We've been going for hours. You risk injury the longer we continue."

"I need to get it right." I shake my head, ignoring Athena's refusal. I can do better. Why stop now?

"You are, by far, one of the best warriors we have. The others may not see it, but I do. It is the reason I train with you. We are done for the day. I will see you tomorrow." Athena sends me a sly grin as she places her weapons back on the weaponry wall—a wall stacked fifteen meters high with artillery from all over.

I let out an annoyed sigh. "One more round."

"Elena, we are done for the day. The training ring will be here tomorrow. We will meet at our regular time."

"I am the daughter of Ares," I snap.

Athena turns on her heels, eyeing me with the same look I've seen men fall to their knees over. "And I am the goddess of war and strategy. I have duties to attend to." Without another word, she turns, untying the thin leather strap holding her hair, letting the long, silk-like black strands fall down her back.

I turn stealthily to do the motions on my own. Just because Athena was leaving didn't mean I had to.

Athena's voice fills the hall as she says, "Do not even think about sparring on your own." Her voice startles me from my stance. "I will see you tomorrow." I let my head sink in defeat. She knows me too well after she picked me to train with her two years ago. "Go back to your quarters. Or visit Apollo."

I'd rather work until the brink of collapsing unlike most of my fellow trainees who usually left early. It makes sense in my mind to practice unforgivingly. I practice as if I am actually in battle at all times. My vigorous practicing is bringing me closer to my goal.

I place my sword on the stone weaponry wall, ensuring it's secure in its hold before walking back to the center of the ring. I lift my face toward the open sky. I always make an effort after training to do this. I let the sun heat my cheeks and let the light cascade in to warm my body and soul. It clears my mind of whatever anxieties I may have.

The hum of birds in the distance and the rustle of the wind through the leaves of nearby trees create a song I find soothing after training. I stand like this until I feel content in my efforts. My gaze slips down to my calloused hands, still shaking slightly from training. I can still feel smaller anxieties bubbling within me, waiting to grow stronger. Like a snake waiting for the perfect moment to strike. My hair falls from its hold and hits right above my rear.

"I am not what they say I am. I am strong. I am fierce. I lead with compassion. I am a warrior. I can do this."

CHAPTER 2

The smell of lilacs and citrus fill my nose as I enter my townhouse. I light the candlesticks in my living room and hang my himation on the rack by the door. It took years of saving to get a two-bedroom place like this. It isn't much, but it's mine.

I hustle up the stairs to my bathroom and fill the tub with warm water. There is nothing like the warmth of the water soothing the aches of my muscles.

As the sun begins to sink over the horizon, I can't help but smile as I look at the city buzzing with life below me. Everything feels peaceful. It seems as though my mind becomes quiet. Even if it is just for a short time, it feels peaceful.

I remember how simple my life was when I was a child. The only worry I had was what game I would play that day. And after all the games, my nanny would sing me a lullaby and tell me I'm destined for greatness while brushing out my hair every night. I miss her.

It isn't until the sun has disappeared below the horizon that I realize how cold my bath has turned. I stand, grab the towel sitting on the quartz counter, and wrap the warm cloth around myself. I drain the water from the tub, then make my way back to my bedchamber.

"I should have known you were bathing."

I nearly jump from my skin. "Good gods, Apollo. You scared me. What are you doing here?"

"It's obvious, isn't it?" The blond man grins while placing his hands behind his head as he perches atop my bed. "It's been too long since I've seen you."

I can't help but grin. "I was with you two nights ago. Surely you haven't forgotten. We were in your bed until the sun crested the horizon."

"No, certainly not." Apollo smirks, then slowly makes his way to my front. Like the rest of The Twelve Olympians, Apollo came down from the Mount every night to immerse themselves in dancing, drinking, or even the occasional romantic entanglement.

He grabs my toweled hip in a gentle embrace. Apollo was always a man I had admired from a distance. He is sought after by many, yet he rarely obliges in such affections. But for some reason, he chose me.

"I'm surprised you came here."

"Is it hard to believe that I would come here? I get rather bored in my dwelling." His grin deepens as he pulls me into his chest. A sharp pain bursts from my side, and I try to hide my wince. "What is it?"

"Nothing." I hurry from his grasp and play it off as though

I need to dress. "I went harder in training than I realized. Let me get changed into some real clothes."

"You're always training too hard. Why not give yourself a break?" Worry drips from Apollo's words as he sits atop my mattress.

"Because I can improve. There are faults in my combat skills that need fixing." I keep my tone as steady as possible and fasten a light blue robe at my waist with a matching ribbon.

"That's bullshit," he counters, standing to meet my startled gaze. "Athena says you're one of the best warriors she's ever seen or trained. I'm sure your father would agree if he weren't busy with the wars the humans are launching on each other."

"You've talked to Athena about me?" My eyes grow wide as I hurry toward Apollo. I grab his muscular forearm in my hand. It means so much to me that he was speaking with others about me. Partially because it means he is thinking of me elsewhere.

"Of course, I have. I want to know how your training is going since all you talk about is improving. Athena agrees that you will run yourself ragged before you accept that you are an amazing warrior." He smiles and he brushes my arms lightly.

"I'm not an amazing warrior if my arms shake when I lift a sword at the end of training each day. My father's arms never shake when he lifts his sword or spear."

"Would you listen to yourself? You're comparing yourself to your father, a full-blooded god, the god of war. Of course, his arm doesn't shake when he lifts his sword. That's what he does." Apollo's demeanor softens. "When are you going to stop killing yourself to be perfect and finally accept that you're already great?"

Great, not perfect. "I know my limits. And I won't stop. Even after I reach my goal." I'm annoyed that he doesn't understand. He helps rule. The people of Olympus accept him.

"So that is what this is all about? Your need to prove yourself as worthy enough to lead armies with Athena? To finally earn a spot in our ranks?" I stay silent but keep glaring. "Elena, she knows you're strong enough. It is not in her control. When the time comes she can recommend you all she wants, but it's Zeus's call in the end. What will you do if he refuses?"

I walk to the place where I left my wet towel. "Should Zeus refuse," I huff, "I will train harder until he is forced to listen."

"And if that doesn't work? Will this life that you're so comfortable fitting into—being able to live in Olympus worry-free with the rest of us unlike the other demi-gods—not be enough for you?"

I tense and instead of meeting Apollo's eyes, I keep my eyes on the city below me. I'm afraid they will betray the truth. I don't want to think of a life where I wouldn't meet my goal. The same goal that would finally make me worthy to all the gods, including the one who's disapproval influences all others: Zeus. I've never thought of a life without leading the armies.

If I never meet that goal, I will never be content with my life. No matter how many nights I spend with Apollo.

CHAPTER 3

I wake to the sun warming my cheeks through the open window and a warm body flush against my side. A smile pulls on my lips when I find Apollo sleeping peacefully. Sometimes, he sneaks off in the night while I sleep, but here he is, sleeping with my bed sheets covering his naked body.

I slip from his grasp without waking him. A relieved sigh leaves my mouth when I realize I was successful. I stride to the bathing chamber to wash up and throw my hair into a braid. I retrieve my discarded robe from the floor before I stroll downstairs to the kitchen.

As I walk through my sky blue and white living room onto the patio, I pop a piece of apricot into my mouth. I cherish the silence of the mornings when the sun is beginning to grace the horizon. Everything feels serene. A feeling I strive to feel often. Occasionally, I get it, but it is always short.

A CURSE OF HONOR

The shops are beginning to open in the distance, so I quietly go back into the kitchen to make a small plate of fruit for Apollo with a note:

Going to the shops. Need more apricots. Will try to be back before you depart. If not, I'll come visit you after training.

To make sure I do not wake Apollo I grab a pale yellow peplos from the clothesline and ensure it is secure at my waist before I head to the shops with a small, wicker basket.

By the time I am on the cobbled road, the streets are bustling with fellow city dwellers and shop owners. Children's laughter, greetings from old friends, and other occasional shouts of welcome fill my ears. The smell of fresh-baked bread and pastries fill my nose, making me want to indulge in a second breakfast, but I stride toward my favorite shop in the quiet corner of the main road.

As I grab the handle of the door, Aphrodite strides out with her own wicker basket full of pastries in hand. I take a step back and hold the door, "Pardon me."

"No, pardon me. It was I who was not paying attention." She smiles before bidding me goodbye and I walk through the door.

"Elena! I was wondering when you'd be coming back in," the shop owner calls welcomingly. The shop is small and smells of spiced apples and has a cozy feeling inside. The shop owner decorated it with small knick knacks given to them by those who had ventured to the mortal lands at the gods' request.

A smile plays on my lips. "Well, you should have known it would be me. I ran out of your famous apricots."

"You're in luck because I pulled a fresh batch this morning. I saved you a few." Stella grins, then places a large basket on the counter between us with a thud.

"Good gods, Stella, I don't think I need that many." I laugh. Stella is a descendant of Demeter which naturally gives her a green thumb, but I have never tasted better apricots than Stella's. Yet, the amount she is trying to give me could last weeks and possibly spoil before I reach the end of them.

I've always admired Demeter's work and it appears some of her strengths has trickled down to her descendents. As it has for all of The Twelve's descendents in the city. As a demigoddess who is half-immortal, I only received a fraction of my father's strengths. It wasn't until I was twenty-one and stopped aging that those strengths went into full effect. That's when I started my training with Athena.

Her laugh is bright. "Oh please. You'll be through these in a week. Besides, if you don't want all of these, you can give some to Apollo."

I roll my eyes as her smile turns to a smirk. "You are unbelievable."

"What are friends for? Speaking of friendship, do you think you could spare some time to go out with one of your dear old friends?" Stella raises her eyebrows enticingly.

"I'm not sure. I told—"

"You told Apollo you'd go see him after training?" Stella surmises. "Come on, just once. We haven't spent an evening together in ages. And that's saying something since we're immortal."

"I suppose I can spare one night," I say with a fake sigh. It truly has been ages since Stella and I have spent time together outside of her shop. She grins widely with bright, gleaming eyes. "You're lucky I was with him last night. Now, if you'll excuse me, I need to take this enormous basket of apricots home before training."

"I'll see you tonight! Meet me here!" Stella's shout chases me as I make my way to the door of the shop.

I look at the rolling hills below me. Hundreds of colors fill the city thanks to the nature surrounding it and the clothes displayed by the local businesses. The city drops off into mountains and hills that eventually run into bright blue waves in the distance.

By the time I arrive home, my cheeks have grown slightly pink from the rising heat of the day. I set the basket of apricots on the counter and pour myself some water. The plate I left for Apollo is empty and placed neatly in the sink.

I bound upstairs, but Apollo is nowhere to be found. I'd be lying if I said I was surprised by his absence. He never waits for my return. He has many responsibilities with The Twelve, which hold his presence most days and even some nights. But part of me wishes he had stayed.

I force myself to dress for training in the specially designed peplos for combat that features loose fitting breeches beneath them. The long walk to the stadium means I have more time for my mind to plague me. Usually, I use these thoughts as fuel for my fight, but it doesn't help if those thoughts come at an unwelcome time. It feels like a violent sea during a fit of Poseidon's rage.

You will never amount to anything.

Step.

You are nothing but a weak demi-goddess.

Step, step.

You should quit while you're ahead.

Step, step, step.

I make my way deeper into the arena and see the stares of some of the men. As I pass, they lean into each other, whispering. I school my face to not give them the satisfaction of knowing what their comments do to me.

"You're early, princess," a voice mocks from the weaponry wall.

Disgust lines my veins. "I've told you enough times not to call me that, Deimus."

"She has a bite today." He offers a spiteful smile. "Tell me, princess, why is it that you come here day in and day out?" Before I can utter a response, he continues his speech. "Surely it's not because you think you're going to be offered the position to lead armies." He chuckles roughly. "That is why you do it, isn't it? I've got news for you. You will never get that position. It doesn't matter how many hours you train with Athena. Zeus will never let a demi-goddess lead the armies."

I scoff. "You think he'll choose you or Phobus?"

"We are full-blooded gods. Besides, he's already asked Father if he has a preference." Deimus smirks cynically. If I wasn't so taken back by the news of Zeus's newest inquiries, I would knock the grin right off of my brother's face.

"You're lying," I challenge through clenched teeth.

"Am I?" He shifts his weight to the front of his toes and leans closer to me, his hot breath dampening my cheek. He's so close I can see his stubble facial hair is the same ginger hue as his hair. "Or can you not accept that you will never get the opportunity to lead armies with Athena because you are nothing more than a weak demi-goddess?"

"Enough!" Athena booms from the entrance of the training arena. I back away from my estranged brother. I have a close bond with Athena, but even I know not to invoke her anger. "Deimus, your training session is over for the day. I would advise that you leave the ring immediately."

"Yes, of course," he nods stiffly, then knocks into my shoulder harshly as he passes. I force my hand to remain where it is rather than rub the spot he struck just to keep him from getting the satisfaction he wants.

"Oh, and Deimus..." Athena pauses.

"Yes?" He pivots to look back at us.

"If I hear you are speaking to her like that again, I will ensure *you* are the one never to lead on a battlefield. Are we clear?" Athena's tone is firm and her nostrils flare in anger. His eyes widen at Athena's threat, but he nods before he departs the arena.

"Are you alright?" Athena pulls my focus back.

Deimus knew how to shake me up. He was the god of fear, after all. Regardless, I give my best fake smile I can muster. "Never better."

"It's preposterous how he and Phobus speak to you," Athena grumbles.

"What else are siblings for?" I brush it off. I don't have the heart to say that it isn't only my siblings that speak to me like that. Being the only half-immortal raised in Olympus City, I find myself the center of attention for The Twelve. But those who hold me in high regard are few and far between.

DELANEY NICOLE

Athena's green eyes capture mine. "You are stronger than them. We know it. Your father knows it. You were lifting swords above your head before either of them were able to pick up a spear. Your ability to lead with compassion alongside your strength sets you apart."

"I know." I nod while taking a steadying breath and forcing myself to believe her claim.

"I want you to show me exactly why it is that I've chosen to train you."

I take one last steadying breath. "Okay."

CHAPTER 4

I stand in front of my mirror, smoothing out the lavender peplos I'm wearing for my evening with Stella. It dips low on my chest, allowing for some view of my cleavage. A slit runs up my right thigh. Aside from clinging perfectly to my chest and hips, the robe cinches at my waist as well. It is a bit scandalous, but the way it flatters my body makes me not care that much.

Strapping my sandals to my feet, I feel nerves bubbling low in my belly. I promised Apollo I would visit him this evening, but I won't. Instead, I'll be out with Stella. I depart from my home, and the night air is a bit cool.

A gust of cool wind sweeps through the city, causing bumps to erupt on my exposed skin. That was strange. Demeter ensures Olympus maintains a comfortable temperature to keep the plants alive, which makes those of us in the city comfortable.

I don't have time to question it as I approach Stella's door. "Stella!" I knock. "Stella, it's me."

"It's open," Stella's muffled voice sounds from behind the shop door. I open the door. "I'll be out in a second. I'm fixing my shoes!"

"Don't worry about it. I knew I'd have to wait on you." I giggle, leaning against the counter. I can count on one hand the number of times Stella was on time for something.

"Not all of us have the luxury of having special romantic relations with one of The Twelve. Us commoners must take extra measures if we want to catch the eye of one of them in hopes of having a relationship like yours," Stella says as she descends the stairs that lead to her home above the shop. She's wearing a blue peplos that cuts low on her chest like mine. The light shade of blue complements the darkness of her skin nicely.

I roll my eyes. "I am not in a relationship with Apollo."

"Really? Then what would you call it?" Stella leans against the shop counter.

"We are enjoying each other's company."

"Right, each other's naked company. Was that your idea or Apollo's?"

"Um..." I pause, trying to figure out a reply she would accept. It had been Apollo's idea to keep things the way they were. I agreed to enjoy his company, when I could, and not complicate things with my training. I will have time for love after I succeed. "Shouldn't we get going? If we don't hurry we won't get good seats."

"You don't even know where we're going." Stella chuckles as I hurry to the door.

"We aren't going to The Muses?" The Muses is always Stella's go-to.

"Oh, fine. Let's go. But don't think I don't know you changed the subject to avoid answering my question about Apollo." Stella points her finger accusingly and I stick my tongue out at her.

The Muses is just down the road from Stella's shop so it takes no time to get there.

"Go get our seats! I'll get the wine!" Stella shouts over the loud music. The Muses is bustling with people who want a night just like ours. The dim light of the candle-filled chandeliers create a mystical atmosphere that I love.

I work my way through the crowd, noticing the lingering stare of men I've seen around the training arena. They want a response from me, but I give them no reaction. Good or bad. I will not be the one to give them satisfaction.

I pass a gaggle of women surrounding Dionysus—who dons a feline-like smirk at the attention he's getting—in a booth before finally making my way to the back balcony of the Muses. As usual, I found my seat unoccupied. It overlooks the rolling hills to the city's west, giving a view of the moon's light across the river flowing between the hills. It's often ignored because this back balcony isn't as renowned as some other parts of the hall. Perhaps that is what I like about it. It also lets Stella and I talk without having to yell at eachother.

"Get this, Calliope gave us a bottle for free because one of her comrades gave her one of my apricot tarts, and she loved it! She said she's never tasted anything so decadent. Can you

DELANEY NICOLE

believe it?" Stella exclaims as she plops down by my side before pouring two tall glasses of dark, red wine.

"That's great, Stell!" I smile, snapping out of whatever thought train I had been on as I took hold of my glass.

A bright, promising smile spread on Stella's lips. "Here's to letting go for the night."

* * *

THE SUN PENETRATES my closed eyes, drawing me from my deep, drunken slumber. I rise slowly, looking around with squinted eyes to find that I fell asleep in the clothing I wore at The Muses. My head pounds as I stand up. I suppose drinking two bottles of wine has that effect. I briefly remember deciding there was no need to change the same way I decided there was no need to sleep under the blankets apparently.

I am thankful Athena canceled my training for the day due to some important meeting she had. It's already mid-day based on the bright sun's placement in the middle of our cloudless sky.

"At least the room isn't spinning anymore," I mumble, rubbing my wounded eyes on the way to the bathing chamber to get ready to go to Apollo's estate. After all, I owe him an apology.

When I leave, a powerful gust of wind sweeps through the city for the second time in as many days and a chill runs through my body. The gust makes me notice how chilly the air is.

Walking past multiple people proves they've noticed the

strange change in the weather. Everyone has weary eyes about the shift in the atmosphere, myself included. It is almost as if a storm is brewing.

"We should get the children inside. I don't want them getting sick," a brunette woman says to her husband as I pass them.

I hug my himation tighter to my body when the goosebumps don't leave my skin on their own.

Apollo's home is placed on the city's outskirts to see the hills to the west and the sea to the east. He once said he chose this spot because it allows him to see the sun rise over the mountains and sink over the blue waves. A stunning view no matter the day or time. Here, the road turns from cobblestones to packed dirt lined with various colors of wildflowers. The hum of birds is louder. The rush of water from the river and distant falls makes its appearance in the ears of the road's travelers.

Artemis's estate is just a ways down. Apollo and his sister have always been quite close. However, things are different when I am around. Artemis acts differently. It isn't anything new, but I get the impression that Artemis hasn't taken a liking to me.

I hope she isn't here today. If only because it will give her more ammo to hate me.

The guards at the entrance allow my entry without any trouble. They know my face by now thanks to my frequent visits. But when I knock on the vast oak doors, the knocks vibrate throughout my body. It's silly, but I hope he isn't upset with me for not showing up last night.

Finally the doors open, and Artemis steps out, expressionless as ever. It appears as though the face she wears with The Twelve is permanently stuck on when I am around.

Swallowing my pride, I ask, "Is your brother present?"

"He is in the back practicing his archery," she answers indifferently.

"May I?" I motion to enter the house. She opens the door a few centimeters more, granting permission for my entrance.

I pass the goddess and walk straight through the large foyer, through the formal sitting room adorned with sun accents, by various bows Apollo used in the past, and his prized lyre. I keep walking until I make it to the back of the estate.

There, firing arrows at targets is Apollo. I can see from here that the white chiton he is wearing is draped very loosely over his body.

"He's been out there all afternoon," Artemis says, peeking over the edge of the couch she sits on to watch him.

"Is something pestering him?" I inquire, stealing another glance at him.

She shrugs. "Not that I know of. Apollo won't tell me anything. I went out there a bit when I arrived, but he stayed quiet."

"Do you think he'd tell me?"

"Doubtful. If he won't tell me, then he most likely won't tell anyone."

I turn back around to see Apollo approaching the house. My eyes lock with his for only a moment before he gives a small shrug and moves to put his bow away.

I walk through the glass door and try to catch up to him. "Apollo."

He stops. His back is glistening with sweat, and he straightens at the sound of my voice. "What do you want, Elena?"

"I came to see you." My eyes rake over his muscular back as I speak. His tanned skin looks like honey in the sunlight.

Apollo lets out a sarcastic laugh before walking again. "Go home, Elena."

I'm taken aback by his coldness. "Have I offended you?"

Before I know it he's towering over me. "Where the fuck were you last night?"

"I—"

"What? Did you find someone else to warm your bed for the night?" He mutters through his teeth. His breath warms my neck and cheeks. A bead of sweat drips from his golden hair and onto my forehead.

"Of course not," I answer. I should have known he would be angry about last night. "Stella wanted to take me out, so I agreed."

"Oh, Stella..." he replies in mock amusement. "And tell me, where did you and Stella go?"

I swallow. I'm afraid to break eye contact with him. "We went to The Muses. I'm sorry."

"I waited for you. Meanwhile, you were out drinking wine, doing gods know what with gods know who."

I remind myself that acting rashly will only make things worse. But that doesn't stop the way my fist tightens and my fingernails carve crescent shapes into my palms. My next

DELANEY NICOLE

words come out harsher and louder than I intended them to, "I wasn't with anyone!"

"Am I supposed to just take your word for it? Because that clearly can't be taken seriously." Apollo's voice heightens, "And you were quite eager for my advances when I met you at The Muses."

The blow hits me hard, and Apollo knows it. He was the first and only man I had ever slept with. It had been the start of whatever strange relationship this is.

"I apologize for not coming to see you last night," I whisper, wiping my wet cheek. Another tear falls down my cheek as I meet Apollo's green eyes. His jaw clenches and unclenches, his chest rises and falls at a slower pace. But he says nothing.

"I'm going home."

"Elena, wait..." Apollo mutters then grabs my wrist to stop me. He scans my face before he drops my wrist entirely and lets me leave. I try hard to keep my composure as I make it back through the glass door where Artemis is now standing.

I'm almost entirely through the room when Artemis says, "You're one of the strongest, most compassionate warriors Athena has ever seen. You are the daughter of Ares. Yet you let him speak to you as though you are nothing more than a defenseless damsel."

I turn to look at Artemis with tear-filled eyes. I don't give her words time to sink in before I leave the estate.

CHAPTER 5

"Push," Athena urges. "Come on. You've got it. A bit more."

I raise my sword with my right hand, using my left for my shield. I drive my shield up, meeting my opponent's sword in a clash of metal. I drop down and sweep my leg, which knocks my opponent off their feet. I stand with my sword placed at my fallen adversary's throat.

"Well done, Elena." Athena grins, then walks to the center of the training ring. I place my weapons on the ground causing another cloud of dust to join the air.

"Remind me why I'm sparring with trainees and not you?" I ask, breathing deeply with my hands atop my head to get my breathing back to normal.

"Because I asked her to," a man calls from behind me. I straighten immediately. I'd recognize that husky voice anywhere.

"Father!" I smile and hug the god of war eagerly. "What

are you doing here? I thought you were busy with the human wars."

"Zeus called upon me for some business, and I wanted to see how your training was going. Gods know your brothers are so proud of anything they do that I get an update from them daily. But you, my favorite daughter, I hear nothing of." Ares flashes a bright smile, a smile I've regretfully heard too much of from some of the women in Olympus.

"I told you she was progressing nicely," Athena beams as she's approaching us. "But, to answer your question, Elena, I had you spar with one of our top trainees to show you how advanced you are compared to the others since you don't believe it when I tell you. That should be proof enough that you are not destined to be one of our guards like some of the trainees."

"She is improving, much more than her brothers, whom I watched over yesterday." My father nods at my side. "Don't tell them I said that. I'm afraid their egos would never recover and I would never hear the end of it."

I try to stifle my laugh. Athena keeps a prideful grin on her face when she says, "I can assure you that I tried to have one of them spar her today, but they didn't oblige my requests."

"That's too bad. I would have loved even a chance at bruising their egos." A picture of beating my brothers in combat runs through my mind. It dwindles, however, when I remember they are full-blooded gods and I am beneath them.

My father laughs. "It wouldn't be too hard. But I have other reasons for watching your training."

"Do you think it wise to tell her here?" Athena motions around the vast arena. Other trainees are in the hall.

My brows pull in as I watch the interaction between my father and my mentor. It is as though they are having a conversation with their eyes.

"Right, I suppose it should be said," my father scans the arena, "in a more private space."

"Have I missed something?" I ask, having grown tired of feeling like I am in the dark about an important issue.

"Nothing you won't know soon enough. I'll leave you two to catch up," Athena says before making her exit.

"Let's have dinner at my home this evening. I have a few things to speak with you about." My father has a tiny glint in his brown eyes that almost looks like excitement.

"I'd love to. What time should I arrive?" It has been ages since my father and I had any quality time together. Contrary to what most think, Ares was a wonderful father as a child.

"Dusk is fine."

At that, I headed home to wash off the dirt and sweat from my skin.

* * *

"I SHOULD HAVE KNOWN you would arrive early," my father jokes, opening the door for me.

I grin as I step inside. "You were the one that taught me that—"

"A warrior that is late might as well hand their sword to

their enemy. War waits for no one." He chuckles. "Dinner's on the terrace."

His estate is like Apollo's in size. However, my father lives along the coast. His estate also includes a training ring, both inside and outside the house. Ever since I was large enough to lift a sword I'd spend morning, evening, and night in them training until my muscles shook from overexertion.

My father and Athena acted strangely at the end of my training session, so to say that I am itching to know why is an understatement. My mind is running wild with the possibilities of what the news could be as we make our way onto the terrace.

"What have you been up to, other than training, in my absence?" He asks as we sit down at the table overlooking the vast blue ocean.

"You know…the occasional outing with friends, staying in some nights to read past oracles and legends…" I say, swirling the wine in my glass before I slowly take a sip. It was sweet and slightly sour on my tongue.

"The occasional lovemaking with Apollo…" my father adds nonchalantly.

I choke on my wine, slapping my hand to my mouth to keep it in. I look at him with wide eyes. My cheeks burn with embarrassment.

"You don't have to be embarrassed. I've had my fair share of lovers," he teases.

"I'm well aware. It is still not a topic I'd like to discuss with my father," I say, trying to regain my composure. My father was never ashamed of his romantic conquests. A fact I wish I did not know.

"Fair enough." He chuckles while he carves into his dinner. It looks like the lamb my nanny used to make me. Growing up, my father hired a woman from the city to care for me when he was busy with wars in the mortal realm. Miss Alexandra was almost a mother figure. She looked after me until I was sixteen when she fell in love and married a shop owner, after which I felt guilty for keeping her from her husband, so I relieved her of her services. I still visit her from time to time.

I take my first bite and lemon, rosemary, and garlic hit my tastebuds. A hum leaves my mouth at the delicious bursts of flavors. It was just like Miss Alexandra's.

"Now," I say between bites, "are you going to tell me what you started to say while we were in the training ring? Or should I start guessing?"

"You're needed in court tomorrow," my father mumbles as if it were nothing more than a regular request. And perhaps for him it was.

I cough through my words when I say, "I beg your pardon?"

As casually as the first time, he replies, "You're needed in court tomorrow."

"I don't understand. I haven't done anything." My hands grow clammy in my lap. Everything I've ever done flashes before my eyes. I'm trying to find any reason the courts would call me before them.

"Relax, you haven't done anything. You aren't in trouble. At least I hope you aren't," he teases. I meet his teasing with a scowl. "It won't be in front of everyone. I won't even be there. I know the specifics, but not everyone does. Your purpose for being called before The Twelve are to be kept quiet for as long as possible."

"I'm not in trouble?" I repeat.

"No. But I need you to be ready to go to court tomorrow morning. I'll meet you outside your place if you'd like."

"I'll be ready." I nod, taking a thick gulp of wine to help ease me with this new information.

"Wonderful! It will be nice to see how your home is coming along. After all, I haven't seen it since you first purchased it," he says, taking a swig of his drink that was much stronger than the wine I'm drinking. I find it strange how fast my father is able to move on from my request in court. I mask my nerves by finishing my glass off and refilling it.

"Speaking of being away." I grin before taking a bit of my lamb. "Tell me about the mortals and their wars."

THE MORNING CAME MUCH FASTER than I expected. All night, I tossed and turned. My mind wouldn't turn off. Everytime I felt like I might fall into a peaceful sleep, my mind flashed dozens of questions about why my presence was requested.

Seeing the sun rise over the horizon, I crawl from my bed on a few hours of sleep and slip on one of my white peplos and secure it to my waist with a delicate gold chain that my father gifted to me years ago. I braid my hair then carefully wrap it around my head to form something resembling a crown.

I take a deep breath, steadying my nerves as much as I

can. I look pretty, at least in my eyes. Then I go to meet my father.

I open the door to find him wearing a crimson chiton, which somewhat matched his hair. His tanned skin looks like it's glimmering in the early morning sunlight. Even though I saw it last night at dinner, it was still odd to see his hair free flowing. I've grown so used to seeing it restricted by his war helmet.

He scans the first level of my home when he steps in. Nerves bubble in my belly at his inspection. After I started training with Athena, my father admired my devotion to my training and gave me an allowance since my schedule made it hard to have a job. If it weren't for him I wouldn't have anything.

"I must say you have used the money I have given you far better than you brothers who resort to buying the pleasures of women."

I feign sickness, "Thank you for that lovely imagery."

My father chuckles, "Sorry. Are you ready, my dear?"

"I don't have much of a choice." I smile tightly, feeling a new bundle of nerves churning in my stomach.

"Nonsense, you have a choice. I will say, however, that refusing this wouldn't go over well."

"Well then," I hook my arm around my father's, "Shall we begin our journey?"

"That's the spirit." My father's grin is proud.

He leads us from my home to an awaiting chariot. Only two of my father's horses—Aethon and Conabus—pull his gold-reined chariot. The other two must still be in the stables. As a child, I would sneak off to the stables to see

DELANEY NICOLE

them. Surprisingly, the fire-breathing beasts took a liking to me.

Lucky for me, my brothers weren't present in the chariot, which I'm surprised by, seeing how they make an extra effort to stick to our father's side when he is in the city.

"Remember, you are not in any sort of trouble. If anyone were, it would be your meddling brothers." My father chuckles, trying to lighten the mood outside the throne room. It is where The Twelve Olympians do most of their bidding regarding the humans. It is where Zeus and Hera sit upon their thrones to oversee all. And now, I am being called.

"I don't want to think about my brothers right now," I murmur. The last thing I want to think of is people who think I am lesser because of my origin. Right now, I need to step into my power, and show them that I am exactly as Athena claims.

Suddenly, a guard steps out of the throne room. "They are ready for you."

The Twelve know how to defend themselves should a threat occur, but the palace atop Olympus and their private homes are protected by guards. The guards are those of former trainees chosen to protect rather than fight in the armies.

I shoot a nervous look at my father. He must have noticed my panic stricken eyes, because he takes hold of my arm. "You're going to be fine. Remember it's just Demeter, Zeus, and Hera. I'll be out here when you are done."

He doesn't understand why being in Zeus's presence makes me uneasy. Nonetheless, I nod before turning to the guard at the door. My stomach tightens when the doors open.

"I am strong. I am fierce. I lead with compassion. I am a warrior. I can do this," I repeat over and over as I pass each limestone pillar.

The throne room is entirely carved out of the finest limestone. An artist painted the ceiling with a fresco of the gods watching over the mortals. The open columns allow the chill of the outside air and warmth of the sunlight to leak in and cast a light upon the gods and goddesses' seats. The room smells like flowers and near each window, sits snapdragons each a bright rose color.

This is where the mortals believe the gods dwell. In reality this room only serves as a portal that allows The Twelve to watch over them when necessary.

My focus pulls to the opposing side of the throne room. Zeus and Hera sit upon their thrones. They sit higher than the others to signify their importance as the King and Queen over all. The other seats for the other ten gods and goddesses are empty, except one—Demeter's. Just like my father said.

I swallow the lump in my throat and stop in front of the raised seats. I bow my head to those on the thrones before me.

"Your majesties," I say, breaking the silence that surrounds me. Though Zeus and Hera are gods, Zeus has made it clear that they should be regarded as royalty to those lesser beings in Olympus City.

"You may stand," Hera says, and her monotone voice rings in my ears.

I lift my head, taking in their appearances. Hera wears a

DELANEY NICOLE

sky blue, flowing robe with a golden crown atop her brown hair. Her lotus scepter sits idly in her left hand. Zeus is wearing a white chiton that almost matches his ice blond hair and beard. Demeter wears her typical green peplos, accenting her naturally pale complexion and blonde hair.

"I do believe," Hera begins, meeting Zeus's eyes, "it is time to start."

Zeus moves his gaze to meet mine. "You are being sent to the Underworld."

CHAPTER 6

My stomach drops into my shoes. My mouth fills with cotton. "I don't understand. Have I done something?"

"Relax, darling, you haven't done anything," Demeter responds, drawing my attention away from Zeus.

"Quite the opposite," Zeus says, though he seems reluctant to admit it. "We've heard from Athena that you are quite the up and comer. Your father holds the same opinion."

"I don't believe I'm following. Why does that mean I'm being sent to the Underworld?" A lump of nervousness forms in my throat at the prospect of being sent to that horrid place.

"We have a task for you." Zeus grins, but his grin doesn't make me any less uneasy.

"A task?" My brows pull into a line. It doesn't make sense to me. Why am I receiving a task from The Twelve when I am still in training?

DELANEY NICOLE

"Yes, and we'd like you to keep it confidential. We don't want the specifics to spread in the city." He nods.

"I understand." My hands are growing clammy the longer I am in here.

Zeus looks slightly mischievous. "I'm sure you've felt the temperature change. And the slight chill to the wind?"

"I have." I nod.

"It is only a fraction of what the mortals have felt. The mortals are experiencing temperatures lower than they ever have. They are not suited to weather this change. Their crops are dying at a substantial rate. They are catching and spreading diseases at a much higher rate. The mortality rate is rising."

"Why have there been changes? I've never heard of such drastic changes," I say, giving a short glance to Demeter. This is her expertise and yet she looks pained. Meanwhile, an ache is growing in my chest at the thought of the mortals growing sick due to the cold and lack of food. It reminds me of my mother.

Zeus sighs before saying, "As you know, Demeter is responsible for keeping the agriculture fruitful for the mortals. And with that, the temperature."

I catch Hera shooting a sidelong glance at Demeter while Zeus is speaking. It is easy to see Hera's disappointment in the goddess.

"Before you ask why the mortals are suffering at my hands, I will tell you," Demeter says, then takes a steadying breath. "My daughter, Persephone, has been taken by Hades. We have begged for her return, but he has refused. I simply cannot continue my duty effectively without her in the city. I refuse."

My heart goes out to Demeter. I can see she is hurting in her daughter's absence through her sunken eyes and frailer frame then I remember. But that does not change what she is doing to the mortals.

"This is where you come in," Zeus interrupts. "You are being sent to the Underworld to bring Persephone back. You cannot make it obvious what you are trying to do. You are to go to the Underworld, become a part of my brother's court, gain Persephone's trust, and bring her back."

"Why will Hades believe I am in the Underworld?" I ask. Surely, they had worked out some sort of plan. The god of the Underworld is no fool. He will be able to sniff out a scheme meters away if I am not careful.

"We will tell him that you are part of our military ranks and we sent you because we have found some discrepancies in some of our previous war accounts. It will improve your understanding of our army's history because the Underworld library has better record keeping. I have encouraged him during our brief discussion to let you stay in his court so you will not have to do much traveling to the library. In reality, you will be in close proximity to Persephone, which is what we need. You will have eight weeks to complete this task. That way you have enough time to avoid suspicion and gain their trust."

I nod and release a breath. That seems like a logical excuse and timeline.

"And if I fail to bring Persephone back?" I ask. The hard

DELANEY NICOLE

part of this task is going to be getting her out without Hades noticing.

"We will not get into the specifics of what would happen if you fail. However, there is something I'd like you to try. Think of it as another part of the task." A wicked grin appeared on the king's face. Confusion lined the goddesses' faces. It is clear that Zeus has not told them this part.

"I'm listening." I nod.

"We have seen an increased number of human souls collected each day even considering the recent devastation brought on by Demeter. We believe it to be the work of the Children of the Night."

"Children of the Night?" My brows furrow.

"They are a group prophesied to take the souls of humans, all but killing them. They are mighty. I usually don't bother dealing with the business of my brother because death is inevitable for mortals, but this is different. The gods have not approved the souls to be taken before they are.

"And we believe that their leader is using Demeter's loss of control as a cover up to increase the number of souls he takes. He is claiming the lives of these mortals at an increasing rate." My eyes slowly enlarge. No one goes against the order of the gods. Even Hades—who was not considered a part of The Twelve as he resides outside Olympus—only ever takes the souls pre-approved by The Twelve. "I can see you understand why this is troubling. I have reason to believe their leader is a man by the name of Thanatos."

"Zeus, this is not—" Zeus raises his hand, silencing Hera.

"The second part of your task is to grow close to Thanatos. Do whatever you need to gain his trust. That

A CURSE OF HONOR

shouldn't be too hard considering your bond with Apollo." My cheeks start slowly burning with embarrassment at the same time a feline smirk marks Zeus's lips. "Should Hades or Persephone refuse her return, your task is to take Thanatos. It is unclear whether we can kill him, but even if you find out you can, he must be brought here alive. He is one of my brother's minions, and likely his most trusted due to his significant power. So, we will hold him captive just as Persephone is. The loss of that much power in his court should make Hades release her. After all, he wouldn't want to lose his precious new toys."

I cannot believe what is being asked of me. This is a great responsibility. "I don't understand why you need me to complete this task. I'm a demi-goddess."

"Yes, we are well aware of that," Zeus mutters. He failed terribly at hiding the disgust in his words.

"We chose you because of the high respect Athena, and others, have for you. Athena says you are the strongest we have in our ranks. After careful discussion," Demeter cast a short glance at Zeus and at Hera who gave her a subtle glimpse, "we have decided that, should you succeed, we will give you the spot to lead the armies alongside Athena."

All the air in my lungs seizes. It becomes hard to swallow. Shock flows through my veins from head to toe. "What?"

"This is what you want, is it not?" Zeus moves his electric-blue eyes to focus on me.

"That is all I've ever wanted," I admit in a more eager tone than I meant to show.

Zeus still looks mischievous as ever when he says,

"Should you accept this task, you will leave in two days. Hermes will transport you to the Underworld."

Demeter chimes in, "Do you accept this task?"

I stand in utter shock, breathing deep to calm how ecstatic I feel on the inside. It is an honor to have this task bestowed upon me. A beam of sunlight spread across my face as I met the stare of the gods before me. This is the start of something. Something much higher than the acceptance of a task.

"I'll do it."

Zeus claps his hands together. "Wonderful. I would advise that you use the next two days to finish any training you may need. Remember, only a few of The Twelve know. We'd like to keep it that way. Do not tell anyone."

"I understand." I nod. The excitement of today's news starts buzzing in my stomach. I feel invincible knowing that Zeus picked me over my brothers, or anyone else. I feel seen. Like I finally matter to them.

"You are dismissed. Best of luck to you," Zeus says, then waves his hand to open the doors behind me.

I bid them farewell, allowing an excited smile to come across my face when I approach the doors. Before I pass the threshold of the throne room, Zeus's voice fills the air, "And Elena?"

"Yes, your Majesty?" I turn at my hips, looking back at the two goddesses and the god.

"Watch out for the Children of the Night."

CHAPTER 7

"I can't believe it. I didn't think I'd ever be given the honor of completing a task for The Twelve," I say through deep pants while shielding myself from Athena's strikes.

Athena grins. "I told you it would happen."

"You did. I still didn't believe you." I chuckle, turning around to distract her before driving my sword forward. It would have been a perfect killing strike had this been a real fight.

"You distracted me," Athena states, holding her head high.

"Maybe."

"I see you've taken up one of my signature moves," Athena says with a satisfied smile despite her heavy breathing.

"It's not one of my favorites. My favorite is the one I used when I sparred with the other trainee." I raise my arms above

DELANEY NICOLE

my head to open my airways, letting the dusty air filter deep into my lungs before pushing it back out.

"That one is effective," Athena says, placing our swords and shields on the weaponry wall. "Your father wanted me to tell you that he would like your presence at dinner tonight. He said it would be normal time."

"If you happen to see him before then, tell him I'll gladly join him." I'm happy my father requested my presence for dinner since I leave for the Underworld at tomorrow's dawn.

Athena walks back over to me and places her hand on my forearm. "It has been an honor to train you. I do not doubt that you will succeed at this task in no time."

"Thank you." It felt oddly comforting to me that Athena gave me such kind words as my mentor.

"A word of advice: Hermes does not take kindly to waiting on others. And though he knows vast amounts on all the realms, he does not like to be bombarded with questions."

I chuckle. "Noted."

"You're going to do great." Athena wraps her arms around me for a hug. This is a first for us, but it feels nice. "I must be going. I have other business to attend to. And Elena, do not forget your compassion while you're down under."

I stand in the center of the arena watching Athena make her exit.

* * *

As I climb the stairs to my father's estate, I can't help but repeat Athena's advice in my head. "Don't forget your

44

compassion while you're down under." I wonder if she meant something, or if she was simply telling me to stay true to who I am as a fighter.

Pushing my worries from my mind I knock on the door to my childhood home. It is a bit odd to be having dinner with my father so soon after the previous one. However, his stay has been longer than usual.

"Elena, there you are," my father grins and opens the door wider. "I thought we could eat out on the terrace again. It was your favorite place to dine as a child."

"That sounds lovely." I hang my himation on the rack in the foyer. The wrap matches the blush color of the peplos I've chosen.

We meet the setting sun with its cascading shades of pink, blue, and purple across the sky upon our entrance to the terrace. It's beautiful, and yet it brings me pain and maybe a little anger knowing it is the work of Apollo. The waves in the ocean are gentle, creating a calming hum for the ears of anyone nearby thanks to Poseidon.

"Are you ready for your journey tomorrow?" My father pours a glass of dark red wine into the glasses on the table.

"I don't think anyone is ever truly ready to go to the Underworld. Other than Hades, of course. But I am excited and ready for the reward for completing the task. Do with that what you will." I shrug, then raise my glass of wine in front of me for my father's traditional toast before the meal.

"To finally reaching your goal." He raises his glass with pride gleaming in her eyes.

"Elena, I wanted to give you something before your departure tomorrow. I've had this since you were born, but I

DELANEY NICOLE

wanted to wait to give it to you." My father pauses and pulls out a small necklace. "It was your mother's. She made me promise I'd give it to you one day. I thought now would be a perfect time."

I take the necklace from my father's hand, eyeing the dainty gold chain with a small ice blue gemstone atop a larger opal stone. My eyes start to sting. This necklace is the only thing I've ever had that was my mother's. It is the only connection I have to her. "It's beautiful."

"Your mother was a beautiful woman." A somber expression marks my father's face at the reminiscence of his former lover. "May I?" He inclines his hand to assist me in putting the necklace on.

I nod silently, handing the dainty piece of jewelry back to my father. I look out at the ocean, holding my hair to one side. It is hard to describe what I feel. Sad for the mother I was never able to meet since she died a few minutes after my birth. And happiness that I now have a piece of her.

"There." My father sits back down at the table. "You look beautiful. Like she did when she wore it."

"Will you tell me about her?" I move my gaze back to him, toying with the charm of the necklace between my fingers.

"I could." Ares's eyes trail out over the sea with the smallest of smiles on his lips. "She was beautiful. The most beautiful woman I've ever seen. I thought so the moment I saw her. Her eyes were the lightest blue, like ice. Her skin matched her pale hair. She could light up a room with her laugh. She showed compassion even to those she disliked. So many lack that ability, as I'm sure you know.

"I fell in love with her, which caused problems. It was

frowned upon to have relations with mortals even if Zeus has done it numerous times. She had a husband she was forced to marry. A husband she warned me would cause problems should he find out about our affair. We ignored him. I told her I would protect her should he find out." The smile on his face was growing, warming my heart as I thought of the love they shared.

"I don't think I'd ever been happier in my life than when I was with her. We were happy. We were in love. Then, one day, she told me she was pregnant. I knew it was my child because I could feel the connection to it like a tether pulling me in. She was terrified her husband would find out. I remember like it was yesterday. I told her I would protect her and the child, you, no matter what."

My father let out a sigh before continuing, "We planned for her to tell her husband it was his child. I told her I would help her in any way she needed me to. And that was that.

"Until your mother went into labor, then things took a turn. It took a toll on her body, more than expected. I knew she wouldn't make it. Her husband was away, which made it possible for me to be there with her.

"She used all of her strength to get you here. When she held you, I saw a light in her eyes I'd never seen. It made my chest ache because I knew it wouldn't last long. Your mother knew it as well. She made me promise I would take you to live in Olympus with me and keep you safe. I knew you were unique. After all, you were hers. I would've fulfilled any request she had because that was how much I loved her. She took the necklace from her neck and made me promise to give it to you when the time was right.

"I stayed with her. You were in her arms until her last moments. She passed with a smile on her face. She was happy even in her last moments," my father finishes, moving his eyes back to mine.

I hadn't realized tears were falling down my cheek during his tales. My mother sacrificed her life to give me mine. I will never be able to thank her.

I wipe the tears from my cheek. "She sounds lovely."

"She was. I see a lot of her in you."

"I'm not sure I am worthy of such a declaration." I meet my father's eyes and find them softened.

He stands gracefully and extends his arm toward me to escort us in. "You will achieve greatness beyond what some of The Twelve can even begin to imagine."

"But what…what if I'm not ready?"

I latch onto him, and we stop at the threshold of the house. "The question is not whether or not you are ready. It is whether you want to be ready."

Silence falls between us before my father finally speaks again. "I know how you must be feeling right now. Your task requires a lot. But you are the strongest warrior in training. It is why you were selected. You have the strength to fight those that get in your way. You will accomplish great things. But that starts with this task."

"I know." And I do. I know this is the only way I will be able to lead with Athena. If I fail, I can kiss any hopes of commanding the army goodbye. I won't let that happen. I will go to whatever lengths to ensure I succeed, including—

"Father?" I turn, hoping for a little more information.

"Yes?"

"Do you know anything about the Children of the Night?"

A deep sigh leaves my father's mouth, and he drags his hand over his face. "I cannot share that much because I do not know enough about them. But I have heard tales. I believe I may have seen one of them on a battlefield before. She was ruthless. And—"

There is something he is not telling me.

"Father, what is it?"

He shakes his head, deflecting, "It is getting late. You should prepare for tomorrow."

I place my hand on the door, stopping it from closing. "Anything you keep from me now may end up harming me later. You, of all people, know I need all the information I may obtain before I leave. Otherwise, I am entering a den of vipers blind."

My father opens the oak door. "Their leader, Thanatos, was the one that took your mother's soul."

There was no stopping ice from rushing through my veins.

CHAPTER 8

My entire walk back to my home, I think about my mother. I'd give anything to meet her once, to thank her. I also can't keep control of my rising anger and disgust for Thanatos.

I hurry to my bed-chamber, untying my peplos and letting it fall around my feet as I pass the threshold. I slip into a soft silk nightgown and as I secure the gown around my waist, a knock sounds on my door.

I meet eyes with Apollo and feel slightly annoyed at his presence. "What are you doing here?" I don't need him coming to make me feel any worse.

"I came to see you," he responds quietly, then enters my room.

"So you've decided to visit your demi-god whore?" I roll my eyes as I put the peplos I wore to dinner in the hamper.

"You know I don't think of you like that." Apollo walks in, closing the gap between us.

"I don't think I do. You hurt me during our last encounter." I fold my arms over my stomach. The previous days distracted me from what Apollo had said to me, but seeing him now, reopened the wound.

"I came to apologize. I had no right to react the way I did." He steps closer and he brushes my forearm in a feather-light graze. Goosebumps erupt on my skin and I silently curse myself for reacting to his touch.

"You're right. You didn't." I move toward my window to put distance between us.

"Please, Elena, let me apologize." Apollo grips my arm, stopping me in my tracks. It isn't tight, but it's enough.

"Let go," I mutter through my teeth.

"Elena, please, don't let this be how your last night in Olympus is." He loosens his grip and closes the gap almost entirely. I tilt my head back to meet his green eyes, and my breathing shallows.

His head dips to the right of my head. "Let me apologize." His lips press lightly against my neck. "The way I know how."

I suck in a breath as his tongue connects with my neck for a second time. My head lolls back, giving Apollo more access. I want to give in, but I also want to stand up for myself. "I can't do this."

"Just tonight?" His breath cascades on the soft skin of my neck. I know what it will mean if I let this continue. He wants to do this. He wants to be with me. He is making an effort to be with me. Who am I to deny him?

I slowly bring my head up and my eyes meet Apollo's heavy lids. My hands grip his muscular biceps.

In what feels like an instant, my lips meet his. His grip on my hips tightens, and he pulls my body against his. His kiss is hungry, dominating. I find his hair and pull it at the roots. A guttural grunt comes from his throat,

Apollo walks us back to the bed. As the backs of my legs meet my bed, he starts removing my thin gown. I am quick to remove his chiton.

My back meets the soft mattress, and Apollo's lips trail the line of my jaw, dipping lower to my neck again. My head falls back as I grip his shoulder and hair. Between my thighs is throbbing, and wetness begins to pool.

Apollo descends my body and a gasp leaves my mouth as his tongue meets the peaks of my breasts. He looks up with a cheeky grin. "Has someone missed my touch?"

Instead of answering, I pull Apollo forward, meeting his lips again. He hovers just over me. The ache between my legs deepens.

"Apollo," I mutter between deep pants.

His eyes lift to mine. His hands are one either side of my head. A slight grin lines his lips. "You're eager tonight."

Before I give a snarky comment about how he was the one that sought me out, a moan escapes my lips. His thick length pushed into my core and my grip on Apollo's shoulders tightens.

"What am I going to do when you're in the Underworld?" Apollo says through his heavy breaths. His thrusts are slow, tantalizing, and profound.

All I can think about is how I need him.

"Apollo," I whine. He knows that slow strokes feel like torture to me. I meet his eyes while a smirk spreads across his face.

Apollo bends down, meeting his lips with mine. I meet his hunger-filled kiss. His tongue lapses across the seam of my mouth. His tongue meets mine, and another whimper escapes my throat as his thrusts quicken.

Apollo smirks into our kiss, moving his lips down. His right hand skims the length of my thigh and wraps my leg around his waist. My head falls back onto the pillow beneath my head. My back arches while a moan leaves my lips. I can feel a tightness coiling low in my belly.

"Remember me when you're in the Underworld. Remember this," Apollo mutters as he lifts his head to look at me beneath him. The look in his eyes is the reason I let him continue tonight. It makes me feel...It makes me feel cared for.

Apollo rolls his hips as I pull him back to my mouth. Another grunt leaves his throat when I pull at his roots. That coiling continues to tighten in my stomach, closer and closer to snapping. His strokes are growing sloppy.

The arm that had once skimmed my leg now kneads the stiff peaks of my breasts. A short gasp leaves my lips at the unexpected stimulation.

In what feels like seconds, the tightness that has been coiling in my stomach releases. My head falls back, my back arches, and a moan of Apollo's name falls from my lips. My body shudders beneath and around him. Apollo quivers atop me with a sharp groan a few thrusts after.

We fall silent, panting heavily. A thin layer of sweat coats us. Apollo falls to my side, the sheet draping our lower halves.

A smile lines my lips as I turn to face him. His arm wraps

around my waist, and he pulls me flush against his body. I rest my cheek against his chest. My fingers trace his muscled stomach idly.

"What will you do while I'm in the Underworld?" I move my head to look up at Apollo.

"I'll do what I've always done. Do my business with The Twelve and train," he answers, tracing my arm with his fingers like I was doing to his stomach.

"You won't seek another in my absence?"

Apollo shrugs. "I didn't feel a need before. Why would I now?"

A small flutter fills my chest. I am the one he has chosen. He wants no one else.

"What will you do without my presence in the Underworld?"

"The same as you, I suppose." I shrug. "I can't imagine there'd be any reason to change that."

CHAPTER 9

I awake before the sun crests the horizon. I turn to see the bed is empty. Apollo is gone. I'd be lying if I said I was surprised.

But last night felt different. At least I thought it did.

I climb out of bed and head to the bathing chamber. I brush my hair and let it air dry against my back before I meet Hermes. I feel oddly calm, as though I have finally accepted that this is the only way I will be able to accomplish what I need to. Any belongings I wanted to take with me to the Underworld had been sent last night, courtesy of Hermes. I fasten two halves of a laurel wreath in the sides of my hair, pinning the front pieces beneath them out of my face. With one last scan of my room, I walk down stairs. It seems strange that I won't be returning tonight or the next night.

I leave into the chilly morning air. At the top of the hill that looks over the city I see Hermes observing the city that would soon be waking.

Hermes' long hair is strawberry blonde and shines in the sun. He is wearing a typical white chiton and the winged shoes the mortals always depict him in. He turns when he finally takes notice of my presence on the hill. His brown eyes meet mine before he speaks.

"You're late."

"Am I? I believe it was agreed upon that we would meet as the sun began to rise." I point to the sun that is now rising over the horizon. "I hardly think it fair to be accused of running late when I am, in fact, one time. I should not be held accountable for you arriving earlier than agreed."

A hint of a grin spreads on Hermes' face. "I was told you had snark. Nice to see you hold a similar attitude to your father."

"When you grow up with brothers like mine, you learn to bite before you are bitten."

"I believe that is a solid philosophy to live by." He grins, flashing his white teeth. "I'm afraid we must be going. I am a busy man."

"As you wish." I nod, ignoring the nerves in my stomach.

Hermes holds his arms out before him, waiting for me to move closer. After a second of hesitation and a final deep breath, I allow him to scoop me into his arms. His right arm holds my back as the other hooks under the bend of my knees. It is a far more intimate hold than either of us want, I'm sure. But it is the only way I can get to the Underworld unless I want to pass through as the mortals do, which includes having to pass a three-headed dog among other creatures that guard the Underworld.

I hold tightly to Hermes's neck as he flies. I remember

Athena's warning about Hermes not being fond of being asked questions though he knows more than anyone. But it doesn't stop my curious thoughts.

"May I ask you a question?" I move my eyes to his cheeks.

His jaw clenches slightly before relaxing. "That depends. What is the question?"

"Why were you assigned to transport me?"

"Because I am the only one that can move freely among all of the realms.That is also the reason I am the liaison for The Twelve. They tasked me with transporting you because I can get you there in record time. If you were to travel like the mortals, it would take you much longer to arrive in the court than they can afford. Not to mention, Hades's guards."

"I see."

I haven't paid attention to our journey until I notice we are flying toward a large pit in the ground. There is only darkness on the other side. My breath catches as we dive toward the pit.

A few seconds later, I allow my eyes to open in the slightest degree, looking above Hermes's head to the pit now seemingly above us. I look down to find land divided by four rivers.

We were in a realm of eternal night—the Underworld.

My heart quickens in my chest as my eyes roam the vast land beneath me. "Can I ask another question?"

Hermes lets out a short huff. "Were you not warned that I do not like being bombarded with questions?"

"I was."

"Then why are you continuing with your inquiries?" He looks at me with a pointed expression.

DELANEY NICOLE

"Because if I were to cower and heed every warning I received, I wouldn't be where I am now. I wouldn't be on a task for The Twelve. Besides being a man that deals in secrets, you have valuable information that I'm sure most do not know," I say without any nervousness in my voice.

Hermes lets out a defeated sigh, causing a sense of pride to fill me. "What is your question?"

"What do you know about the Children of the Night?"

Hermes's lips flatten into a thin line. He contemplates his answer for some time. "There isn't much I know of them. That's why Zeus has asked what he has of you and given you a warning."

A nervous knot forms in my stomach again. The messenger of the gods—the one who is supposed to know more than anyone—knows nothing of the people considered to be my most significant threat. I know hardly anything about them other than they are ruthless, and that their leader was responsible for taking my mother's soul as well as others.

"I do know, however..." Hermes pauses, setting me down on a stone step. We are outside of Hades's court, and my stomach bubbles with anticipation of this task. "That you should be cautious when around them."

I swallow the lump in my throat, nodding in agreement at Hermes's warning. Being out here feels much different than in the training ring. In the arena, if I messed up, I could start over or try again another day. Out here, I have this one chance. If I mess up, it could very well be a death sentence.

"I will walk you to Hades's throne room to ensure you are

acquainted with whom you need to be. Then I will leave you to return to Olympus."

I eye the large palace in front of me. I take a deep breath, reminding myself that this is how I will meet the goal I've always wanted. "Okay."

Hermes holds out his arm, waiting for mine to latch on. He refrains from speaking until my arm is linking with his. "And so, the fate of the mortals hangs in the balance."

CHAPTER 10

My eyes roam the walls with each turn in the corridor. Each division is lit with torches, shedding dim light on the various sculptures and paintings lining the light gray stone. I wonder if this is an old design. Surely if this were new, The Twelve would renovate the acropolis atop the Mount to emit their power as this does for Hades. Perhaps I have it backwards. The acropolis is the newer structure and the Underworld is outdated. I'm sure that is the case. Olympus would never be caught without the upperhand, even with such a miniscule thing as architecture.

Either way, it is regal in every way imaginable. Deep arches form doorways. Glass panes painted various hues mark the ends of each corridor. The height of the stone ceilings rivals that of towers. A crimson rug runs across the length of the floor. It is shocking how different everything is.

Instead of panicking, I force myself to take note of every possible escape route, should I need it. Hermes stays quiet at my side. Occasionally, I discreetly look over to find him gazing at the vast land to our left.

"We can't be far. We've been walking for ages." I look up at Hermes's face.

A mischievous glint fills his eyes. "Hades loves his security measures. And he's a man that likes a view."

"A view?" My brows wrinkle in confusion.

"You'll see." He lets out a small chuckle as we turn the corner of another dark corridor. In the middle of the hall stands two guards. "Gentleman, we have business with Hades."

The men before us don't move, instead, they stare at the wall behind us without seeing. Had I not been able to see their chests move, I would believe them to be statues. In fact, the longer I look at them, the more their skin looks white as stone.

"Why aren't they moving?" I murmur.

"Oh, right. Here you go." Hermes says with a cocky smile as he places two gold medallions in their palms. "Go buy yourselves something pretty." The guards quickly move to the side, holding their blank stares. Finally, they pull the large, arched doors open, allowing entrance to the throne room.

"Is their behavior not peculiar to you?" I whisper once Hermes and I pass the threshold.

"They're like that with everyone. There's a rumor that Hades granted their souls a new body, but the catch was that they had to serve as palace guards," Hermes whispers back.

"Hades granted their souls another body?" My eyes grow

DELANEY NICOLE

large, so large that I can tell the whites around my eyes are entirely visible to anyone that looks.

"That's what—"

"Hermes! How wonderful to see you again," a voice booms from the opposing end of the throne room.

"My dearest Hades, how are you this fine decade?" Hermes grins, then pulls me forward toward the god of the Underworld.

My eyes find the windows lining three out of four walls, which nearly reach from floor to ceiling. The view shows four rivers separating the Underworld into different sections, each having its own characteristics.

"Never a dull moment in the Underworld." Hades smirks. He sits next to Persephone in a chiton the same dark blue shade as her peplos. His muscular arms brace each side of his seat. His dark hair is left free flowing at his shoulders. I watch as his eyes bounce between Hermes and me.

My breath catches as my eyes connect with the man standing at Hades's side. He has skin that resembles that of teakwood with bulky muscles. His dark, midnight-colored hair is down like the other men in the room. His eyes are dark but different than Hades. He is very handsome. A sword is fastened securely at his side, and my eyes roam from the blade back up to his face. The grin he has when my eyes move up makes it seem as if he knows what is going through my mind.

"So I've heard," Hermes says. His voice draws my focus back in.

"And you must be the great Elena we've heard all about." Hades turns his head in my direction.

62

I hold my head high as I speak, "I am."

"I can't wait to see if you live up to the reputation you've gained atop Olympus," Hades's tone turns tantalizing. A threat or an invitation?

"Hades," Persephone murmurs at his side as if to warn him. At first glance, she doesn't seem as though she is being forced to sit. Rather, she looks comfortable. Her golden hair falls down her shoulders from a crown adorned with dark, midnight blue and white flowers. Her hands sit upon the arms of her chair, but her left hand is intertwined with Hades's.

"I'm just having a little fun, darling. Besides, I'm not going to do anything. I can't, however, promise that the others won't." He moves his hand to show the other at his side.

I stay trained ahead of me, not letting it appear that the cocky god is getting to me. No matter how much his bravado makes my eyes want to roll.

"How rude of me. Let me introduce you. To Persephone's side, you have Hypnos. Next to him, you have Keres. I'm sure you remember her, Hermes." A mischievous smirk lines the lips of them both. Keres has pale skin like that of the moon and she wears a dark blue peplos that dips low on her full chest and a slit that rides up her thigh. Hypnos has tanned skin like Hermes, and his hair falls just above his shoulders. His chiton is the same color as the woman at his side.

"You don't know much about them?" I mock in a whisper at Hermes.

"It's a long story, which includes lots of wine and a party hosted by Hades," he murmurs.

"To my side," Hades's voice booms again, "is Thanatos."

DELANEY NICOLE

My stomach drops as my gaze shoots to the man I had thought handsome moments ago. He is my second target. I try my hardest to hide my disgusted glare. He is responsible for taking my mother's soul. He is the reason I grew up without a mother.

"And together, they are the Children of the Night."

Feral grins emerge on their faces. Something tells me it isn't pride that makes them act this way. There is something animalistic about them. They have no remorse for the strife they have caused. Much like I will feel no remorse when I bring Thanatos back to Zeus alongside Persephone.

"Now, Hades, don't scare the girl," Hermes says as if he is speaking with an old friend. Hermes is known for dealing with secrets. But how many secrets did he have of his own?

"Don't worry. Elena will be taken care of." Hades turns his head back to Hermes. "We'll allow her to complete the task as Zeus asked."

"Very well." Hermes nods. "I'd love to stay and chat, but I'm afraid I must be returning to Olympus."

"Don't be a stranger, Hermes. You're always a welcome visitor. I'm sure Keres agrees."

"Goodbye, Hades," Hermes replies as he begins to leave, refusing to acknowledge his comment.

"Goodbye, Hermes," the god grins.

"Goodbye, Hermes," Keres replies in a tone that is dripping with feral desire.

I watch Hermes exit the throne room. With a click of the door in the silent throne room I turn back to face those on and around the throne. I'm officially on my own.

"Now that that's over, I'd like to let you know that the

library is still in the process of being prepared for you. You should be able to start your task within the next few days. I was given very few details about your goals by my brother. He assured me you would fill me in."

"I'm supposed to go over the army's archives to ensure everything matches up. Unfortunately, we've run into a few discrepancies up on the Mount, so Zeus sent me here to find missing archives while also learning a deeper history of the armies," I say with a steady voice.

"I see. It should be ready soon. Until then, we will have dinner this evening with the court, and we invite you to join us. We do expect you to be there as our guest of honor. But we would understand if you need time to... adjust." Hades smirks defiantly.

"How could I resist such a generous invitation?" I smile so forcefully my cheeks begin to hurt.

"A guard will escort you to the room we've set up for you during your time here. You may go. We'll have another guard retrieve you when it's time for dinner."

"Thank you." I give a curt nod and turn toward the door. I clasp my hands in front of me. I've never wanted to get out of a room faster than I do right now. I want to be far from Thanatos and the other Children of the Night.

"Elena," Hades calls out.

"Yes?" I turn to face the god on the throne.

A devious smirk pulls at his lips. "Welcome to the Underworld."

CHAPTER 11

Standing in what is to be my room during this task causes the weight of everything to finally sink in. The room is pretty spacious but dark. It's only lit by a sliver of moonlight coming through the windows. A king-sized bed adorned with plum-colored silk sheets sit in the center of the adjacent wall. The four posters around the bed are curtained with a sheer fabric to pull down when sleeping. On the wall opposite the bed, sits a couch and two chairs centered around a small tea table. Curtains line the large windows, each drawn back and the same shade of dark purple as the sheets.

I walk over to the corner of the room where a full-length mirror stands. It is crafted from the finest metals and embellished with various flowers. It's opulent.

I am so transfixed on studying the mirror that I hadn't even noticed a note sitting on the table behind me until I saw it in the reflection of the mirror. I pick up the letter.

Elena,

I hope you feel welcome. I'd love for us to chat. I know how hard it can be when you first arrive. Until then, I hope you accept these Moonlight Roses as a welcoming gift.

Persephone

The roses are a shade of deep blue like the night sky. The flowers seem to glimmer with a silver glow when touched by the moonlight. I've never seen anything like it. They are beautiful.

The room is lovely too, but no number of lavish gifts or rooms can change why I am here. I won't fall for their deception. And to start, I need to get close to Thanatos, gain his trust, and take him to Zeus, no matter how badly I want to kill him myself.

With that fresh on my mind, I walk to my bathing chamber to have a look around before getting ready for dinner. The chamber is lavish. There is a large tub next to a grand window. The water that runs from the sink and the bath is warm. Bath salts and lotions line the counter. It is clear Persephone wanted me to receive a warm welcome.

Once done with my inspection, I lather my body in a sweet lilac-scented lotion. I style my hair in a similar way in which I previously had it, simply fixing the wind-blown pieces. However, instead of my white peplos, I throw on an ice blue one. The blue brings out my eyes and matches the small jewel on my mother's necklace. I haven't taken it off since my father gave it to me. Finally, I sheath the ivory and opal dagger my father gave me a few years back to my thigh, carefully concealing it from the eyes of others.

A knock sounds on the door, startling me from my

routine. I open it with caution by hovering one of my hands over the handle of my dagger in case I need it.

"Who is it?" I ask as I peek through the crack. It's an unfamiliar man. My hand clasps around the hand of my blade.

"I am here to escort you to dinner," the man states.

I realize I can only be so cautious since I have not seen or met enough of Hades' court to know if he's telling the truth. I take a breath, reminding myself that I have my dagger if all else fails. I open the door fully and glance around my room to ensure I have everything. "Very well."

The guard keeps his gaze ahead of him, hardly paying me any mind. I look around the corridors, taking in the various forms of art that stretch from paintings to sculptures. We walk silently for some moments. The art changes styles with each new corridor we pass through. I never thought of Hades as an art lover, but I suppose even the keeper of souls has his interests.

Occasionally, my glance shifts to the guard. Even through his chest plate and other armor, I can tell he is built with lean muscles. I also know, however, that does not affect his fighting capability. He must be skilled to have been selected as one of Hades's guards.

"May I ask you something?" I say, finally breaking the silence.

"That depends," he responds shortly.

"On?"

"On what you ask."

My lips purse. "How long have you been Hades's guard?"

"Longer than you've been alive, I'm sure," he responds flatly.

I decide not to respond, though there are plenty of questions I want to ask. I refrain from pestering the man any longer. There will be time for that later.

My guard gives a silent nod to the guard standing at the dining hall doors. With this, the doors swing open with a rush of air, revealing a vast room with an oversized table sitting in the middle.

At the table's head sits Hades with Persephone at his left. "Elena, how lovely of you to join us," Hades grins but I know he is taunting me with the way he stares at me. He's trying to see how far he can push me. "We saved you a seat next to Persephone."

My stomach churns as Keres and Hypnos watch every step I take like animals calculating the perfect moment to strike.

"On behalf of all of us, we're excited to have a visitor that isn't Hermes," Persephone says when I sit beside her.

"Thank you for the kindness you've shown me," I respond sweetly. The lie tastes bitter. I look around, noticing the empty chair next to Hades signaling the absence of Thanatos. "Shouldn't there be one more joining us?"

"You've noticed Thanatos's absence. I'm afraid he might miss dinner. He's out on business," Hades says, rubbing his hands together on top of the table.

"I'd hardly call it business," a voice sounds from somewhere in the corner.

Hades's feline grin widens. "You made it."

"The souls of the damned didn't put up much of a fight today. And I promised I'd make an appearance. I wouldn't want the guest of honor to get the wrong impression."

Thanatos emerges from the shadows. He winks in response to my acute scowl.

I find it challenging to hide my disgust. This is the man that has robbed innocent mortals of their lives. And he shows no remorse. He takes pride in it. He is a monster.

"Good day, I assume?" Hypnos inquires from my right side.

"I didn't experience any serious challenges if that's what you mean," Thanatos responds, taking a swig of red wine in his chalice as if we were discussing the weather.

"Nice to hear you didn't meet another like Sisyphus, brother," Hypnos chuckles. My brows furrow. I don't particularly care about getting to know those around me, but his comment does make me curious.

"I'm not going to be put in that situation again."

"We're glad you made it in time," Persephone says. "Hades, don't you think it's time we begin our welcome feast? I'm sure Elena is starved after her journey."

With a clap of his hands, several cooks enter with various plates and trays in their hands. In what felt like the blink of an eye, the table before me fills with food and then the room is empty, save the dinner party, once again.

"Let the feast begin," Hades says.

Keres and Hypnos are quick to fill their plate with small pieces of everything in the spread. I sit unmoving. Persephone scoops a mixture of what looks to be garden-fresh vegetables and delicate filets. The only other person who hasn't made a move to make a plate is Thanatos. His eyes track my every move just as I am doing to him.

"Is there something wrong with the food Elena?" Hades asks with a morsel of filet tucked in his cheek.

"Goodness no. I was only trying to figure out what to indulge in first." I give my best fake smile I can manage in the presence of such dismal company.

"Don't be scared. Our chefs are some of, if not the best chefs there are," he grins.

"Don't be scared, darling. It won't bite," Thanatos adds sarcastically as he begins filling his plate.

Darling. I meet his eyes with a sharp glare. I've had years of experience dealing with men like him. He is arrogant and prideful. I'll have him on his knees.

"Elena, what is it you did in Olympus? It seems odd that I never made your acquaintance," Persephone inquires.

"I train with Athena. Then I visit my father or return home," I say before bringing the chalice of wine to my lips. I take a deep gulp, tasting of rich sweetness. I do not wish to divulge much information to these people, even if it is Persephone who asks the question. For all I know, they have put her up to this.

"Hermes has talked about a certain god finding an unlikely companion," Hades says with a mischievous grin. Unease burrows within my stomach. "How is Apollo?"

Thanatos's eyes lock on me. The other two Children of the Night pause their conversation to eavesdrop on mine. Unease filters through me further. I'm not sure why they act as though they've never heard of The Twelve since they work for Hades. He may not be an official member but he associates with them when necessary.

"He's... um..." I pause. It is hard to describe my relation-

DELANEY NICOLE

ship with Apollo. Some days we appear as though we are in love, a happy couple. Other days it is as if a switch goes off, and we are fighting, saying that we are nothing more than someone to warm each other's bed. "He's doing well."

"It's nice to hear he's still doing well. What of the others? Artemis? Athena?" Persephone inquires.

"I don't speak with Artemis often. Athena is doing well. My father too," I reply before taking a bite of the roasted vegetables, hoping it would be enough to deflect another question

"My, I don't believe I've spoken to Ares in quite some time. I should invite him for dinner in the future," Hades says pridefully.

"Ares? He is your godly parent?" Keres ventures. Her tone is icy as she speaks. I nod, not knowing what else to do. "I would have believed you were a descendent of Aphrodite. In fact, I did. Your resemblance to her is uncanny. Of course, I've only seen her in passing."

"My mother was a mortal. Ares was the one who fathered me. I've been told I look like her."

"And a good fortune that is. It would be a shame if you looked like your father." Hades took a deep gulp of wine before refilling his chalice.

"Hades!" Persephone snaps.

"What can I say? I'm just living up to my reputation." He smirks and eyes the woman at his side.

"Your reputation is leading the Underworld as a fit ruler, not acting like an ass," she counters.

I choke on the wine I was trying to drink. Chuckles emerge from the Children of the Night at my side. I am shocked that such language came from Persephone. It isn't a peculiar thing for vulgar language to be used by The Twelve or others, but it is strange coming from the woman rumored to be one of the kindest goddesses.

"Now that we have all been re-introduced to the true nature of Persephone. Let's have dessert." Hades brushes Persephone's comment off as though it were nothing.

"Is it the recipe you received from The Fates?" Hypnos asks.

"It is. It's one of the best ones we have. It would be shameful if we didn't share it with our guest," Hades says, beaming.

"The Fates?" My brows furrow. I've never seen them but Apollo talks about how often they irritate Zeus. The sisters that believe they are above him and therefore do not listen to him. But I don't understand how they pertain to the Children of the Night.

Hades nods. "I learn many things from them. The Fates give me insight into the future, sometimes to prepare for massive entries of new souls. Other times it's just to show me anything interesting they find. This building, for example, will not become a popular style for another few thousand years. Nevertheless, I think it's delightful."

"I noticed this wasn't an acropolis, but I would have never guessed this would be from the future. What exactly are buildings like this going to be used for?" I ask, eyeing the high ceilings. I hope my inquisitions will aid me in finding out how they are connected to The Fates.

"The Fates said the mortals would call them castles. They'll be used to house kings and queens alike. They'll be

DELANEY NICOLE

palaces similar to those in Greece, but this darker look is much more my style."

"Yes, Hades, we know you are dark and mysterious. You don't have to remind us every day," Persephone says, feigning a groan before taking a short sip of her wine. I find it hard to keep my laugh contained.

"You seem to be showing off more than usual this evening. Is it because you want to appear tough for our guest?" Hades says with narrowed eyes. "I can recall a few times in which you didn't have such a harsh tongue. Rather you were using it to scream my nam—"

"Hades!" Persephone interrupts, drawing deep chuckles from Thanatos and Hypnos.

Keres rolls her eyes while bringing her chalice to her mouth, "Men..."

"Tell me about it," I mutter.

"Elena, before we forget," Persephone began, "there is a training ring on the floor below us in the east wing. You are free to use it whenever you like. Have one of the guards escort you."

"I'll put it to good use, thank you." I give Thanatos a warning glance of deviance. "Thank you for the warm welcome."

"Believe it or not, the Underworld is not the scary place it is chalked up to be." I can tell there is truth in her words. "I am going to retire to my bedchamber. I hope everyone has a pleasant evening."

"I will join you, my dear," Hades calls after her.

"I know you will. You cannot spend an evening without me after all," the goddess responds as she passes the threshold of the dining room. I must say, Persephone's hidden snark is amusing.

"Someone's quick this evening." Thanatos is slouched in his chair with his legs hanging off the arm of one side.

"She acts that way when she wants a special form of treatment. Excuse me." Hades stands from his seat, bidding everyone a goodnight before exiting the dining hall.

I toy with my cake-like dessert, feeding a spoonful of some sort of whipped cream in my mouth. If I were not surrounded by cold-hearted murderers, I might have hummed at my satisfaction of the dish.

Keres and Hypnos toss me a glance before looking at their brother. I feel no inclination to speak with them. I don't have to know them to know I don't like them. They appear to share a similar feeling. So, I do what anyone in my situation would do. Leave.

"It was lovely meeting the three of you. I hope to have more interactions like this during my stay." I offer a tight smile to each of them. Without looking back, I walk out of the dining hall and back to my room with the same guard as before. I already feel more familiar with the passages to and from my bedchamber. Soon, I shouldn't need an escort. Or at least I hope I won't have one.

After arriving back in my room, I light the candles on my bedside. As I move to burn the other ones, I stop in my tracks. Something is wrong. Silent, I unsheathe the dagger from my thigh.

"Have you not heard of knocking?" I say into the darkness. I am willing to bet my life that it is one of the Children of the Night.

"Where's the fun in that?" The figure emerges from the dark corner, their face dimly lit by the candles.

"What can I help you with at this late hour, Thanatos?" I ask, keeping my tone strong and voice steady. Disgust grows within me.

"Do you believe that I do not know what you are doing?" he asks, pacing the stone floor ahead of me.

My stomach twists for a fraction of a second before I will myself to stop. There is no way he knows. "I do not know what you are speaking of."

Suddenly, my back is on the harsh stone wall and weight bears down on my chest, and a sharp coldness meets my neck.

"Maybe this will clear it up." Thanatos pushed the blade in his hand harder on my skin. A bead of blood rushes to the surface of my neck. His breath warms the exposed parts of my chest.

Disgust and anger take over my body. I hate him. I hate him for the way the candlelight shadows his chiseled jaw to the way he stands centimeters from my face. Everything about him makes my hate for him grow stronger and more resilient. "Like I said. I do not know what you speak of."

"Do you think it isn't obvious that you seek to gain Hades's trust to use what he tells you against him with Zeus? It is no coincidence that you were sent after Lady Persephone's arrival. It is no coincidence that you were sent after my siblings and I took permanent residence in the Underworld…" He pauses, fuming in his stance over me. "Do not think for one second that I do not know what you are doing."

I swing my arms around before Thanatos has time to

regain his composure and break his contact with my chest. With the same agility, I flip, pushing him harshly against the wall and press my dagger to this neck.

"You come into my room and threaten me with a dagger? It's a first, and it will also be the last." I dig the dagger deeper, drawing blood from his neck. Thanatos leans his head forward, inching his face so close to mine it grows hot from his minty breath.

"Not likely, *Princess*."

My distaste for the man in front of me topples over. "What do you want from me? To admit my guilt? That will not happen even if you were right in your accusations?"

Another power struggle knocks me back into the wall and my dagger falls from my hands. My neck is met with a warm hand. My chin is pushed up by Thanatos's grip. My eyes are forced to meet his. Our breathing is heavier, and our eyes study each other.

His eyes have a dark shade of gold. His eyebrows are harsh in his expression, but they are the same color as the dark curl that fell to his forehead during the struggle.

He leans in. "I came to give you a warning. Hades is a dear friend of mine. If you do anything to bring him, or my siblings, harm, I will not hesitate to end you."

Thanatos releases his tight grip on my neck. I lightly touch my throat and glare at the man walking toward the door. I will deliver his end.

"I am not called the bringer of death for nothing, my dearest Elena."

CHAPTER 12

I tossed and turned all night. I was fighting the urge to seek out Thanatos's room and slaughter him or simply stay alert in the case that he tried the same. I couldn't keep my mind at ease.

I knew I would be challenged by Thanatos but it was still shocking. I need to be alert at all times.

I need to train.

Jumping from bed, I find the appropriate clothing and pull my hair back into a braid, making sure the end is secure for the activities I plan to do.

As I step out of my room, I find a new guard, he keeps his unseeing stare on the wall at the side of my head.

"Do you mind escorting me to the training ring? I'd like to relieve some stress," I ask.

"I've been told to escort you to breakfast before allowing you to go into the training ring. You are to eat a proper meal before training to keep your energy up," the guard says. His voice is deep, husky even, but in all honesty, I am surprised he is talking.

"Who gave this order?" I challenge.

"It is an order that came directly from Hades, miss."

"Very well." I sigh. "You may escort me to breakfast."

With a simple nod, the guard pushes off the wall and walks down the stone corridor. With alert eyes, I notice the more intricate details of the palace. There are things I wasn't sure I'd ever seen before.

"May I ask you something?" I say to break the silence between the guard and me.

"Sebastian warned me of your inquiries."

"Sebastian?" My brows pull.

"He was your guard last night."

"And may I know your name?" I inquire, angling my body to face him as we walk. He seems much friendlier than Sebastian.

"You're a curious little thing aren't you?" The dark-skinned guard says with amusement filling his eyes.

"It is only proper that I know the name of the guard I am trusting to keep watch over me. Even if it's for a short time."

"Your attitude reminds me of Ares." My eyebrows raise in surprise and he chuckles. "Yes, I know your father."

"How did you know—"

"I am wonderful at reading people, miss."

"Be that as it may, you still have yet to answer my question," I add.

The man stops, turns abruptly, and opens the door to the dining hall. I hadn't realized we had arrived. "The name is Leon."

DELANEY NICOLE

"See, that wasn't all that hard, Leon." I say facetiously. I am still on edge as I enter the dining hall. I am more at ease around Leon though. In all honesty, he reminds me of Stella. They share the same sarcastic spunk.

The inside of the dining hall, lit by the eternal moonlight of the Underworld, contains practically every breakfast food imaginable. From breakfast crepes to meats and fruit. It was all there. I sit down at the unoccupied table.

My eyes wander over the gray stone columns, up to the arched ceiling while I work my way through my plate of fruit. I must say I am quite glad to be eating alone. I like the quiet around me. It lets me think of all the things I need to do to succeed in my task.

Speaking of, where is Thanatos?

First and foremost, I need to be convincing in the task I fed Hades. I also wouldn't mind a history lesson on The Twelve and its armies.

The Underworld kept accounts of every soul and important matter regarding themselves. However, I'm not sure who has been doing that. Hades made it clear that the library required preparing before starting my task, meaning no one had been in there for quite some time. Perhaps The Fates do it since they're supposedly all-knowing.

"Leon, you daft devil. I'll remember that next time you want to challenge me," a male's voice booms, then Hypnos enters the hall. He has a bright grin on his face, which turns to a smirk when he meets my stare. "I didn't expect to see you here."

"It is the dining hall, after all," I mutter with a piece of

A CURSE OF HONOR

honeydew wedged in my cheek. I could have sworn I saw a flash of amusement spread over his eyes.

"Fair enough. Don't mind me. Just having a bit of breakfast before today's work; feeling a bit peaky," he replies sarcastically. A common theme for those in Hades's court.

"I was finishing up," I say, shoving one last piece of apricot into my mouth before standing from the table.

"Don't leave on my account," he calls after me. "I don't bite. Although, I can't say the same of my brother."

"Don't flatter yourself." I roll my eyes at Hypnos's arrogance.

"I see you've had the pleasure of chatting with Hypnos." Leon flashes an amused grin.

"Take me to the training ring please," I say.

Leon gives me a mock salute with a firm face. "Yes, ma'am."

"You are getting on my bad side, I was just starting to consider you a friend." I glare up at him.

"We only met this morning."

"Maybe so, but you remind me of a close friend." I shrug. It would take more for me to consider anyone from here a friend.

"Ooo, do tell," he purrs.

"I believe I'll save the specifics of her for a time when you're not being a pest."

"It's a woman?" He leans down rather quickly, his chin hovering over my shoulder. "Is she in need of a companion?"

I train my gaze on the wall ahead of me. "I have a dagger strapped to my thigh. Do not make me use it."

"You know, I might take you up on that offer of friendship. You can be entertaining. Your snark reminds me of Keres."

My head swivels over my shoulder and my feet falter. "Do not compare me to *them*."

A knowing stare fixes upon his face. "You speak of them as if they've wronged you."

"I speak of them as the arrogant, insolent monsters they are," I surmise.

"I see. And what have they done to make you believe that?" Leon inquires. He walks with a cockiness that reminds me of my brothers.

"They take the souls of mortals without so much as a thought to what happens to those left behind. They have no remorse for their actions."

"May I share something with you?" Leon asks as he opens the heavy door to the training room. I had been so lost in conversation I hadn't paid attention to how we got here.

"That depends."

"On?"

"What you choose to share."

"It is a small piece of knowledge I have gained from my time living and working for Hades."

"Then I suppose so." I nod. Any information about the inner workings of Hades's court may be useful for me. "However, that does not mean I will listen to it."

"What a surprise." His eyes flash with amusement. "In all of my years of living, I have found that to find where the truth lies, you must listen to both sides of the story. Sometimes, it is those closest to us that wish us to stay ignorant to benefit themselves."

I stop mid stride to the large fighting ring. Slowly, I turn to face the man I met this morning. Was he implying that The Twelve had lied to me? Keeping me in the dark for their own gain?

"Do with that what you will. I will be outside when you are ready to return to your quarters." Leon closes the door behind him and leaves me alone in the dark room.

I stroll around the training room. I note various forms of weapons on the dark stone walls, very similar to the ones in Olympus. After last night's visitor I want to make sure my hand-to-hand combat is up to par because regardless of how skilled I am wielding a sword or dagger, none of that will matter if I can't defeat my foes in a simple fistfight. Last night was proof enough.

I push the cushioned mass that is used for practicing close combat to the center of the ring with a little more effort than I originally expected. With each punch or kick, I replay Thanatos's words in my mind, which only make me want to strike that much harder.

"Princess."

Punch.

"Darling."

Kick.

"My dearest Elena."

Punch. Punch. Punch.

"I am not called the bringer of death for nothing."

I muster up all of my remaining strength and drive my fist forward. The punching bag topples over with a thud.

Panting, I grip my hips. It felt nice to relieve the pent-up

DELANEY NICOLE

tension I had allowed to build in the short time I've been here.

After steadying my breath, I move the bag back to the place it had been in before. I will figure out what to do with the rest of my day after I return to my quarters. Maybe I could pay a visit to Persephone later in the day.

But as I approach the entrance of the ring, I hear two voices on the other side of the door—male voices. Opening the door, my gaze catches on Leon, laughing brightly.

"Elena, look who I ran into."

My gaze connects with none other than Thanatos.

CHAPTER 13

"Elena, nice to see you. It was a shame you left dinner early last night." Amusement and something that resembles burning hatred flashes across Thanatos's bright eyes.

My eyes move toward Leon who is watching the two of us with an intrigued smile before my eyes meet Thanatos's again. "I felt quite tired after my travels yesterday. I apologize if it hindered you from greeting me how you wished."

"I'm sure we will have plenty of time to make acquaintances during your stay here." His grin deepens as he winks. "I'm afraid I must be off. I have much to do in the mortal realm today."

"Do hurry back. I wouldn't want to miss your presence at dinner." My voice is laced with a ferociousness that only seems to intrigue him more.

"I'll keep that in mind."

"That was quite entertaining. You two should stay near

DELANEY NICOLE

each other all the time. It would certainly give us guards something to do around here." Leon chuckles.

"Just take me back to my room."

* * *

I STAND before the full-length mirror in my room. It took me ages to find what to wear, but eventually, I landed on a pink gown that was already in the wardrobe when I arrived. It wasn't a peplos. In all honesty, I have no idea what to call a gown like this. My guess is that it is from the same era as the palace. It is flowy and pushes my breast higher on my chest because of its cinched bodice. I want to look presentable, being only my second day in the Underworld.

I walk out of my room to find Leon still standing guard.

"You're still here? I would have expected you to switch out with the other one," I say with my hands clasped together at my hips.

"Hello, Leon. How are you, Leon?" The dark-skinned man says facetiously. "Oh, hello, Elena. I'm doing wonderful this evening. Thank you for asking."

My eyes narrow toward the cheeky man. Even though I am beginning to think he isn't going to attack me when I turn my back, I have to admit he could be a real pain in the ass sometimes.

"You think you're funny?" I tut, walking forward without him.

"I think I'm rather hilarious at times," he retorts, falling into pace at my side. "Are you inclined to believe otherwise?"

"I am inclined to think you are a pest."

"Ouch. You know, Thanatos warned me you were quick with your tongue." Amusement flashes across his eyes when I stop him.

"I told you not to speak of them," I grit through my teeth.

"Yes, but I don't like following orders and I get the feeling you don't either. Which is why I think you'd get along quite well with Keres. But, of course, you'd have to get on her good side. Frankly, her bad side has murderous tendencies."

"I do not care about getting on her good side because I have no interest in becoming close with any of them." I march forward.

"Perhaps." Leon shrugs.

"What is that supposed to mean?"

"Oh, nothing. I merely think you are too quick to judge." Leon turns, leading me down an unfamiliar corridor.

"I am not too quick to judge. I form opinions with the knowledge I have of a person. I am completely justified in my assessment of the Children of the Night. Hey," I pause, losing my train of thought when the corridors no longer looked familiar. "Where are we going? This is not the way to the dining hall."

"There are many passages to the dining hall, miss. However, you will not be dining there tonight. Persephone requested your presence while the others are out doing tasks.

"Why has my presence been requested for private dining with Persephone?" I ask. Leon stopped in front of another large oak door.

"I can't be sure. Think of it as girl-talk." He opens the door. "You desperately need it."

87

DELANEY NICOLE

I meet him with a mocking glare before walking through the open door. The room is decorated with midnight-blue and gold furniture. Paintings of the constellations decorate three walls. It is an observatory—a lavish one. The fourth, furthest wall opened onto a large terrace, large enough to fit a decent-sized dinner party. It reminds me of the terrace Stella and I used to sit on back at The Muses. The ceiling was a transparent dome, offering more opportunities for stargazing.

"Wow," I mutter.

"Elena, I didn't hear you come in," Persephone says as she walks in from the terrace.

"No worries," I say, seeing that Persephone wears a gown similar to mine.

"Well, now that you are here, we can eat. Dinner will be on the terrace." The goddess turns to walk back outside, and I follow suit.

"Persephone?"

"Yes?" She looks over her shoulder.

"Are these gowns from the same era as the palace?" I ask. The suspicion was eating me up.

"Yes, they are. Keres and I prefer them over a peplos sometimes. I thought we'd give you the same option. Most of the clothes in the wardrobe we provided you are from the same era."

That explains the training clothes too. Instead of a peplos-like gown with breeches of the same cloth underneath it like what I wear in Olympus, they are a tight fitting tunic with some material that stretches with me—I'm not sure what one would call it—and breeches that match it.

"Wow," I whisper, walking out on the terrace. It looks out over two rivers that divide the Underworld. Growing up, I was told it divided the realms of the souls. Each realm a soul remained in for eternity was decided solely on how the person spent their lives. Souls that remained kind and just were kept on the upper levels, dwelling in either the Elysian fields or the Asphodel Meadows. Judging by the healthy landscape, I'd say the terrace we now stand on overlooks a piece of them both.

"This is one of my favorite places to come and sit." Persephone looks out over the vast land in front of us. The field and meadows are filled with flowers and greenery. It looks as though she has blessed the land herself.

"I had no idea it looked like this down here. I was told—"

"You were always told that the Underworld was filled with fire and despair. Yes, that's what my parents told me as well. That is what most are told. They are told to fear this place. While some parts contain fire and torment souls of the damned, it is quite different from what most believe. Hades never tells anyone differently. He likes to keep what is good a secret. Because, frankly, he knows that when a good thing comes to the attention of many, it is ruined by greed." Persephone pauses, looking as though she is reminiscing on a different time. "He sees that all the time. Even in his brothers."

"I see where he is coming from," I mutter, my stomach currently twisting in a knot because I am tasked with taking not one but two things away from Hades. Even if only one of them is good. I feel as though my task is going to be much harder than I originally anticipated. "There are

DELANEY NICOLE

rumored to be four rivers. Are they not visible from this side?"

"No, they are not. You can see them, along with Tartarus, on the other side of the palace," Persephone says as she sits. I join her across the table still admiring the view.

Without so much as a snap of the goddess's fingers, chefs appear, placing bowls of delicious smelling food in front of us.

"I had the chef prepare one of her specialties, chicken orzo soup."

"It smells amazing," I say, grabbing the spoon at my side as the delicious aroma fills my nose. As soon as the dish meets my tongue, I taste splashes of lemon zest and garlic. "It is amazing."

"I'd hoped you'd like it. Some days when I miss home, I ask the chef to make it," Persephone says with a satisfied smile as she takes her first bite.

We bask in comfortable conversation about things like gardening and places we loved to visit in Olympus. It appears Persephone likes Stella's shop too.

"Do you miss home often?" I ask as we finish our meal. This is my chance to find out how Persephone truly feels about staying here. This will decide how I go about my task for Zeus and The Twelve.

"Occasionally," she says.

"Do you think you'll return?" I ask, following Persephone to the edge of the terrace where she tends to a small bundle of flowers. It's roses similar to the ones I was given upon my arrival.

"I see where this conversation is headed," Persephone mutters. "Elena, do you see these roses?"

I nod, unsure of how this relates to her return home.

"They are moonlight roses, meaning they only grow in the presence of moonlight. Shortly after my arrival, I was given the seeds for these flowers from Hades. He told me he acquired them from Selene. When I first arrived, I was furious, and I fought him whenever and however I could. But he gave me these seeds and told me he wanted me to feel at home. When he gave me the flowers, I realized he was the first person that ever wanted to try to make me feel comforted." Persephone's gaze turns to mine.

"I do not expect you to understand. I am simply telling you why I found a home here," the goddess clarifies. She turns back to the fields and meadows in front of us. "In Olympus, I am known as the kind goddess, the happy one. I could never be anything different and it made me scared when I felt anything other than those two things. I found a home here because there is a man that loves me despite what I keep buried deep from others.

"Hades embraces it. He shows me it is okay not to be sunshine and rainbows all the time. He loves me even when I do not fulfill a certain duty. He doesn't love me just so I can complete a task for him. He lets me be. And for that, I will love him forever."

I meet Persephone's emerald gaze with a strange feeling emerging in my gut. Before I can even begin to utter a word she continues, "So the answer to your question is no, I don't think I will ever return to Olympus. This is my home. *He* is my home. And I will recommend that you do not try to convince me otherwise."

I am at a loss for words. I have never felt love like that. I have never felt at home the way she describes it. And I am not sure I ever will.

I also realized something I am sure Zeus and Demeter failed to consider. Persephone is in love with the ruler of the Underworld. It is going to make my task that much more complicated. But I don't want to worry about that. Either way, I need her to trust me.

"So it's true then?" I finally speak, snapping Persephone's attention back on me. "You grow used to the eternal night thing?"

The goddess's face softens, and the grin that pulls on her lips meets her eyes. "Yes, you do. Only if you're there to welcome it."

CHAPTER 14

A knock sounds on the door, drawing my focus from my daze, "Come in."

"I've come to send word that the library is now ready for you," Sebastian states flatly.

"Best be getting to it." I glide across the room, not forgetting to grab the forged ledgers I was given from Zeus and Hera to make my story appear plausible. "Thank you for telling me, Sebastian."

Leon was away for a few days. We've become close acquaintances in our time together, maybe even friends. However, I won't be admitting that to him.

"You're welcome, mis— how did you know my name? He looks down at me with such a puzzled expression.

"A dark-skinned guard whose name rhymes with Creon gave it to me." I walk forward with the guard's guidance.

"I should have guessed it was Leon. That man doesn't

DELANEY NICOLE

know how to keep his mouth shut." Sebastian shakes his head. "Did he say anything else about me?"

"Only that you have an extra toe on your right foot." I shrug, keeping my stride at Sebastian's brisk pace.

"I can't believe he told you about that. He barely even knows you," he mutters in annoyance.

"I was only joking." I laugh. "He only told me your name because I asked. Although, it is quite funny now that you've admitted you have an extra toe on your right foot."

"Ah, he told me you could be witty from time to time." He gives an almost genuine smile. "Nice to see you're living up to your reputation."

"Leon talks about me?" I ask, feeling an uneasy bubble form in my stomach.

"Yes. Sometimes it's with Hypnos or Keres. I'm sure he has with Thanatos, but he's been absent in recent days," Sebastian says, not knowing the panic he is slowly instilling in me. I feel my eyes grow wide in my head. I hope Leon did not tell them the things I say about them. It would most likely blow my cover. It could ruin my plans.

"All good things, I hope," I reply nervously, running my newly clammy hands against my hips.

"Just things like, 'it's good to have someone that can hold their own around her again,' nothing bad," Sebastian says.

We make our way down a candle-lit spiral staircase until meeting a sizable wooden door embellished with various carvings in the dark corridor. Images of creatures roaming at the side of mortals fill the wood, spanning from beasts I was well aware of to those I do not recognize. Sitting above the door is another carving, only this time they were words.

"The truth lies with only those willing to seek it," I read aloud.

"I wonder what it means," Sebastian murmurs under his breath.

"What do you mean?" My brows furrow.

"The inscription changes for each person. Usually, it pertains to what someone needs to hear most."

I look back toward the inscription on the wall.

"Anyway," he claps his hands together, "Hades has said you are free to use anything inside. I will be out here if you need anything."

I nod my thanks before entering the dark library. Once the fireplace is lit and the table candles are aflame, the expansive library comes into view. Shelves upon shelves stretch from floor to ceiling are filled with books. Moonlight floods into a dark corner the firelight fails to reach from a large glass window.

At the center table, I find a small stack of books and a note.

I'm not sure precisely what you'll need, but this should be a start.

Hades

I sit down in the cushioned chair and pull the first book from the stack, which causes a small red one to fall to the floor.

I pick the small book off the floor and place it back on the table. I will get to it eventually, but I want to start in the order Hades gave me the books. I open the first old, tattered book in the stack. At first glance, it appeared to be a regular book, but upon further examination, it is an account of every god and goddesses' origin dating back to the titans. Hades brought me back to the literal beginning of everything.

I already know the history of the gods and how they came to rule, but this new perspective made me enthralled with my reading. So much so that I hadn't even realized how much time had passed.

I read in silence until a chill spreads through my body and the hairs on the back of my neck stand up. Unease filters through me. My gut is rarely wrong, and right now, it is telling me I am no longer alone.

"Hello?" I speak into the seemingly empty library.

A gust of wind flies past me, smelling of mahogany mixed with slight hints of lavender. It smells familiar, too familiar.

Quietly, I unsheathe the dagger from my thigh. "I know you're there."

A shadow moves from a dark corner of the library toward the door. I throw my dagger. The shadow comes to an abrupt stop before it can reach the door. My blade is stopped mid-air by a tan hand.

"Dagger throwing? That's new." A bright sparkle is present in Thanatos's eyes as he examines my blade.

"You're back," I retort, sitting back in my seat. My attention is still on the man across the room. I hadn't seen him since our run in with Leon in the corridor. Persephone mentioned he was tending to urgent business during our daily talks. His absence only made it easier to form the second half of my plan. The part that will make him fall at my mercy.

"Did you miss me?"

"I wish you'd stayed away longer."

"Ouch. My feelings." He clutches his chest with my dagger still in his hand. "I'm wounded."

"Poor thing." I pout. "Give me back my dagger or more than your feelings will be hurt."

"I don't know." Thanatos twirls the blade between his fingers. "I've grown fond of it. I may keep it for myself."

My eyes narrow at the man I loathe more than my brothers. "Why are you here?"

"I commented on you missing at dinner, and Persepone insisted I bring you something to eat." He pointed to a plate of steaming food on the table in front of me. He must have put it there when I was distracted by the wind.

"Sebastian couldn't bring it down?" I ask, folding my arms across my chest.

"Sebastian is no longer outside," he states as he admires the way the opal of my blade glimmers in the firelight. "I sent him off for the night. It's just you and me down here. Please, eat. I wouldn't want you to grow famished."

"Is this your way of trying to poison me?" I lean back, carefully watching as he inches closer.

"If I wanted to kill you, I'd do it with my hands," Thanatos remarks.

"Is that a threat?"

"Think of it as a promise."

"Why not kill me now? There's no guard. No one is close. You could get away with it." I incline my head to meet his gaze.

Thanatos leans forward, bracing his hands on the table, until he is inches from my face. "Where's the fun in that?"

A cascade of mahogany fills my senses. I stand and lean

forward until Thanatos and I are nearly touching. My eyes stay locked on his as I speak slowly, "Why are you here then?"

"Once Persephone and Hades get an idea in their head, there is no changing their minds. Unfortunately, when I was told to bring you food, I was also tasked with helping you in whatever fake scavenger hunt you're on." He pushes back from the table.

A short laugh leaves my lips. "As if I'd ever let *you* help me. And it is not a fake scavenger hunt. I have been tasked with learning about the armies and finding any discrepancies between the accounts here and the ones from Olympus."

Thanatos turns his head as he leans back lazily in the chair at the opposite end of the table. "I get the feeling you don't like me."

"What gave you that impression? Was it when I held a dagger to your neck? Or when I threw it at your face?"

A wide smirk spreads across his lips, revealing the dimple in his right cheek again. "We're going to have so much fun together."

"Not likely," I mutter, dipping my head back into the book I had been reading.

After a few moments of silence, save the crackling of the wood in the fireplace, I look up to find Thanatos sweeping his gaze over the bookshelves.

"Are you going to come in here every time I'm researching?"

"As I said, when Hades or Persephone make up their mind there is no changing it. It would not go over well if I didn't follow through on their request." He shrugs.

"So you're going to sit in a chair and do nothing while I read through all of these books?"

"I won't be doing nothing. I'll be plotting how to kill you when you eventually make your move against Hades." There's a mischievous glint in his eyes.

"Lovely." I meet him with a similar expression.

"You're welcome to do the same. Although, it would most likely be a waste of that pretty little imagination you have."

"I will."

Amusement flashes in his eyes and the dimple reappears. "Promise?"

I let out an annoyed huff. "I was wrong about Leon."

"Oh?"

"He's not the pest. You are. It will only make killing you that much more relieving."

"Ouch," his tone dripping in delight. "I must say, though, 'pest' is tame compared to some of the things I've been called."

"Let me guess," I pause, standing to place the books back on an open shelf. I can't focus on anything with him here. "Arrogant? Bastard? Maybe a mixture of those. Or there's always a classic, ass…"

"Those do seem to be ringing a bell."

"While I think your presence is oh so precious, I'm afraid I must cut it short. I'm going back to my quarters," I say, heading toward the door.

Before I can reach the door, a tan hand with a large white scar across the top grasps the handle. My eyes sweep from the scar, up the arm, to Thanatos's face. For a moment, I could have sworn my heart stopped.

DELANEY NICOLE

"May I help you with something?" I mutter through my teeth.

"You need an escort," he states plainly.

"And you—the person that creates fantasies in his mind of how he's going to kill me—are going to be my escort?" I challenge.

"Don't act like you don't have similar fantasies of killing me, princess." He winks and I roll my eyes. "But yes, I will be escorting you because there is no guard, and you do not know your way around yet. Not to mention, you never know when a random creature or rogue soul will decide to roam the halls."

I know he's right. I don't know my way around the palace well enough, and there is no way of getting out of this. "I feel like you are lying about the last part, but fine, lead the way."

CHAPTER 15

"After you," Thanatos says as he opens the heavy oak door.

"A gentleman? How lovely that would be if it weren't tainted with homicidal tendencies."

"What can I say? Chivalry is in my nature." He falls into a stride at my side.

I keep alert, discreetly looking over my shoulder every few seconds to ensure Thanatos isn't drawing one of the swords at his hip.

"Just so you know—"

"Shh." Thanatos stiffens, then pushes me against the cold stone wall, putting his hand against my mouth while the other braces the stone behind my head.

"Don't shush me," I mumble through his hand as I try to push his hand away. It was one thing to tell me to be quiet, but to physically cover my mouth? He is intolerable.

His finger moves over his lips, signaling for me to hush

DELANEY NICOLE

yet again before he points down the hall. I look from the man in front of me toward the opposing end of the corridor. There, a beast with a lion's head, a goat's body, and the tail of a dragon turns the corner—a chimera.

I've never seen one. I've only heard legends. I always thought it was a tale parents told their children in Olympus to make them eat their vegetables. They were monsters. With one pass of their fiery breath, they could take down a village. And now, I am standing before one.

My eyes shoot back to Thanatos who is slowly taking his hand from my mouth. I am skilled in fighting people but seeing a beast I believed to be a legend in real life is terrifying.

"What are we going to do?" I whisper

"We're going to split up," he whispers, looking back at the corner the beast turned.

"Split up? There is a chimera roaming the halls, and you want to split up?"

"Don't tell me you want to stick to my side now."

My eyes narrow. "This is not the time for your jokes."

He rolls his eyes. "Fine. We're going to split up so I can distract it. You will go the other way. Either way, this thing has to get out of the palace."

"How did it get in?"

"Creatures of the Underworld find their way into the castle sometimes. That is why you are supposed to have a guard with you at all times, like I said in the library, which you didn't believe coming from my mouth," he says and sends me a pointed look.

"You never have a guard with you," I say, crossing my arms. "It wouldn't be because I am a woman, would it?"

"What? Of course not. It's because..." He pauses, glaring at me. "This is not what we need to be focusing on. I will head in the direction the chimera went. You go around the other corner."

"But, Thanatos, I don't—" He has already disappeared around the corner. "...know where everything is." I sigh and walk down the other corridor. "Well, this is wonderful."

A pin drop would echo throughout the entirety of the castle. I keep my eyes peeled for any disturbances. It feels like ages since I departed Thanatos's presence. And yet, I haven't heard anything.

A lion's roar breaks out from somewhere in the corridors. It sounds like Thanatos found the chimera. Cries erupt as I run toward the noise. I want to be able to say I fought off a chimera when I return to Olympus. Besides, I can't let Thanatos have all of the fun. A man's yelling pulls my focus from the suits of armor lining the corridor. The chimera is backed against the wall on its hind legs while Thanatos avoids its fiery breath. Its mouth snaps centimeters away from his head.

That was close.

Too close.

I reach for my dagger, planning to throw it at the beast, but my hand grabs an empty sheath. "Shit."

Thanatos still has it.

As if the chimera knows I'm unarmed, it slashes a deep gash in Thanatos's arm. Thanatos releases the beast, clutching his forearm. I don't have time to worry about him though because the monster is charging straight towards me, bearing its sharp teeth, waiting to sink them into my skin.

"Elena, go!" Thanatos shouts. I stand frozen. Fear creeps further in my veins with every step the chimera takes towards me. It's nearly here. I can't move. Everything in me is shutting off. A few more seconds and the chimera will be on me. Every instinct is screaming at me to move but panic claws at my throat, claiming every nerve for itself. Rendering me useless. "Elena!"

I jump out of the way, narrowly missing the chimera's sharp jaw. As my body falls to the ground, my hand touches cold metal armor. It's a suit of armor. No, not just a suit, an armed suit. I look back to find Thanatos battling the chimera against the wall yet again. How did he get to this end of the corridor so fast? I don't have time to think when the beast lets out another long pull of its fiery breath.

I yank the dagger from the suit beside me. My hands shake from the nerves the chimera invoked. Taking a deep, steadying breath, I focus on my target.

The blade spins as it flies through the air. The chimera won't know it is there until it is too late. Whizzing past Thanatos's ear, the blade flies into the mouth of the beast. The lead blade kills it almost instantly.

Thanatos sags. His wide-eyed gaze flies in my direction. "You." He pauses to catch his breath. "You could have killed me."

"I was aiming for your head," I mutter, pulling the blade from the beast's mouth before cleaning the blood from it with its fur.

"I'm glad you missed."

After placing the used blade back in its armor set, we begin our journey back to my quarters. Thanatos said he'd take care of the corpse once I was back in my chambers.

"Just so you know," I looked up at Thanatos, noticing his attention was already fixed on me, "even if you have possession of my dagger, I am trained in hand-to-hand combat. So whether my opponent holds a weapon or not doesn't affect me."

He lets out a small chuckle. "I would expect nothing less."

"Meaning?"

Before I realize what is happening, my back meets cold stone for the second time this evening. Thanatos's non-injured forearm presses hard on my chest. However, he holds no weapon in his hand this time, and he's keeping his hands in fists far from my neck. Still, it deeply annoys me.

"Meaning when we do inevitably throw punches or swipe swords at each other, I know you will put up a fight. You will make me work hard for my victory." His eyes roam across my face. "However, I am not one for unfair fights."

"I save your life, and this is how you repay me?" I let out a short chuckle. This man will never fall short of ways to vex me. "How noble of you to not be a cheater."

"Why would I need to be? I give my enemies advantages and I still come out victorious in the end. Besides, you've already said you meant to aim for my head rather than the chimera. It is a stroke of luck that you missed, and I am still standing before you."

"Maybe you haven't met your match yet," I challenge, ignoring his jab about my dagger throwing.

I watch his jaw clench and unclench several times. I'm

DELANEY NICOLE

working on his nerves, and I enjoy it. "What's wrong? Scared I'm right? Scared you'd lose to a miniscule demi-goddess like me?"

"I hope you're able to keep that same spirit when punches and blows are thrown." He releases his grip on my chest. A rush of relief fills my chest at the lack of pressure.

Before he turns to walk away, Thanatos stops. "Here's to keeping it a fair fight."

In his hand an opal and ivory dagger glimmers in the moonlight—my dagger.

I take it from his hand and revel in the feeling of its weight in my hands. He slowly walks down the quiet stone corridor. I can't stop the words before they fall out of my mouth, "One more thing."

He stops in his tracks as I place my hand on the door, opening it slightly. "I don't miss."

CHAPTER 16

hanatos

I DEPART Elena's room feeling strange. She admitted that she saved my life on purpose. I don't believe I've ever felt like this. This—confused.

I stole her blade. She saved my life in return. I am trying to wrap my head around it. We've been at each other's throats since the beginning, yet she killed the beast instead of letting it kill me.

The words *I don't miss* rang in my brain as I approached Hades's door.

"Thanatos, what can I do for you this evening?" Hades's eyes enlarge when he sees the blood on my arm. The gash is shallow enough to heal on its own. I find it rather annoying

DELANEY NICOLE

that it ruined my favorite shirt though. "Tell me our guest is still alive and breathing."

"She is." I sit in a chair across from him.

Hades's lip pulls up on one side as he places his feet lazily on his desk. "What does this visit pertain to then?"

"There is a dead chimera in one of the corridors," I say, picking the dried blood from beneath my fingernails.

"What?" Hades's eyes grow wide for a moment. "How does a dead chimera end up in one of my corridors?"

"Elena and I found it when I was walking her back to her quarters. I was trying to get it out, and it wasn't working out so well. The beast ended up dying." I shrug in my seat, leaving out the specifics. I catch the inner part of my lip between my teeth, gnawing at the flesh. Why did she save me? She has to have an ulterior motive. And I must figure out what it is.

"I will instruct the guards outside to keep a more careful watch of the entrances." Hades grins with bright mischief after a few minutes of shared silence, "How is your pairing going? You and Elena I mean."

"The usual threats and arguing." I smirk, thinking of our interaction before we left the library.

"Shame the two of you don't get along." Hades meets my smirk. My eyes narrow. Hades is always up for meddling.

"If it makes you feel any better, she was the one that killed the chimera."

His eyes flash with bright amusement. "She saved your ass."

Annoyance floods my veins. Hades's reaction is why I tried to refrain from telling him in the first place. "Oh, please. She is, as the mortals put it, 'all bark and no bite.' The only reason she had the chance to kill it was because I was fighting it off long enough for her to grab a dagger."

"Seems as though I've struck a nerve." He chuckles.

Standing, I begin my walk out of Hades's study. "Tell Persephone I said hello."

"Good night, Thanatos."

In the empty corridor, I go back to running tonight's events through my mind. *I don't miss.*

No matter how hard I try, I can't stop thinking about the look on her face after the dagger missed my ear. It was relief. It was shock. It was calm.

Even after washing the blood of the beast from my skin I knew I couldn't wash the memory of tonight from my mind. No matter how hard I scrubbed. The more I think of it, the more annoyed I grow. I didn't need her to save me. I didn't need saving. I was fine then, and I'm fine now. I don't need saving.

CHAPTER 17

lena

IN THE TWO days since the chimera, I haven't been able to think of a viable reason why Thanatos chose to return my dagger. He claimed it was to keep the fight fair. But if the roles were reversed, I would have kept it. It would have given me an upper hand.

So why did he give it back? I hope it wasn't because I saved his life. I saved him because it would take all the fun out of doing it myself if the beast had. I haven't been able to stop thinking of that altercation.

The scent of lilacs and vanilla fill my nose as I immerse myself in a warm bath. The warmth of the water slowly eases my tense muscles. I soak in the steamy water until it begins to grow cold. Dressing in a lavender gown, I walk to my door. To my surprise, a face I haven't seen in days waits for me.

"Leon!" I grin.

"That was much more enthusiastic than I was expecting. Did you miss me that much?"

"I will not feed your ego further by agreeing." I raise my chin slightly before walking on toward the dining hall.

"I'll take that as a yes." He winks when I roll my eyes. "It is nice to know I'm missed among the ladies."

"That is why I refuse to feed your ego. Besides, I do not speak for all women. Plus, I see you as nothing more than a friend." I look up at him with teasing eyes.

"Aha! You admit we are friends," he beams.

"I could go back to thinking of you as a pest if you'd like," I offer, raising a brow.

"On the contrary, I think it's nice to have you not wanting to ring my throat. Although that, I suppose, is reserved for Thanatos."

I step toward the doors of the dining hall, keeping my gaze forward. "Careful, Leon. Even if I admitted I think of you as a friend, comments like that will make me want to remove your tongue."

"There's the Elena I've come to know and enjoy." Amusement floods his face as he opens the wooden door for me.

"It's good to have you back, Leon."

"It's good to be back."

In the dining hall, Keres and Hypnos are speaking quietly to each other at the table. They pause when I take my usual seat.

"Elena." Hypnos nods politely.

"Good morning." An awkward silence surrounds us. I hate the feeling. It's like my every movement is being analyzed.

"I must applaud you for saving my dear brother against the loose chimera," Keres says, finally breaking the awkward silence.

"It was the least I could go. It certainly didn't look as though he was going to win that battle," I say, scooping fruit onto my plate.

"I will say, Callan does not like admitting when he has been bested—" Hypnos clears his throat, stopping Keres from continuing her sentence. My brows pull together as confusion fills me. Callan? Did she just call Thanatos, *Callan?*

"We should be going. I've promised Keres time in the training ring," Hypnos says, standing from the table with his sister at his side.

I watch in confusion as they hurry from the room whispering. Why did Keres call Thanatos Callan? And why did Hypnos rush them off once she did?

"Elena! How wonderful to see," Hades's voice booms through the dining hall. "Persephone and I were just having a conversation about you."

"All good things, I hope."

Persephone takes her seat across from me. Hades sits down at the head of the table at Persephone's side.

"I was just saying it's nice to have another person here that I can call a friend," Persephone admits. Something within my chest warms. It feels as though things are different in the Underworld. Friendships...genuine ones come easy.

That is something I found very hard in Olympus until I met Stella.

"I have to say, I agree."

"I must add that there are others who have a different view," Hades chimes in between a mouthful of his breakfast.

My brows lift in surprise. "And who, might I ask, is speaking not so fondly?"

"Hades, do not start anything this early in the morning," Persephone warns.

"I had a chat with Thanatos after the chimera snuck in. I checked to ensure he was meeting my request in assisting you. And he…" Hades chuckles, "he told me of your verbal threats toward him. I find them rather amusing. He, however, tells me that you are, 'all bark and no bite.'"

My tongue slides across my cheek while a chuckle of disbelief passes my lips. "And where," I meet Hades's stare, "might I find him now?"

"Thanatos is a busy man." His smirk widens slightly. "However, I believe I heard talk of him and Hypnos wanting to spar under the stars."

"How marvelous," I say in a sweet tone laced with death. "If you'll excuse me, I feel the need to do some training."

I walk with a purpose toward the door of the dining hall. If he truly believed I wouldn't put action behind my words even after saving his life, then he is in for a wicked treat.

"Hades, I told you not to start anything this early," Persephone scolds from the table.

"Darling, it's been a while since we've had any entertainment like this." Hades's tone is still dripping with pleasure.

Determination and hatred burn through me as I throw

open the doors. Leon is standing near the wall. His eyes widen slightly when he catches sight of my demeanor.

"Elena," he speeds after me, "what is the matter?"

"The matter is that I have left a certain Child of the Night unchecked for too long. It's time I show them exactly why I am a favorite of Athena's and what the daughter of Ares can do."

"So you're going to storm in and pummel him? Do you honestly think it will be that easy?" He asks while quickening his step to try to stop me in my tracks. "Because if you do, you are more foolish than I originally thought."

I stop and half turn to catch the guard's alarmed stare. "I hope he fights back."

Leon raises his arms in surrender. This is something I need to do. "Fine, but don't say I didn't warn you."

"I do not need your warning," I grit through my teeth and march forward.

I burst through the door and catch a short glimpse of Keres leaning against the wall. Hypnos stands near the weaponry wall drinking water. In the center of the room, stands Thanatos. His back stays turned to the entrance until he hears my heavy footsteps.

I push hard on his shoulders, which makes him step back with a confused expression.

"I save your ass, and this is how you repay me?" I shove him again. "All bark and no bite, huh?"

"You've been talking to Hades," he states.

"I may have let something slip," Hades says as he enters the training room with Persephone at his side.

"You can't let us have a normal day, can you?" Persephone scolds.

"Darling, I think you're well aware that there is no such thing as a normal day in the Underworld," he says.

I turn back to Thanatos. "Well, what do you say about testing who is really all talk?"

"Careful, princess, that's a box you might not want to open," he teases.

"Brother, you can't say she doesn't put action behind her words, then proceed to do the same," Keres says from the wall. Her tone is more relaxed than I thought it would be. Given our past interactions, I'm half surprised she's taking my side. Or perhaps she's hoping to see me be pummeled by her brother.

"Careful, sister. You might bruise our brother's ego by being right," Hypnos challenges, then walks to her side.

Thanatos's glare shifts toward his siblings, then slowly, his head turns back to me. A mocking smile fills his face but it does not meet his eyes. "If you insist."

"Please don't kill each other," Persephone mutters, bringing her hand to her face.

"If you must make that rule, my lady, then I suppose we will call it a match when one of us lands a spot that would be a killing blow if we used full force," Thanatos says while offering me a sword from the weaponry wall.

"Are you sure you want to start this?" Thanatos went into his ready stance.

"Seems like a question you should be asking yourself," I say before swinging the heavy sword in front of me.

Thanatos leans back before the sword could cut his arm.

A calculating chuckle leaves his mouth. "That would have hurt."

"My apologies. I'll make sure I get you next time." I drive forward again and have to twist to avoid Thanatos's blade.

Swords clash and blows are ducked. Each of us throw calculated blows, just not calculated enough to beseech the other.

It is as though we are dancing in the ring. I take a step back and use my sword to shield myself from Thanatos's. While he regains his footing from his failed attack, I lunge to the side, slicing through the air at an angle to strike his open side. Damn. He dodged it just in time.

Each of his swings forces me further and further back. He's forcing me into a corner. By the time I realize his tactic my back meets cold stone in a harsh thud. His knee slams into my ribs and I lurch forward. The air knocks out of my lungs for a second and I hold my sword diagonally in front of me to block him until I can regain control of my breathing.

"Can we take bets?" Hypnos's voice fills my ears. There is a crowd of spectators, which includes Hades, Persephone, Hypnos, Keres, Leon, and a few other guards.

Deciding to block out the noise around me, I focus on my fighting. Despite my efforts, my breath remains heavy. My sweat is glistening, making my stray hairs stick to my neck. I watch Thanatos's every move in order to block his blows. I will be damned if I allow him to win because I wasn't paying close enough attention. And I'll be damned if he gets me against a wall again. Athena trained me better than that.

"If you give up now, no one will hold you accountable.

They'll understand," Thanatos purrs, his attention locked on me as I stand tall again.

I scoff. "If I didn't know any better, I'd say someone sounds scared. Trying to end the fight early to escape losing to a woman?"

Thanatos takes hold of my arm and spins me around until my back is flush against his chest. His arms wrap around my neck and he says, "You are far from miniscule."

My eyes catch the group against the wall. Hades, Hypnos, and Leon look almost pleased. Persephone's lips are pursed. She almost looks worried. Keres, however, is unreadable. She holds my stare. But then, she offers me a short nod. Is she encouraging me? No, that's impossible.

"I know some that would argue with you." I drive my elbow back with such force that Thanatos's grip around my neck loosens. I turn and swing a harsh blow that Thanatos barely dodges.

"Careful darling, that was a close one." He flashes a bemused smirk.

"Quit moving, and maybe I'll finally best you," I jest.

Thanatos shakes his head. He swings his sword quickly, making me pay more attention to dodging than swinging.

"She's losing," Persephone says.

"You can't say it's all surprising. My brother is death," Hypnos states matter-of-factly.

"Keres," Persephone says again.

"Give it time, Persephone," Keres states calmly.

I block them out again. I'm forced to crouch lower and lower to the ground.

Thanatos brings his sword back to deliver a powerful

blow. His amber eyes shine brightly in the moon-lit training ring. His muscles flex while holding the heavy sword. A single curl twists on his forehead with sweat.

I sweep my leg out and meet his calves. His sword clambers out of his hand. As he falls, I drive upward and hold my sword to his neck.

"Seems as though our winner has emerged," Hades says while ushering everyone to follow him out.

While the others leave, I stand silently over Thanatos. We're both panting as I keep my sword at his neck.

"Was this," I pant, "enough action for you?"

Thanatos's jaw clenches. He grabs the blade, and he fixates on me towering over him. In a blur, I am knocked from my feet. Ice-cold shock floods me.

Standing at my feet is Thanatos, but he is different. Large, feathered wings the color of midnight protrude from his back. They stretch far past his arm span. Each intricately placed feather almost glistens in the moonlight. They are a wonder.

"What..." I begin, my eyes roaming the wings before moving to his face. "How—"

Thanatos storms out of the ring, slamming the door behind him.

I try to process what had just taken place. I won the fight, but that equated to nothing compared to what I saw.

I let out a small huff. "Wings."

* * *

"YOU'RE QUIET TODAY," Leon says.

"Just thinking," I mumble.

"Are you thinking about your victory? I must say it was quite surprising."

"You could say that," I say. I can't get the image of Thanatos's wings out of my mind.

"His ego will be bruised for quite some time." He laughs.

"My goal was achieved then." It made me quite happy to think about the arrogant man's egos being bruised by my victory.

"Send word when you're done with your reading. I will retrieve you."

"You aren't staying down here?"

"You are trusted enough to stay here by your lonesome. You are given a guard in the event that a rebellious soul or monster decides to roam the halls," Leon states calmly as if that was a normal occurrence for me.

I nod, remembering my encounter with the chimera, "Good to know."

Leon chuckles at my wary expression. "Besides the chimera you and Thanatos ran into, it hasn't happened in quite some time, but we like to take precautionary measures. Have fun with your reading."

I enter the great library again. The fireplace lights upon my entrance, casting the same warm light through the room.

After lighting the candles on the tables, I grab the books I had been reading through the last time.

I had just finished reading through the story of Athena's creation when a thud sounded at the door. My gaze snapped toward the noise to see the door opening slowly and in walked Thanatos looking as though he was trying to be quiet.

"It appears you've lost your touch," I say, resting my chin in my hand.

He whirls around. "I have not lost anything."

"Keep telling yourself that," I say as I dive back into the origin story of The Twelve, or rather The Olympians as they were known back then.

"Are you still angry with me?"

"I'm not anything with you." I pause and watch him as he sits in the same chair as the last time we were in the library together. "I wasn't aware that I was fighting a bird."

A loud laugh billows from Thanatos's mouth. A laugh I must admit I was not expecting. "I don't think I've ever been called that before."

A small smile forms on my lips until I catch myself. "There's always a first for everything."

Thanatos holds my gaze. His eyes roamed my face for some time. I could have sworn they even fell to my lips for a few short moments. "Yes, I suppose there is."

Thanatos sits silently in his chair while I read. I can feel his gaze on me. Suddenly, he leans forward and grabs a book. I look up from my book about the origin of Aphrodite. "What are you doing?"

"I was tasked with helping." He shrugs. "You're reading so I suppose I should too."

I hold his stare for a moment, debating whether I care about what this sudden desire to read means or not with my bottom lip between my teeth. Finally, I nod. "Okay."

CHAPTER 18

hanatos

"You are quite literally the most annoying being I believe I have ever encountered." Elena scowls at me.

She knows what her words do to me. "That is not what you were saying earlier."

I lean into her neck, sucking on the soft spot beneath her ear. A sharp gasp leaves her lips as I take hold of the back of her head.

"Callan."

"What is it you want from me?" I ask, pressing my lower half against hers. The smallest whimper leaves her lips. She bites them before I press harder. She's toying with me. And gods if that doesn't make more blood rush to my cock. "Use your words, Elena."

DELANEY NICOLE

"You know." Another whine escapes as I move her on my hips. My hand skims up her thigh, past the dagger she keeps strapped there, to her backside. "You know what I want."

Her eyes are heavy with lust, almost glassy. She wants this badly. And I want her to tell me exactly what she wants. I need her to do it fast.

I roll my hips, knowing I rubbed that bundle of nerves between her thighs because a low moan leaves her lips. "I need you to be more specific."

"I want you, Callan. I want every part of you," she says as her hands glide between us. I can't stop the groan that parts my mouth when her delicate hand begins tracing the outline of my hard cock. "Especially this part."

I startle awake and search my room only to find it dark and empty. Sweat is glistening on my chest as I try to catch my breath.

I just had an erotic dream about Elena. I am not even attracted to her, no matter how much the hardness of my dick may suggest that as of now. I would have the same reaction to a dream like that about anyone. It has nothing to do with Elena.

I continued to tell myself this as I made my way to the dining hall for an early breakfast. A sigh of relief passes through my lips when I find only my brother in the hall. I do not know if I could handle anyone else's presence at this moment.

"Good morning, brother," Hypnos says. "You're up early."

"I couldn't sleep," I say as I plop into my usual seat before fixing myself a plate.

"Is everything alright? It is not like you to have trouble sleeping even when your time in the mortal realm is taxing."

I take a deep gulp of the wine provided. "Yes, everything will be alright. I'm sure a round in the training arena will do me good."

"Would you like me to accompany you? Or perhaps I could have Leon fetch Miss Elena. Your brawl was quite the show—"

"That will not be necessary," I snap. I regain my composure after seeing my brother's enlarged eyes. "I would like to train alone this morning. Thank you for the offer, brother."

Not waiting to hear my brother's response, I leave the dining hall as quickly as I can. I need something to relieve me from this strange feeling.

* * *

THANKS TO TRAINING, I feel ready for the next few hours of reading with Elena. I stop just in front of the large doors, looking up to read the inscription again.

Fighting for those you hold closest will prevail above all else.

It serves as a reminder of my duty to protect my family every time I enter the library. It is empty and dark. I busy myself lighting the candles on the tables and pulling the books she's been reading from the shelves.

"You're early today." Elena's voice fills my ears, and I get a flashback to the dream that drew me from sleep this morning. *"I want you."*

"I finished with my other tasks, so I thought I would come down early," I say, hurrying to sit in my seat.

DELANEY NICOLE

Elena eyes me with a concerned expression. "I guess we can get to work then."

"Marvelous idea," I say, grabbing the first book in the stack and flipping to a random page. I do not dare look up to see what Elena does.

Elena reads about whatever member of The Twelve she was on now. I find myself watching her read in peaceful silence. I can't seem to take my eye off of her. Her delicate finger thrums the pages, and I am yet again pulled into my dream where her fingers traced the outline of my hard cock. *"Especially this part."*

"Thanatos..." she says. "Thanatos?"

The harshness of my name falling from her lips the second time pulls me from my trance. "Yes?"

"Are you actually going to read with me or was that some lapse of judgment the last time we were in here?" she asks as she assesses me with a pointed look.

"Yes. But I'm feeling a bit ill today. I should take my leave for the evening. I will tell Leon to escort you to your quarters when you are ready," I say.

I rush out of the library. As soon as the heavy door clicks shut, I release a harsh breath. "I need my head examined."

CHAPTER 19

lena

"You may come in," I yell.

Leon's dark hair peeks through the door. "Persephone has asked to see you again."

"By all means, lead me to her," I say.

In my short time in the Underworld, Persephone has only shown me kindness and respect. But she also isn't afraid of hitting me with the harsh truths either. She speaks like a true queen.

As Leon and I walk to the star-gazing room, I notice a portrait of Hades sitting in his throne on the wall. I stop and examine the brush work of it. How even an oil paint rendition of Hades radiates darkness and power. The artist somehow captured the way fire dances behind Hades eyes, just waiting to erupt with the smallest inclination of displeasure. His dark beard is trimmed neatly and his shoulder length hair combed just as uniform. His dark gray chiton adorned with crisp gold clips somehow solidifies the regality of it all.

"Wow, it's beautiful," I say, in awe of the work.

I turn to see Leon gazing at the art with the same appreciative eye. "It was done by an artist close to Hades."

"What used to be there?" I ask, pointing to the bare spot next to it. From the other corridors I've traveled down, Hades is too keen to detail to leave such a large spot empty like this..

"Some other random piece of art," Leon answers after we start walking again. "If I'm not mistaken a portrait of Persephone is supposed to go up soon."

As we turn the corner, I can't shake a question I've had since I realized how deep Persephone and Hades' connection really is. "Leon?"

"Yes?"

"If Persephone is the daughter of Demeter and Zeus, and Hades is Zeus's brother, wouldn't that make him—"

Leon chuckles before saying, "No, Elena, Persephone is not fucking her uncle. Zeus and Hades have no actual relation. They call each other brothers as a familiarity. The only connection they have is Poseidon. Poseidon and Hades share the same mother while Poseidon and Zeus share the same father."

"Good to know," I nod, feeling slightly relieved.

"Glad to be of service."

When I enter the blue and gold room I see Keres lounging lazily in one of the blue-velvet chairs.

"Hello," I say timidly. Something about Keres incites fear deep within me. It runs so deep, I'm unsure where I start and where it ends.

"You do not need to be afraid of me," she says. I gulp when one of Keres's fingernails morphs into a sharp talon. "I have no intention of harming you, unless you give me a valid reason."

"Keres, I warned you about your threats," Persephone says shortly. It eases the tension in my shoulders.

Keres rolls her eyes. The talon is gone and her hands look human again. Maybe I hallucinated it. "You take the fun out of everything."

Persephone whirls, snapping her eyes toward the woman in the blue-velvet chair. Keres raises her arms in surrender. "I was joking. You know I enjoy pestering you."

A satisfied smirk lines Persephone's lips as she turns back to me. "Sorry about her. We're still working on the friendly aspect of her existence."

I smile at the jab. "It's alright. I'm used to such words. Besides, I use similar methods with others."

I find the interaction amusing, mainly because Keres knew not to test Persephone. Perhaps it is Persephone I should be scared of rather than the Children of the Night.

"Like with my brother." Keres readjusts in the seat.

"Yes, your brother does receive quite a bit of it." I nod.

"Don't stop on my account. I enjoy seeing his ego taken down a few notches. It's been too long since someone chal-

DELANEY NICOLE

lenged it the way you do. As long as that is the only thing you are challenging." Keres shoots me a warning glare at that.

A small flush of relief flows through me. But it only goes so far at the threat she kept laced in her words. She may not be plotting to kill me in my sleep but she will certainly try when I make good on my task against her brother.

"I thought it would be nice for the two of you to become acquainted. What better way than sharing a meal overlooking the fields?"

"You're forgetting that not all of us spend our days looking at fields of flowers nor consider it fun," Keres says, seemingly more focused on her nails than the conversation.

Persephone raises her middle finger toward Keres. I find it hard to contain my giggle. It is quite funny to see a goddess known for her kindness and beauty using such vulgar gestures.

"And you try to teach me about being friendly," Keres teases.

"Perhaps, she's picked up on your habits," I say with an inclined brow as I take a seat across from Keres.

"She has a point," Persephone adds.

"Fair enough," Keres says.

Trays of small cakes and cups of different wines are carried in by the chefs. I have never seen such a decadent spread. I have heard of spreads like this being at parties thrown by The Twelve, specifically Dionysus, but I had never seen it for myself as I was never invited to such parties.

"Are you alright, Elena? You look as thought you've seen a ghost," Persephone says. "Although, that would not come as a shock here."

"No, it's just that I've never received such treatment in Olympus," I say, feeling myself grow timid as both Keres and Persephone look at me with puzzled expressions. "Never mind, it's a bit silly."

"What do you mean?" Keres asks as she grabs a small cake.

"Things like this," I motion to the spread before us, "were only ever in parties thrown by The Twelve. I was never in attendance at such parties."

"Surely a child of Ares would have been invited?" Persephone asks, then takes a short sip of deep red wine from her chalice.

"Others were." I nod. "My brothers were."

Persephone's brows scrunch, her face contorts in confusion for only a moment until it finally smooths in a pained understanding.

"What is it?" Keres inquires, looking toward Persephone for an answer.

"I never received an invite to the parties because my mother was not a goddess like my brother's," I say, realizing how ridiculous the whole situation sounds.

"But you're as much a child of Ares as they are," Keres says.

"I am, but their mother is Aphrodite. My mother was a mortal. I'm sure you're familiar with Zeus's distaste of the gods mingling with mortals," I say while it looks like Keres is radiating anger from her seat. Surely, she is not angry on my behalf.

"Doesn't Zeus have relations with mortals quite often?"

"He does." Persephone nods. "That's one thing about the

king of gods, he will set forth rules he expects everyone to follow except himself."

"So you are not invited because you are born from a mortal and fathered by a god?" I nod at Keres's inquiry. "Yet Zeus takes pride in his children that are born both demigods and goddesses?"

Persephone nods. "I've always hated my father's hypocrisy. Elena, I'm so sorry. I had no idea how bad it was in Olympus."

"There's nothing you could have done, Persephone. It's an unspoken rule. It's only like that with me because I was brought to the city when I was only minutes old. Typically, for a demigod or goddess to live in Olympus, they have to prove themselves worthy. They must become heroes. I have not. So some view me as entitled because of it."

Most expect the life of a demigoddess living in the city of the gods to be remarkable. But this was the first time I have ever told anyone about my life in Olympus even if it was a tiny piece.

Keres eyes me skeptically in silence. I can't quite decide what she's thinking and part of me doesn't want to know. Finally, she breaks the silence after pouring herself a tall glass of wine. "Olympus seems like a pretentious hellhole."

I giggle, then a genuine laugh bursts from my mouth for the first time since I arrived in the Underworld. Persephone follows suit with a light-hearted giggle.

"That wasn't a joke." Keres looks between the two of us as though we've gone mad.

"We know." I laugh and clutch my stomach. "We're laughing because it's true."

A CURSE OF HONOR

Keres looks suspiciously between us before her own laugh filters through the air.

* * *

I ENTERED the library to find the candles lit, the books stacked neatly on the table, and the man I was told to be careful around sitting in one of the old chairs reading.

A small flutter disrupts my stomach. I stop dead in my tracks when I realize a small grin has formed on my lips.

What is wrong with me? This is Thanatos, the man that brings death to mortals. Mortals like my mother.

"You're here early," I say, trying to mask whatever momentary insanity passed through me.

"I figured the sooner I got here and prepared everything for you, the sooner you could finish reading and I could get away from you," he says, looking up from his book.

"Charming," I say sarcastically.

"I try." He winks. The silence that follows is tension-ridden as we wait to see who will crack and speak first. So far, we are both winning.

I am growing restless, so I resort to tapping my finger on the edge of the book to give myself something to do.

Thanatos huffs as he drops his book on the table. "Would you like to go on a walk around the palace?"

"Why would I do that?" I ask. Secretly, I revel in my victory over him in our silent competition.

"Well, no one can get anything done with you incessantly tapping." He motions to my finger, which is still tapping the old book. I still my finger.

DELANEY NICOLE

"As if anyone could get anything done with your constant shuffling," I counter. It was true. Every five seconds, he was shifting in his seat.

"Ugh! You are an impossible woman." He rolls his eyes.

"And you're an arrogant man just like the rest of them," I snap, then I return to my book slightly annoyed. I try to read, yet find my mind focusing on anything but the words on the page. I drop the book and let my head fall on its pages in defeat.

"Come on." He waves at me to stand then he glides gracefully across the room.

I follow at his side through the dark corridors. I can see through the windows that we are walking past the Elysian fields and the Asphodel Meadows I often look upon with Persephone. "Where are we going?"

"You will see when we get there," he says.

"You're not taking me somewhere to kill me, are you?"

Before I can take another step forward, my back meets cold stone, and a warm hand wraps around my neck. A devious smirk marks Thanatos's lips. "If I wanted to kill you, I would have done it by now."

"I suppose I'll take that as a comfort," I say as I try to look down at his hand wrapped around my throat before meeting his eyes. His hand isn't squeezing. It is more or less sitting there.

"Take it however you want, darling." His eyes flash with something darker. "But don't pretend you don't enjoy it when I have you against a wall."

I scoff as I try to keep the heat in my cheeks at bay. "Let me go."

"As you wish." Thanatos releases me.

We walk in silence again. I spend the next several minutes trying to collect myself—the nerve of him. If either of us like it when I am against a wall, it is him.

"Can I ask you something?" I ask, feeling a wave of confidence.

"I suppose."

"How do you do it?"

The space between his brows creases. "Do what?"

"How do you do what you do?" I ask as we walk out onto a large balcony. The landscape is much different than that seen from Persephone's balcony. Here, the land on one side seems to be dead. On the other side, it dives deep into the ground, looking as though someone set fire to it. "You know, taking the lives of mortals?"

Thanatos's head sinks. He studies his feet, but his voice is almost a whisper as he says, "It's what I was made to do."

"That's your excuse? That you're made to do it? You're made to take the lives of innocent mortals?" My tone sharpens as I wonder if he would say the same thing if he knew about my mother who died before I could even meet her.

"You can believe I'm a monster. It doesn't affect me anymore." His eyes are harsh as they meet mine. "It's what everyone thinks. That's why my siblings and I joined Hades's court. He's the only one that sees us as more than monsters as you clearly see me."

"What makes you a monster is that you take those that aren't supposed to be taken."

A sharp laugh comes from Thanatos. "Is that what high

DELANEY NICOLE

and mighty Zeus told you? Darling, let me tell you this, I do not answer to any god. I answer to The Fates. No god—no matter how bad Zeus wants to believe he is—is above The Fates."

I stand completely stricken by the information. "I– I don't understand."

"Of course not." A huff leaves his mouth. "You were spoon-fed information about my siblings and I being evil, were you not?"

I don't have to speak for Thanatos to realize he is right. "But you do take the souls of mortals. You kill them."

"I only take the souls of those that The Fates tell me to. I bring them here, and their souls are transported to wherever they belong."

I don't know what to say. I choose to look out over the rivers ahead of us. I need a moment to collect my thoughts. Nothing makes sense. "Where are we?"

"We are overlooking Tartarus and the rivers that surround it. It's not a pleasant place. It's all darkness. It's what mortal children and even adults are taught to fear about the Underworld." He pauses, placing his arms to lean on the balcony. "But it's one of my favorite places to look out on."

I look out over the vast land before me. Tartarus is where the souls of the damned go. There is a part of me that I keep buried from everyone that finds it comforting knowing the darkness is all around, rather than on the inside.

I turn towards Thanatos. "Does it ever bother you?" His eyes catch mine, and it is like I am seeing them for the first time. They are like pools of warm honey even in the darkness of the night. "Taking souls?"

"It used to." He leans against the balcony again. "It still does sometimes."

"Sometimes?" My face scrunches in confusion.

"Usually when the mortal's family is near. Seeing them can take a toll. Or if the mortal was pure and kind."

"And what of those in war?"

"I can't take all of the credit for that. Deaths like that are brought on by Keres." My stomach drops. That's why I feel uneasy around her. She must be the one my father thought he saw on a battlefield. "She is the bringer of violent death. She also doesn't do it on her own."

My confusion must be obvious because a knowing grin spreads on Thanatos's face. "She can shift and split into two. She can take the forms of monsters. But she rarely does that."

I feel my eyes grow more expansive than they've ever been. That explains the talon she flashed me earlier. "What?"

"Yes. But as I said, she doesn't do it often. She only does it when she needs it most."

"But why? If she has the ability, then why only use it sparingly?"

Thanatos seems as though he is contemplating telling me the truth. "It's for safety." He decided to elaborate more. "Abilities like Keres's draw the attention of those who want to use it as a weapon. Some try to capture us in hopes of using us against their foes."

"You've been captured?"

"Yes. In a small sack, actually," he says. "That's why I

DELANEY NICOLE

started training, to keep an incident like that from happening again."

"Wait." My face lights up, recalling a small remark I heard my first night here. "Was that what Hypnos meant when he mentioned Sisyphus?"

Thanatos huffs. "Yes."

I laugh. It is amusing to picture the strong man at my side being trapped inside a small sack. Each time I imagine it, I laugh again.

"Go ahead, get it out. Laugh all you want."

"I'm sorry. It is comical to picture you trapped in a tiny sack."

"Are you really, though?" He looks back at me with a skeptical expression.

"Am I what?"

"Sorry?"

I try my hardest to hold in my laughs. "Not really."

Thanatos chuckles with a full smile that shows a dimple in both of his cheeks. My laugh dissipates as my gaze falls upon the smiling man next to me. He is smiling from an interaction with me.

I clear my throat, trying to keep my mind clear. "I ran into Keres and Hypnos the morning of our brawl. Keres was applauding me for saving your ass, but she called you a different name, Callan..."

Thanatos stiffens. His jaw tenses for a moment before he finally says, "It's a second name. The three of us wanted names separate from the ones that carry dark reputations. I chose Callan. Very few call us by our second names. Only those we trust are allowed to call us by our second names."

I don't know what to do with this information. But it makes me wonder..."If Keres is the goddess of violent death. What of Hypnos?"

"He is the god of sleep."

I'm not particularly surprised. Hypnos seems different than his siblings. I just didn't know how different. "And you?"

His jaw sets. "I'm the god of peaceful death."

It feels as though the wind has been knocked out of me. If what Thanatos says is true, then what Zeus told me is a lie. He isn't the monster everyone portrays him to be. None of the Children of the Night are. Well, Keres is technically.

"Are you alright?" Thanatos asks.

I nod despite feeling queasy as the weight of this realization hits me. "I need to return to my quarters."

"I can walk you if—"

"No." I back up and try to keep my breath steady. "That's quite alright."

I speed walk back into the palace. I need to get away from him.

"Elena!" Thanatos's voice fills the corridor. I turn my head over my shoulder and watch as he tries to catch up to me.

I keep walking. I have to get away. I ignore his calls until I finally reach my door and slam it shut when I reach the other side.

"Elena, are you alright?"

I say nothing. I wait until I hear his footsteps leave. It takes several minutes, but eventually his steps move farther and farther away until I no longer hear them.

When I'm sure he's gone, I poke my head out of the door. I quietly enter the deserted corridor and speed toward Persephone's room.

I skid to a halt and hide behind the corner when a guard passes the other end of the hall. I quiet my panicked breathing as much as I can until I know he's gone.

I knock as quietly as I can on Persephone's door so as to not draw the guards attention back here. I keep knocking until Persephone opens the door with furrowed brows.

"Elena, is everything alright? What are you doing here at this late hour?"

Before she can say another word, I take a step in and wait for her to close the door. I twist my fingers around each other with my nerves and Persephone's expression turns more worried by the second. "Elena, what has happened?"

"We need to leave."

"What—"

I grasp her shoulders in my hands, hoping my urgency will transfer to her. "Don't you see it is all a deception. They want us to believe their lies so that they can continue their vulgar behavior. We can leave tonight. No one has to know."

"No."

"Persephone you are not listening. They are deceiving everyone. They are monsters. We must—"

"No!" Persephone shouts. I startle at her abrupt tone, my hands falling from her shoulders. "You have crossed a line."

"But—"

"If anyone is being deceptive, it is you, Elena. Am I wrong?"

I gulp, afraid my words will betray me.

Persephone levels me with a harsh stare. "I am not going anywhere. I have told you once, and I will tell you again. The Underworld is my home now.

"We have granted you permission to use our facilities for the task you were given. I suggest you continue your research without meddling in my affairs or you will come to understand why the Children of the Night—however monstrous you believe them to be—know not to test me. Are we clear?"

I find it hard to speak after her scolding but another authoritative glare from Persephone draws the words straight from my lips. "Yes."

"Good. Now I suggest you go back to your bedchamber."

I nod, letting my head hang as I make my way to the door. But before I can make it out, I turn. "Persephone, are you going to tell Hades?"

Skepticism fills Persephone's eyes. "Not this time. I want to give you another chance to see the Underworld for what it truly is. But do not mistake my kindness for weakness. If you pull a stunt like this again, you will not only feel my wrath, but Hades as well."

CHAPTER 20

hanatos

It has been days since I've seen Elena. She's been avoiding me. But that ends now. I stop behind a wall near Elena's quarters when I hear Leon's voice.

"Elena, dinner is ready for you in the dining hall. And before you ask, no, none of them are there. Specifically, Thanatos."

I let out a puff of air. Is this how they interact when they're alone? I must say, it is much different than Leon claims it to be.

Elena scowls as she steps into the corridor. "That is not what I was going to say."

"Really?" The pair begin to walk in toward the direction of the dining hall. I follow, wanting to see if she will mention what happened on the balcony. "What were you going to say then?"

"I was going to comment on how you barged into my room as if there wasn't a possibility I was dressing."

"That would have been a treat to see." I can practically hear the grin in his words.

Elena's head whips back toward him. "You're a swine."

Fair point.

He chuckles. "You wound me."

"That just means you know it's true."

I find myself having to fight a grin. This woman has a fire within that I've never seen. It's mesmerizing.

Leon's focus draws to Elena. "Why did you walk out on Thanatos the other evening?"

I feel my breath drawl tight. Elena appears to have had the same reaction.

"I…" she sputters.

"He told me what happened after he asked if I had spoken to you," Leon says. So much for not selling me out.

"He shouldn't have told you," Elena murmurs, quickening her steps. I can't explain the slight pain I feel in my chest at how dismissive she is.

"But he did." Leon matches her stride. I slow. The more this conversation keeps going, the more I don't want to hear.

"I didn't ask him to."

Leon speeds forward, stopping Elena in her tracks. I stop much further down the corridor. There is a chance I will miss what they say, and maybe I like that.

"But he did. Now I know how you feel toward him and how he feels toward you, but can you at least try to see what

DELANEY NICOLE

I'm getting at? He told you about his past because he wanted to prove he isn't what you think. He's never corrected someone before."

I feel my blood pound in my ears. Leon is right. I've never bothered to correct someone on how they see me. What is it about this girl that drives me so mad?

"Excuse me. I have a meal waiting for me."

Trying to speak with her now will only do more damage than good. I turn and begin to walk back to my quarters before Leon's voice catches me.

"You've lost your touch, Callan."

I turn with a grin. "Losing my touch? I think you've been drinking too much wine, Leon."

"I can see it in her eyes, you know," Leon adds, "She believes what you told her."

My jaw tightens. "Yes, but she doesn't want to believe it."

"Give her time, old friend," Leon says.

* * *

I LAY atop my bed for what feels like ages, then it occurs to me. It is a shot in the dark, but if she is there, it could mean that Leon is right. Jumping from my bed, I speed toward the one place I hope she will be.

As I arrive, I feel a breath of relief fill my lungs because, there, standing on the balcony I showed her days ago, is Elena.

"I'd hoped to find you out there," I say, fearing her reaction to my presence. I don't want her to run again. I want to

A CURSE OF HONOR

know what I said that made her feel she needed to leave my presence.

"It's peaceful," she murmurs, then she leans on the balcony railing.

"That's why it is my favorite part of the palace. It's dark, but it's peaceful darkness. It's welcoming, like home," I say, resting my forearms on the stone railing.

Elena stays fixed on the scene before us as she says, "Believe me, I know the feeling."

What darkness could a girl like her have? I want to know, but I know not to press to hear more. It isn't my place.

She continues anyway. "I grew up as the only demi-goddess in Olympus City. I constantly hear comments about how I do not deserve my place in the city since I did not earn it. They say I am a weak demi-goddess that will never amount to anything. I try to use their insults as fuel in my training. At the age of five, I decided that I would not only be better than all of the warriors, but I would lead them. They would answer to me."

"You were a strong-minded child," I say as I envision her as a young girl wielding fake swords.

"I was."

"You still are strong-willed. But a child should never be forced to grow up too fast. It makes the world seem to lose its luster," I say before catching Elena's gaze. Her eyes are bright with life, but something darker lurks deeper.

Elena forces her focus back to the fields ahead of us. "Yes, well, it only prepared me for what I would experience later in life."

"Meaning?"

Elena takes a deep breath. I'd like to know what lurks beneath the surface of those pretty eyes and defensive shell. "Life on Mount Olympus isn't as glamorous as The Twelve, mainly Zeus, want people to believe. If you're a woman, you're more or less expected to run a storefront. Men are expected to join the army. Obviously, some women join too.

"Athena has been working on building an army of women. But right now, we are few and far between. Of course, that means the women that do fight are easier to target by the others."

"Is this where Apollo comes in?"

Elena nods. "We met at one of the Muses's taverns. I believe he overheard Athena telling Artemis about the new ranks she was trying to form. I was mentioned, and before the night ended, he approached me."

"Your tone makes me believe there's more to that story." I turn and lean against the stone. She sounds tired but not in need of sleep, more like tired of living the life she had before. It is an exhaustion that comes from the soul. One I can understand.

She takes another deep breath. "A relationship with Apollo is...different. We were happy in the beginning. We could barely separate from each other. For once in my life, I felt accepted. But things started changing slowly. He started changing. He was snappier or quicker to anger. I never knew what caused it. He'd yell, we'd fight, he'd leave, and we wouldn't speak to one another for a few days. But he always made his way back."

My jaw tightens. "Why did you let him come back?"

Her eyes are becoming glassier by the second. "As I said, we were happy once. We are still happy sometimes."

A tear falls from Elena. But I needed to know one thing. "Did he ever lay a hand on you?" The thought of it angers me to my core and it causes bile to crawl up my throat.

She shakes her head. "Not in the sense you're referring to. He is only verbal."

I want to give her time to digest. She's trusting me with this information. In all honesty, I do not trust myself to not say something that will upset her more right now. It angers me to think she's put up with such treatment because he was the first to make her feel accepted.

When I finally feel calm enough to speak, I say, "You have to stop tolerating the numerous lows just for the few, short highs."

Another tear falls down her cheek. "It's not that simple. He was the first to accept me in a sea of those against me."

"That's why you're on this task for The Twelve, isn't it? So they will finally accept you?" I fix my eyes on Elena's face. A crack moves its way through my chest when she nods and another tear cascades down her cheek.

"I've learned a valuable lesson from my years of being around the mortals," I say, catching her eye. Her light blue eyes are filled with pain, rigid like an arctic sea. "Just because someone is in your life doesn't mean they're supposed to be."

A puff of air leaves her pouty lips.

"Have you ever told anyone about Apollo?" I ask. She shakes her head, letting another tear fall. She's trusting me with this like I trusted her with information about my family. I hesitate grabbing her shoulder but the next tear to

DELANEY NICOLE

slip down her cheek makes me forget whatever self preservation I had left. My hand falls on her delicate shoulder and she sags into my touch.

"I ran the other day because I saw my assumptions about you cracking, and it scared me." She stared below us and I raised my eyebrows.

"And now?" I hold my breath as I wait for an answer.

This time, there is no hesitation in her answer. "It's completely shattered."

CHAPTER 21

lena

WE HOLD each other's gaze. Something changed in the way I look at Thanatos. I can't understand what it was, but it is different than before. Whether it is good or bad, I don't know.

Thanatos breaks our eye contact and moves toward the palace. My shoulder suddenly felt frigid in the absence of his warm touch.

"Where are you going?" I call out. A pang fills my chest. He is leaving. I shouldn't be surprised. It's what everyone does.

"Making sure that image is completely irreparable." He extends his hand out to me. My eyes flicker from his face to his hand, then back to his face.

"Meaning?"

My heart is beating rapidly in my chest.

"You're going to have to trust me." He smiles. "I won't let any harm come to you. I promise."

I hesitate for only a moment before I take his hand. My breath hitches. His hand is warm and calloused from training but smooth. It's funny. In my mind, I always pictured his hand to be as cold as ice like his heart.

"I'm going to need you not to freak out, princess," he mumbles. Before I can question him, I am scooped into his arms and held tightly to his chest as he soars into the air. I hadn't even seen his wings come out.

"Thanatos, what are we doing?" I yell over the wind. My arms are wrapped tightly around his neck to relieve the feeling of falling.

"Please, call me Callan."

My breath hitches as my eyes connect with his. "What are you doing?"

"I'm showing you what I do," he responds coolly. He tightens his grip around my body. I can feel his heart beating against me.

"It would have been nice if you'd asked me before swooping me up into the air," I say half-heartedly.

"Relax, we'll be in the mortal realm before you know it."

I stiffen. "The mortal realm?"

I never thought I would be visiting the mortal realm. Let alone with him.

"That's one of the requirements for me to take the souls of mortals," he says.

"I know that. It's just...the last time I was in the mortal realm was when I was born and my mother died."

"Welcome back to your birthplace." Thanatos's breath hits the shell of my ear as he speaks. Each word sends shivers down my spine.

I look around us at our new setting. It is unlike the path I took with Hermes. Small buildings freckle the vast land below. Orange hues pour out of each home from the fires that are lit within them. Herds of animals surround them.

The air was much colder than it should have been in Greece. Though I had never been back to the mortal realm, my birthplace, I knew this was not how it was supposed to be.

"Where are we?" I ask, looking at Thanatos.

"We're in Cyprus, famously known for being the birthplace of Aphrodite."

We are getting closer to the ground on the outskirts of the city. "Why must you collect this mortal's soul?"

With a quiet thud, I am placed back on my feet outside a small home. The bright glow of fire peaks through the windows of the hearth. Purple calla lilies sit near the window. A slight breeze sweeps through, which makes me tuck my arms into my chest.

"You will see when we enter," Thanatos strides forward with his usual confidence.

"You think I'm going in there with you?" He has to have gone mad if he believes I will walk in there with him to watch him take the soul of an innocent mortal.

His amber eyes flash toward me. They appear much

brighter with the light of the fire cascading over them. "It's the only way you'll see that I speak the truth."

With a huff of defeat, I walk timidly toward the door. Thanatos waits at the threshold.

The inside of the home is tiny and proves the owners don't have much fortune. There is a single bed in the corner, a small table, and a kitchen on the other side of the tiny home. The entire dwelling is one room. But even though it's small, something about it feels homey. I can feel the love that flowed through it. It pains me to think Thanatos is about to rip that away.

In the center of the room is a small middle-aged couple. The woman is crouched over the man, dabbing his forehead with a small cloth. He is sick.

"You can come in. They can't see us. It's part of my powers. I'm able to glamour myself, and others, if I feel the need," Thanatos says. He crouches at the man's head. His wife stands, dampening the cloth once more.

I take a few steps forward. "Why must you take him?"

Thanatos takes a short breath. "There's a sickness spreading among the mortals. With the lack of food and other resources available to the commoners, they die."

"Why has it happened?" I already know the reason, but I hope I am wrong.

"Do you not know?" His gaze flicks from the sick man to me. I shake my head, not wanting to believe it until he confirms my thoughts. "Because of the chill, crops have been failing. The mortals are losing the sustenance they need to survive because of it. It started spreading after Persephone arrived in the Underworld."

It felt as though someone had stolen the air from my lungs. It couldn't be. "Demeter."

"Anastasia…" The man's voice is weak.

The woman turns, then brings the cloth to his skin. "Yes, darling?"

"I love you. I always have, and I will even when I am in the Underworld." His voice grows weaker and weaker with each word. His time is drawing near.

"Darling, don't speak like that. You are not dying tonight." A tear falls down her cheek as she grasps his hands between her palms.

I meet Thanatos's eyes. This will be the end for this loving couple. A lump begins to form in my throat.

"My only hope," the man whispers, "is that I will see you again, my dearest, Anastasia."

The sound of the man's dying breath fills the air as Thanatos strokes his cheek—the stroke of death. My eyes begin to sting.

"Chariton?" His wife calls.

"Chariton? No, please. Please come back! Come back!" She wails. Her screams fill the home, rattling my bones as Thanatos stands from the ground.

I force myself to leave the home because I cannot bear to watch the women's torment any longer.

"Elena?" Thanatos's voice is soft. "What is it?"

"Nothing," I mutter while tears streak my cheeks.

His warm hand lifts my chin. "It is not nothing if it makes you cry. What is it?"

"I just—" I sigh. "Watching you, in there, made me realize that is how my mother must've died before I was old enough to form a memory of her."

His shoulders sag. "You know that death is a part of a mortal's life, so I will not bother explaining that to you. What I will say is that if I was the one to deliver her soul, then she did not feel any pain. She simply passed in the most peaceful way a soul can."

His words oddly make me feel better. They were like a comforting hug that healed the longer it sat there. I nod to let him know I understand what he is telling me.

"I was going to bring you with me to deliver his soul to the Underworld, but I do not wish to upset you further. I will deliver his soul, and you will stay here," Thanatos says. "You must stay right here. Do not go anywhere or wander away from this spot."

I nod, feeling a few last tears fall down my cheeks.

With a whoosh, I am left outside of the mortal's home. I stare at the stars above me as a wail from the mortal's wife fills the air.

I turn back to look at the weeping woman, and I feel something I've never felt before thrum inside my body. It feels like waves of despair, anger, and acceptance are sweeping through me all at once. My hands feel as though they are warming, vibrating almost.

Before I know what I am doing, I'm drawn into the house, sinking to my knees in front of Anastasia. I reach out but hesitate when I hear Thanatos say, "Elena, what are you doing?"

"I want to help her," I mutter in a trance-like state. My hands humming with unknown power.

"There is nothing you can do. No one has the power to

help her. We must go," Thanatos urges, sounding sterner though it is muffled in my ears. All I hear is the woman's cries.

"Let me try."

"Elena," he warns.

All goes quiet when my palm brushes the woman's cheek. A breeze sweeps through the air. She is no longer screaming or weeping. Her eyes hold pain but not in the same way they had. There is a new light in her eyes, and that causes a grin to form on my lips. I feel at peace now, no longer vibrating with power or raging with emotions.

"What did you do?" Thanatos snaps, eyeing the scene with panicked eyes.

"I don't know. I touched her." I stood to my feet, finally pulled from the strange trance I was in. I have no idea what I did.

Gripping my wrist, Thanatos edges us to the door. "We must go. We have to tell Hades immediately."

"Has anything like that ever happened to you?"

Thanatos scoops me into his arms. "No."

Without another word, we're soaring. What have I done?

As the night air switched from cold to warm I knew we were close. The closer we get to the palace, the more it feels like my stomach is twisting in knots.

Thanatos sets me down on my feet at the front doors, then sped into the palace.

"Are you angry with me?" I ask, following him.

DELANEY NICOLE

"I'm just trying to figure out what you did." His tone has an icy bite to it.

My steps falter. "You're telling me you've never had an experience like that?"

He stops and faces me. "No. Loved ones of the dead have always been the same. Even if I see them in passing, later on, they always look hollow as if they are never the same, as though they've sunk into despair. What you did is something I've never seen."

"Thanatos?" A familiar voice calls from the end of the corridor. Leon is standing in the hallway. "We must go to the throne room—immediately."

"Has something happened?" I ask, knowing there is no possible way that they have already gotten word of what happened with the mortal woman.

"You'll know when we get there." Leon turns and walks back toward the throne room. "May I ask where you two were? Not trying to kill each other, I hope."

"I took her to the mortal realm."

Leon stops in front of me, almost causing me to run into his muscled back. "We need to hurry."

My stomach bubbles with nerves as we approach the throne room. Any more nerves and I'm afraid my anxiety will never settle.

Leon opens the door with sudden agility. Multiple heads turn toward the door including Hades, Persephone, Keres, Hypnos, Sebastian, and three women I don't recognize. One with light hair, the next with brown-black hair, and the third with fiery red hair.

"Elena, where were you? We all were searching for you."

Persephone rushes forward, assessing me and Thanatos with alarm in her eyes.

"My apologies, Lady Persephone, she was with me." Thanatos catches her gaze.

"Why was she with you?" she asks as she releases me from her hold.

"I showed her what I do. She's hated me for a false impression that she formed in her mind. I thought it was fitting to show her the truth." His eyes sweep over each person in the room. I could have sworn his face grew a shade paler when he noticed the women at Hades's side.

"Have you gone insane?" Keres snaps, then takes a step toward Thanatos. Hypnos comes to her side and holds her arm to keep her from reaching him.

"Never mind that right now," Hades says. "We have bigger things to worry about, starting with what happened while the two of you were in the mortal realm?"

"Has something happened?" Thanatos asks, stepping in front of me. It was a small gesture, but it didn't go unnoticed.

Hades nods. "And now that The Fates have spoken, we believe it may be connected to whatever happened while the two of you were up there." Thanatos meets my alarmed gaze before looking back at Hades. "The truth would be preferred."

Thanatos nods. "I brought Elena with me to show her what I do. I wanted to show her that it isn't the lives of random mortals I take. Everything was going according to plan until—"

"Until I touched the man's grieving wife," I interrupt. I'm not going to let Thanatos take the fall for my actions. "I felt

DELANEY NICOLE

like I could do something for the weeping woman. I don't know what compelled me to do it, but I touched her cheek. When I did—"

"When she did, it was as though the light returned to the wife's eyes. Not the same, but a light nonetheless," Thanatos finishes. "I've never seen it before. It was like she was—"

"Like she was healing," the dark-haired woman finishes.

"Exactly like that," Thanatos says with a nod.

"Lachesis, what if she is the one?" the blonde woman whispers. My eyes enlarge slightly and unease coils in my gut.

The first woman, Lachesis, nods. "I believe that is a possibility, Clotho. Considering what has happened, I think she is."

"May I ask what exactly you two are talking about?" Thanatos asks after taking note of the alarm in my face.

"It is a prophecy, my dear," the third woman says. "It appears that, soon enough, you will find out what we mean." She turns to Hades, her hair whipping with her. "You have nothing to worry about. Now that we know what has happened, we can assure you, Hades, you are under no threat. Everything is falling into place the way it should."

"Thank you, Atropos," Hades says.

"We are glad we could be of help," Atropos meets her sisters, and they leave the throne room.

"Now, would you like to tell us what was so shocking that you had to request their presence?" Thanatos inquires.

Hades faces Sebastian without a word. It feels like ages since I've seen Sebastian. I've grown used to Leon guarding me. "Sebastian, please pull the drape."

With a curt nod, the guard pulls a drape covering three of the floor-to-ceiling windows. Moonlight floods in and mine and Thanatos's eyes grow wide when we see the rivers. There are no longer four. There are five rivers and a new piece of land.

"I don't understand. How is that possible?" I turn to the party behind me.

"We didn't know. The Underworld began to shake, and I watched as the ground separated and water flowed," Hades says. "I immediately sent for The Fates. If anyone knew what this meant, they would."

"What did they say?" Thanatos asks, returning to my side. His body heat radiates against me, causing my breath to catch.

"They weren't sure until the two of you arrived back. Your story confirmed it. But they had an idea because they already had a name for the river and the field that sits next to it."

"And?" I ask. I'm surprised I managed to utter a word.

"It is called the Acheron River, otherwise known as the River of Woe."

"And the fields?" Thanatos asks.

Persephone answers, "The Fields of Mourning for those who were hurt by love."

CHAPTER 22

"Tell me what you want," Thanatos whispers in my ear. His breath warms my neck and ear, feeling too good.

His weight on top of me feels delicious. All I can do is let out a puff of air.

"Is it this?" he says in his seductive whisper, then presses an open kiss under the shell of my ear. The smallest whimper leaves my mouth. Heat is building low in my stomach, begging to be extinguished by him in any way he pleases. "Or perhaps lower?"

I track Thanatos as he moves down my body, placing a kiss on my collarbone, then each of my breasts. He hovers there for a moment and pays special attention to each peak which elicits a low gasp from my lips.

"No, that's not it." He trails his mouth down my stomach until— *Oh gods.*

I moan and my back arches slightly. I grasp the pillow

behind my head, and my ass buries into the soft mattress below me.

"That's it, let me hear you," Thanatos purrs. He licks and sucks at the bundle of nerves between my thighs. I stare into his eyes which are darkened with desire. He lifts his head from his work and says, "Do you want me to stop?"

"No." Another moan leaves my lips and his head dips again. "Don't stop. Don't stop."

I gasp as I awaken. Sweat lines my scalp and back. My room is empty except for me. "What the fuck was that?"

I tossed and turned all night. All I could do was worry that something was wrong with me. And what the hell did The Fates mean by "the one"?

I lay atop my bed, hoping sleep would take me yet again into a—hopefully—dreamless sleep. But it was no use. I could not go back to sleep after that dream. I need to train. So, that's exactly what I will do.

"Elena. What are you doing here this early?" Hypnos asks, halting his motions with his sword as I enter the training room.

I am shocked to see him. The only time I've seen him in here was when Thanatos and I fought. "I could ask you the same thing."

"I asked you first." He scowls before cracking a smile. I find his niceness odd. We've barely shared any conversation since I came to the Underworld.

"I couldn't sleep," I say.

I grab a sword from the weaponry wall, cursing the heat that crept up my neck at the recollection of my dream.

"Ah." He stays in the center as I approach him.

DELANEY NICOLE

"Are you going to tell me why you're here this early?" I ask with raised brows, then I start sweeping through my warm-ups.

"I train early. It keeps others from bothering me. I like silence when I train."

"I take it you'd rather me not be here right now," I say, challenging him. I am not leaving, especially not after that dream.

"I don't think I have much of a choice."

"Good answer." He chuckles at that.

We start a light spar. It is nice to combat against someone without having to use all the strength I have. It reminds me of my training with Athena.

"Are you going to tell me what's going on between you and my brother?" Hypnos asks.

I tense. "Nothing is going on with me and Thanatos."

"Whatever you say." Hypnos snickers.

"I'm telling the truth," I say, scowling at the god before me.

"I won't judge you. It seems to me, and the others, that something may be going on."

"Nothing is going on," I say a bit too harshly.

"Maybe for you, but he's never brought anyone to the mortal realm with him," Hypnos says.

Is he joking? He has to be. Nothing is going on between us. "I think I'm done for the day."

"Elena, our friendship is never going to work if you can't handle teasing," Hypnos calls after me.

"I will see you later, Hypnos," I reply and then meet a

sleeping Leon in the hall. I sneak up to his side, waiting until I'm in the perfect position before I shout, "Leon!"

Leon nearly jumps out of his skin and looks around with alarm. When he finally notices me at his side, he narrows his gaze. "You are evil."

I clutch my hands over my heart to mock him.

His eyes narrow again. "Hades would like to see you."

"What?"

"Hades asked to see you while you were training," he says again, guiding me through the corridors.

"Did he say why?" I ask concerned. Hades has never requested my presence before. What if Persephone told him about the night I begged her to leave with me? My hands grow clammy.

"No. I know the suspense is killing you," Leon says.

"You're evil."

"Maybe." Leon's eyes flash with amusement. "He's through there."

Looking at the large, dark oak door before me, I take a deep breath. I hope it isn't something serious.

"Elena, good to see you," Hades drawls from where he sits at his large wooden desk. Based on the grandiosity of the desk and formalness of the room, I guess that this is his study.

"Leon said you wanted to see me," I say from behind the expensive looking chairs.

"Yes." He opens his mouth to speak before the door opens behind me and stops him. "Perfect timing, Callan."

A low coil of heat forms in my stomach thanks to the

DELANEY NICOLE

memory of this morning. I turn away from him, hoping he cannot sense what is coursing through me.

"You wanted to see me?" Thanatos asks, stopping at my side. Heat radiates from his body and warms my right side. Annoyance filters through me, did he have to stand *there*?

"I needed to speak to both of you." Hades looks at each of us. "I need the two of you to go and check the lands, check if any of the courts were affected by last night's events."

"What?" We ask in unison.

"Hades, you cannot be serious. I cannot take her there," Thanatos objects.

Hades's hard gaze fixates on the man at my side. "I am serious. The two of you will check the lands. You two are the reason they changed, so you will make sure no one was affected by it."

Silence fills the study.

"You will leave now, and if need be, make camp for the night. I do not care how long it takes; you will do this."

CHAPTER 23

"I hope this doesn't take as long as Hades made it sound," I huff as I walk with Thanatos through the corridors. In truth, I don't mind making sure everyone is okay. I just don't want to do it with him.

"Relax, it will not take long. We will gather what we need and be on our way," he says as if this is an everyday thing.

I roll my eyes, dreading having to spend the day with him. I was hoping to avoid him. But, of course, I cannot have that luxury.

I have never ventured to the bottom floor of the palace. Outside snow coats the ground. We pass all of the other turns and doors in the corridor until we reach the very last one.

"Ready?" Thanatos inclines his head, challenging me.

"Open the door."

He does as I say, revealing the palace's stables, which I did

DELANEY NICOLE

not know it had. Black, gray, and white horses stand in the stalls lining the walls.

"What are we doing?" I ask.

"We are getting ready to leave," he says as if he's stating the obvious.

"Yes, but why are we taking a horse? Can't you fly us there?"

Thanatos walks to the last stall with an all-white horse. "No, I cannot. In order to ensure none of the creatures with wings escape the Underworld, Hades has cast a spell on the land. If something tries to fly, they are weakened, so much so, that they die from exhaustion. I am only able to fly in and out because the spell is weaker over the castle."

"Oh," I say, gazing at the horses. "I don't know how to ride. A horse, I mean."

A smirk ghosts his lips. "I'm glad you cleared that up, the horse part. But doesn't your father have horses? Or is that a different member of The Twelve? I can never keep up with them."

I clasp my hands at my hips. "He has horses, but he uses a chariot. I was never taught to ride."

Thanatos looks between me and the reins he's currently holding.

"Then I suppose we will have to ride together," he says, offering his hand.

"You cannot be serious."

"On the contrary, I am quite serious. Did you forget that when I said once Hades gets an idea in his mind, there is no changing it?"

All my self-preservation efforts from this morning begin to crumble. Who have I crossed to be handed such luck?

"Fine." I glower. "But your hands will not wander. They will stay in one spot."

His hands rise in surrender while amusement flashes in his eyes. "I wouldn't dream of anything else."

I almost laugh at the irony of his words, but I stop myself. "Just help me on the damn horse."

* * *

A SEEMING ETERNITY LATER, Thanatos and I are finally on our way through the lands. We are on a cleared path surrounded by heavy woods, a light dusting of snow graces the edges of the path and trees.

"Would you stop pushing your hips into my back," I hiss as I whip my head over my shoulder.

"Would you stop complaining about every time I touch you? We are sharing a horse for gods sake," Thanatos retorts.

"That does not mean you have to touch me every five seconds," I mutter. I knew this ride would only make getting over my insipid dream harder, but every time his hands brush my arms or hips nudge my back, I get flashes of his body over mine.

"That is quite literally what this ride entails because if you haven't noticed, there isn't much room to share. Perhaps if you knew how to ride, we would not have this issue."

He's right. I straighten and choose to ignore him. It is my ignorance that has placed us in this comical situation.

DELANEY NICOLE

"Why must we venture so far out?" I ask while watching the water flow in the Acheron River to my left. The Fields of the Mourning are harder to see through the trees to our right.

"Because the rest of the living members of Hades's court reside on the outer edges of the lands. That way the souls are forced to stay in the heart of whatever field they are assigned. The living members are who we are checking on."

"So we will see the others in the court?" I ask, feeling uneasy. I can see from a distance that we are getting closer to what looks like a small village. Perhaps, the distance is playing tricks on me, and the village is not small. Maybe, it could even rival Olympus. No, that's impossible. Nothing rivals Olympus.

"Don't tell me you're scared," Thanatos teases. His breath passes over my ear and I fight the shiver that erupts.

"I am not scared," I say through my teeth. I ignore the flutter of my stomach when his fingers ghost my ribs. "Stop touching me."

He huffs, and he shakes his head. "You are a stubborn woman. I have never met anyone as menacing as you. I also have never met a woman who has been so offended by my touch that she cannot stand it when my hand accidentally brushes hers."

"How disheartening that must be for you," I say, turning to face him. My face is so close to his that I'm able to see the slight crease on his forehead, and the exact hue of his eyes as he examines me. His breath warms my lips. My eyes dip to his lips and I notice for the first time how lush they look. A small bubble of warmth sits low in my stomach.

I force my gaze up to his eyes but find them focused on my lips. Finally, his gaze wretches to mine. We are so close. It would only take one of us to move forward for our lips to meet.

A rattle in the trees draws my focus away from him. Clearing my throat, I try to steady myself. "I'd like to get off."

"Elena, we are in the middle of the woods. You cannot—"

"I wish to get off," I say with much more ferocity than intended.

"Very well," Thanatos mutters.

He stops the horse and hops off. I take his extended hand before landing on my feet with a thud.

I allow myself to take in the new scenery. It looks peaceful. It seems to radiate similar feelings to the ones I felt last night. But at remembering The Fates' words, I move away from it. I do not know how I am connected to the land, but I'd rather not find out.

"Are you done?" Thanatos asks.

"Not quite," I say while examining a bunch of flowers lining the river. They are beautiful. They look similar to the moonlight roses Persephone tends to, but their color is more blue than purple. "Perhaps, I should bring Persephone back some flowers."

"Elena, she does not need flowers. Get back on the horse so we can continue."

"It will only take a minute," I say.

"Elena, don't touch those," he warns.

"What are you, my father?" I challenge, half turning to face him.

"Just do as I say for once," he orders, giving me a look of authority.

I feel the side of my lips pull up. He's quite funny if he believes I will listen to him. "It is just flowers. It will take a—"

"Elena!"

"Ouch." I clutch the part of my hand that a thorn cut, feeling my thumb grow wet with my blood as I apply pressure.

"No, no, no." Thanatos's words are urgent as he rushes to my side. "Elena, look at me."

"What are you doing? It is a small cut," I say, but worry is etched into his face.

"Look at me. I need you to look at me," he orders. "Whatever you do, stay awake. Do not close your eyes."

"What are you—" I feel weaker and lean more into his grip.

"Shit," he murmurs as he lifts me into his arms. "Elena, stay with me. We'll be there in no time."

Wind rushes around us, and I no longer feel the security of the ground. I look through my heavy lids, watching the trees pass below.

But trees can't pass us, so that would mean...

"Thanatos, why are you flying? You said you can't fly here."

"Because you were cut by a poisonous thorn, and if I do not get you back to the palace soon, you will die."

Something in my stomach dropped, yet it felt distant. Everything feels distant. "But you said, anyone that tries to fly a great distance dies from exhaustion."

"I will take that risk if it means you live," he says. Sweat lines his forehead.

My eyes start to roll back. It's harder to stay awake.

"Elena!" Thanatos's panicked voice faintly reaches my ears. "Stay with me, damn it!"

CHAPTER 24

hanatos

"HADES!" I shout. A small rush of relief spreads through me when Elena stirs in my arms. But the panic returns when she turns limp again just seconds later. "Hades, damn it, get down here!"

"Callan, what are you— oh gods." Persephone runs towards us with panic marred on her face. "What happened?"

"She was cut by a thorn at the edge of the river. I flew her here."

"Are you mad? You know what flying through the Underworld can do!" My sister shouts from across the corridor.

"That does not matter right now," I snap. "Persephone, I need you to send for The Fates immediately."

"I will. Take her to her bedchamber and then you need to be examined."

"I will, but get The Fates here. She's been able to hold on this long, but I do not know how much longer she has. I've seen some people die almost instantly after being cut by those thorns." Persephone's face turns an ashen color when the severity of Elena's situation begins to sink in. I fight the bile that threatens to spill from my mouth.

* * *

"How long has it been since she was cut?" Clotho runs a hand across Elena's cheek. Her skin is visibly clammy.

I pace the edge of Elena's bed, my arms crossed over my chest. "I don't know. An hour maybe?"

"Brother, sit down," Keres orders. "It is a miracle you did not croak on your way back. That was incredibly foolish of you. You should have sent for help."

I roll my eyes and continue pacing despite my sister's wishes. I'm far too anxious to sit.

"I have to agree with Keres." Persephone agrees. "But it was also incredibly brave."

"I do not care if it was foolish. I need to know if she is alright," I snap much harsher than I'd intended. I make a mental note to apologize to Persphone later but right now my mind is too scrambled to think straight.

"Callan," Hades pauses. "Sit."

I sigh, accepting my defeat and pull a chair next to Elena's bedside. My knees bounces rapidly against my elbow.

Each of The Fates take turns examining Elena further. A

pressure builds in my chest each second that passes that they do not speak. She has to be okay. She can't die. Not like this.

Atropos finally breaks the suffocating silence. "She will be fine. She will need rest to let the poison work its way through her system with the help of a tonic to ease her pain, but she will be fine."

"I don't understand. How is that possible?" My brother's brows scrunch when I look back at him. I had not even known he was there.

"It is the bond she shares with Thanatos," Clotho says.

"What bond?" I ask. Unease fills my gut for an entirely different reason now.

"There is a bond between your powers. You bring death, and she brings healing after it. Through that bond, your lives are tethered together. You exist as long as mortals do. And as long as you exist, she will too."

My stomach drops. We can't be bound to each other. Elena hates me. She blamed me for her mother's death for gods know how long.

Silence fills the room for a long moment.

"That is why she was able to survive the poison. You."

IT'S BEEN ALMOST two days since the accident, yet Elena still has not awoken. I've been tormented ever since she went limp in my arms when I rushed back to the palace. Watching her eyes flutter back and her head lull sent a pang through my chest that I thought was going to render me flightless.

Why did she touch those gods damned thorns?

A soft knock sounds from my door. "Callan?"

"Come in," I say with as much strength as I can.

Persephone pushes the door open slightly, then closes the door behind her before gracefully walking to my side. "I haven't seen you since the accident."

"That is how I wished for it to be," I say. Her face looks different than before. Her eyes have dark circles, yet they seem to hold the same bright light as always. Her hair looks slightly unkept, and her dress looks strikingly familiar to the gown she wore the day of the accident.

Persephone looks at my bed-chambers, which have seen better days. I cannot seem to keep it pristine when Elena cannot even get out of bed.

"Talk to me, Callan," she whispers. "Tell me what you're thinking, please."

"It's my fault," I mutter, a sinking feeling fills my gut. "It's my fault she is stuck in a sleeping state. It's my fault the accident happened."

Her hand grasps my shoulder. "Callan, you know that is not true. You saved her."

"You heard what The Fates said..." I pause and bring my hands to my eyes. "I did not save her. She would have lived either way."

"But you did not know that," Persephone adds in her soft voice. "You thought you were saving her. You damn near killed yourself bringing her here. That should not be overlooked."

"Maybe so," I say. "But none of this would have happened if I had warned her rather than—"

"Rather than what?"

"It's nothing," I say, thinking of the moment we shared before the accident. I remember the exact shade of her heated gaze. The way her eyelids hooded when she looked at my lips. "I should have told her about the thorns before she asked to get off the horse. If I had warned her, she would not be in this situation."

"This accident is not your fault. And if we are being honest, I think Elena would have touched those thorns regardless of your warning. You know as well as I do, she is stubborn. She does not listen to anyone she does not wish to." The couch dips at my side, and Persephone turns to face me.

"You may be right, but that does not change the fact that I should have protected her. I know the dangers of this land far better than she does. I should have stopped her. I should have protected her."

Persephone grasps my hand, giving it a comforting squeeze. "Sometimes people do not need your protection. Sometimes what we need is the knowledge that there are people to help us if we need it—that we are wanted."

I nod, not knowing what else to do when silence fills the gap between us again. I think I will always live with the guilt of this accident because I could have prevented it.

I sigh. "Persephone, I have been in agony ever since thinking that she will not wake, that I will no longer get to watch her glare at me or hear her remarks."

"I know. I saw it the moment you ran through the corridors with her in your arms. I saw the fear in your eyes. I saw how deeply you feel for her." She squeezes my hand again.

"You did what you thought was necessary, and she will not overlook that. And if she does, she is a fool."

I chuckle but it feels foreign in light of everything.

"But I must say, no matter how heroic you may have been," Persephone stands and walks to the door, "you were incredibly idiotic. I implore you to never do that again."

She stops as she reaches the threshold.

"But I should let you know that your efforts were not in vain. Hades is speaking with her now."

The weight of the past two days lifts from my shoulders immediately. The agony I have felt ceases, and I can no longer deny what I've been telling myself is not possible for weeks. I cannot deny the relief that fills my body at knowing she is okay. I can no longer deny how I feel.

CHAPTER 25

lena

I LIE IN BED, staring up at the purple fabric canopy. No matter how many times I run it through my mind, I cannot understand how I let myself get here. How I let myself almost die from a flower's thorn. Or how Thanatos saved my life.

"Elena," Hades says, interrupting the silence in my bedchamber. I turn my head and offer the god the kindest smile I can. "May I come in?"

I nod. "You may."

"I came to see how you were doing."

"Much better. But I think anything is better than dying." I try to laugh but it makes my chest ache.

"I shouldn't have made you go," he says with a sigh. "I

should have sent Leon and Sebastian to check on everyone, not you and Thanatos."

"It is alright, Hades. I am fine. I will be back on my feet in no time," I say.

"I wanted to ask how you're adjusting and how your task is coming along?"

My breath catches in my throat, and my hands grow clammy in my lap. Did Persephone mention our interaction to him? She swore she wouldn't. "Everything is fine with my task. Thanatos's help is greatly appreciated."

"Good. How are you adjusting?"

I ponder the question for a moment. "I'd say I'm adjusting well. I've made friends. And Persephone has shown me nothing but kindness."

Hades grins. "Persephone does that. She's a wonderful woman."

"She is." I can't help but notice the sparkle in his eyes when he speaks of Persephone. "You love her dearly."

Hades is quiet for a moment, looking as though he is somewhere else in his mind. It's so strange seeing the god before me—who is known for his envy, pride, and dark power be rendered speechless over the mere thought of Persephone. "I do. I didn't think I'd ever love someone the way I love her. She's everything I didn't know I needed. I'm not sure how I lived before her."

"She loves you too, you know." I enjoy watching the love between Hades and Persephone flow through the walls of this palace. They are such an unlikely pairing. But after speaking with both of them, it is apparent they are meant for each other.

"I don't know why. I never thought I was lovable."

A surge of pity spreads through me. Surely Hades didn't believe he was unlovable. And yet I often find myself thinking the same about me. "Everyone deserves someone."

His eyes fix on me as if he's hesitating to say something to me. Instead of speaking, he stands to take his leave. But not before offering a simple, "Indeed they do."

Silence fills the room again in Hades's absence. I'm left to do nothing but stare at the decoration in my bedchamber and think. I can slowly feel sleep starting to come over me again.

My eyes begin to drift closed when my door opens. I turn and take in the figure that enters.

"Thanatos," I say. His hair is disheveled as if his hands ran through it several times. His clothes are wrinkled, and his eyes are unreadable.

"I, um..." He pauses, letting his eyes fan over me. "I came to make sure you were alright. Persephone told me you had awoken."

A warmth spreads in my chest. It must be the remnants of the tonic The Fates gave me. "Yes, I am well. It was very thoughtful of you to come."

His head dips the slightest degree, yet he still holds me in a fierce stare. As my eyes meet his, my heart sputters and I take deeper breaths. Flashes of that day run through my mind like the panicked look in his eyes, his worry-filled voice, the warmth of his chest as he held me against him, and his curses before I lost consciousness. I also remember when he said, *And I will take that risk if it means you will live.*

"I will take my leave. You must be exhausted. You need your rest," he says, turning away.

"Thanatos," I say.

He turns and looks at me with great yet unreadable emotion etched on his face. "Yes?"

"Thank you." I pause. "For bringing me back."

The right side of his mouth pulls up. "You do not need to thank me, Elena."

CHAPTER 26

"Elena, we're happy to see you out of bed. And you're just the person we wanted to see," Hades exclaims. Persephone holds onto his arm as they enter the dining hall.

"Here I am," I say, although I'm slightly suspicious of Hades's gleeful mood. The last time he entered the dining hall like this, I was holding a sword at Thanatos's neck less than an hour later.

Persephone sits in the plush seat across from me. Hades joins her at her side, admiring the goddess beside him as if he's never seen anyone so beautiful. I haven't seen Hades since our discussion in my bedchamber. Everything seems to be returning to normal despite the new river and landscape of the Underworld. It is as though the others have chosen to ignore it.

"So," Persephone says, "we are having a party in the palace

in a few days. We sent word a few minutes ago. It's going to be a ball, so the attire will be formal."

"And you're inviting me?" I ask.

"Of course, why wouldn't we?" Persephone smiles. She knows how much this means to me.

"You have proven to be a wonderful company," Hades adds, placing his hand on top of Persephone's. "But if anyone asked if I said that, I'd probably lie."

"Hades." Persephone rolls her eyes.

"What? I'm being honest." He chuckles.

"I won't tell anyone you have a soft spot," I tease. I pop a slice of apricot into my mouth. "What's the ball in celebration of?"

"I usually hold a ball for solstice. The longest night of a calendar year is an important event. However, this year, some special news is being announced," Hades says.

"I'm eager to hear of it. But I'm afraid I don't have a dress suitable for a ball."

"Don't worry, I have that covered," Persephone assures.

"Why am I not surprised?" I grin, tossing another piece of fruit in my mouth.

"Because Persephone would not be Persephone if she weren't looking out for those she cared about," Hades replies.

Persephone smiles when Hades kisses her temple, but she looks at me with a threatening stare. It's a warning, or rather a reminder of our interaction in her bedchamber. I gulp and her glare is gone as fast as it appeared.

"That she wouldn't. Excuse me, I have some tasks to get back to."

"Oh, Elena," Persephone calls from the table just as I

DELANEY NICOLE

approach the door. Leon is leaning lazily against the wall outside the threshold. "We'll be having a special dinner with the court tonight. We do hope you attend."

"I'll be sure to be there," I say.

* * *

THE LIBRARY FEELS DIFFERENT. It has the usual dark glow from the candles, but something feels off. I am beginning to think it is the Underworld itself. What was once a place I dreaded is slowly becoming a place I love. Maybe Persephone was right.

"Nice to see you up and about," Thanatos purrs as he emerges from the shadows.

"It's not like I can continue to sit around. I have a task. Now are you going to help?" I ask sarcastically.

"I would never work with you," he retorts, showing a dimple in his right cheek as he sits down at my side. He sits in a different chair than he's sat in the entire time he's helped me. Rather than the one at the opposite end of the table, he's chosen the one right next to me. I don't mind his presence at my side. Another thing that has changed since my accident.

"The feeling is mutual." I chuckle and pick up one of the books I've been reading through.

"Fantastic."

Thanatos and I read separately. I try hard to focus on the book at hand. Intrigue fills me when I trace the jagged edge of a torn page. It was supposed to be a list of all of Zeus's children. However, my mind strays from the vandalism and spins around two things, Thanatos sitting next to me and The Fates.

"What do you think The Fates meant by 'the one'?" I ask, turning to face him.

"I'm not sure." Thanatos flips a page. "But they did say it was a prophecy that posed no threat to the Underworld."

"So, that's it then? I have no way of knowing how I fit into this strange prophecy after I magically changed a woman with my touch and somehow split the Underworld?"

"Relax," he says, then casually walks over to a bookcase with a matching set of books.

"Relax? How would you feel if you were vaguely told you were part of some strange prophecy, and it could change your life dramatically? Oh wait, you are connected to it since, you know, they said our lives are bound to each other." I turn to watch him.

He stiffens. "You heard that?"

I shrug. "I was in and out of sleep."

"Either way, you worry too much," he says. I roll my eyes. "Ah, here it is."

Thanatos pulls a large worn book from the shelf.

"What is it?"

"This," it lands on the table with a thud, "is the book of prophecies. Well, the ones that fit into the present. There are too many volumes to read through them all. If you want to know what The Fates meant, we'd better start here."

"Okay," I mutter. My eyes caught on a small red book that was hidden under the prophecy book. "Did you mean to bring this one?"

His brows furrow, "No, it fell into my hand when I

grabbed the prophecy book. I planned on putting it back when we're done here for the day. What is it?"

"It looks like a journal," I say as I examine the worn diary.

"I'm going to start reading over the prophecies, so you'll stop thinking all the monsters are after you," he says.

"I do not think the monsters are after me."

He chuckles. "Whatever you say."

I open the journal to a random page near the beginning. Something about this book is pulling me toward it.

Dear Journal,

I saw him again today. Though I've been around him for ages, things are different now. We've been sneaking off to the sunny fields while my husband is away. Having his arms wrap around my body when he catches feels as though it's a dream.

I'm afraid a violent storm will be unleashed upon us should my husband find out, but we can't get enough of each other. I think I am falling for him, his smile, the way his eyes sparkle in the sunlight, the way his red hair falls over his forehead, everything.

"Anything important?" Thanatos's husky voice sounds too close to my ear.

"I'm not sure," I scan the passage again, and a strange feeling fills my gut.

"I think we should return to this prophecy book. Unless you'd like to read whatever gossip is inside that thing."

"I do not want to read gossip," I sneer. But when I turn, I find his face centimeters from mine. My nose fills with the scent of minty breath and lush mahogany. His eyes bore into mine, and they grow a shade darker. His eyes roam lower on my face, landing on what I can only assume are my lips. I instinctively look down to his.

His mouth opens a fragment. He leans forward. "Elena."

I clear my throat. A loud crack from the fireplace pulls me back into focus, and I turn my head to the right.

"Right." He coughs and closes the book as he stands. "We can return to the prophecies later. Let's go, we must be getting ready for dinner."

* * *

THE GOWN I put on is ice blue and matches the small gem on the necklace my father gave me before I came to the Underworld, before my task became complicated. My hair dangles down my back, touching the end of my spine.

With one last look at myself in the mirror, I walk toward the door, but stop when the journal I stole from the library catches my eyes. I'm not sure if Hades cares about taking books from the library, but something is different about this journal. I can feel it, almost like when I touched the mortal woman and healed her. It intrigues me.

A sound from the corridor pulls me from my focus on the book, and I start toward the dining hall. When I turn the corner, I'm met with a hard chest.

"Oh, I'm sorry."

I flick my eyes up and see Leon's proud gaze. "You should be."

I rolled my eyes before proceeding. "Oh, please, it was as much your fault as it was mine."

DELANEY NICOLE

"Yes," he says, "but you said 'sorry' to me and not the others."

"Is that what you talk about with the others? While I'm flattered to be the topic of conversation, I must admit, it's a bit boring."

"So you don't wish for me to mention your apology?"

"No, not really."

The table that once reached from end to end of the vast hall was now smaller, more intimate. Hades, Persephone, Keres, Hypnos, Sebastian, and Thanatos are already seated.

"Elena, so glad you could make it. We were sad when you didn't come to the last one," Hades says.

"Hades, don't patronize her. The last time we had a dinner like this, she was still adjusting," Persephone warns.

"While I'm sure you're right, Persephone," I say, sitting down in one of the two open seats next to Keres. "I had no idea there was another dinner like this."

"That's impossible. We told Leon to alert you of your invitation," the goddess counters.

"I'm sure you're telling the truth, but Leon never said anything."

"Was that the bet you won?" Hypnos looks over to the guard at my side. The guards are sitting at the table as though they aren't guards but friends; something I find quite interesting.

"Bet? What bet?" My brows furrow.

"This should be good." Thanatos chuckles and then takes a deep gulp of wine. He leans back in his chair, leisurely bringing his hands behind his head. I notice the way his muscles bulge in his shirt. My mouth runs dry. The memory

A CURSE OF HONOR

of our moment in the library flashes through my mind, how my lips were warmed by his breath and how close we were. That's how close I was to messing everything up. I need to stay focused.

I see a grin forming on his lips as he catches my stare. His eyes shine bright with mischief.

"I'm still waiting." I fold my arms over my chest, bringing my attention back to the table.

"If you must know," Hypnos says, "we had a bet on whether you would show or not. Leon bet that you wouldn't. I tried to give you the benefit of the doubt."

My head snaps to Leon in disbelief. "You withheld my invitation to ensure you would win a silly bet?"

His eyes scan the room before his face becomes more calculated. "In my defense, would you have gone if I had told you about it?"

I sit quietly for a moment. He's right, and I couldn't think of a way out of this. "That is not the point."

The table erupts into laughter. My attention draws to Thanatos. His smile is glowing as it was the night in the library when I called him a bird. I realize that this is the first time I've heard him laugh a real laugh since that night.

This is how life in the Underworld is in reality. No masks. No facade. This is real. Comrades meeting around the table like a family. Guards sitting like friends. But nobody is acting. They are a family. They are friends. I can't help but smile that I am being considered a part of it.

It reminds me of something Hermes mentioned to me upon my arrival.

"May I ask something?" I say.

DELANEY NICOLE

"I don't see why not." Hades places his chalice down.

"When I arrived, Hermes mentioned something about souls taking on the form of guards. Is that—"

"Is that what we are?" Sebastian grins. Leon matches his amusement at my side. "While there are some souls that are guards. We," he waves his hand between him and Leon, "are not. We have souls, and we are living. However, we are much older than some may think. We go back to the Titans."

My eyes grow wide. "What?"

"He's exaggerating a bit," Leon supplies. "We originated somewhere in the downfall of the Titans and the rise of the Olympians—as they were called back then. Originally, we were made to protect the Titans. Zeus, being Zeus, didn't take kindly to that. So, after The Olympians won the war on the Titans, he ordered our executions. Hades, however, was able to bring me and Sebastian to the Underworld before we were taken. Some of us, others we were very close to, did not have such luck. It is my understanding that we are the last two of our kind."

My stomach twists in knots. "I'm sorry, I had no idea."

"Yes, well, we've had plenty of time to deal with it." Leon takes a deep gulp of wine. "Now, who's ready to eat."

* * *

IF SOMEONE HAD TOLD me how much fun I'd have when I first arrived, I would have probably told them they'd gone mad and offer to smite them.

"Would you like me to escort you back to your room?"

Lavender and mahogany assault my senses. I know who

is behind me without turning. "If Leon doesn't mind, then I suppose it wouldn't hurt."

Leon's amused eyes bounce between us. "As long as the two of you don't try to kill each other."

I reply, "No promises," and turn to Thanatos.

We walk closely enough that chills run up my spine when Thanatos's fingers graze mine.

"Are you going to be in attendance at the ball?" he asks.

Why does he want to know? "I believe I have to since Persephone mentioned a gown for me."

"You don't sound excited."

"I just…" I sigh. "I was never invited to parties like this in Olympus. I don't know how to fit into a crowd like that."

Thanatos stares at me like I am an animal on display. It makes me uneasy at not knowing why. But before I can close my door, he says, "Go to the ball."

"What?"

"Go to the ball," he says. "This is not Olympus. The Underworld is home to those that have been outcasted—the misfits. Go to the ball, darling."

CHAPTER 27

I take a deep breath, eyeing my target with predatory precision. I pull my arm back, tightening my core to ground me as I launch my spear through the air. As it whizzes through the dry, cool air, I don't wait and watch it hit its target before I unsheathe the sword at my hip.

I replay the brawl between Thanatos and I in my mind, micking his steps so that I may find his weak spots and use them as my counterstrikes. I may not be eager to fight him again, but the difference in his battle tactics could be useful for me to learn.

I step back with my right foot, turning on my heel and slashing the blade through the air. The sharp, iron blade slices the chest of my faux adversary.

"You will need more than a slice across the chest to fall a faux," Keres's voice wafts into my ears. My head whips to the corner she emerges from. How long has she been there?

"I think it will suffice for now," I say through my pants of breath.

"Tell me, Elena, how many wars have you been in?" Keres asks, her hands clasped behind her back as she slowly approaches me.

I stay silent. If I had it my way, I'd have already fought many wars.

"Hmm, what about witnessed?" Keres inquires again. This time she looks at me more cynically and I shake my head. "I see. Do you know how many wars I've been in?"

"You have been to war?" I ask. I almost cannot believe it. I mean from my previous interactions with Keres, she has never shown interest in fighting or training. Even though Thanatos told me Keres is the bringer of violent death, it's strange hearing her talk of war.

A prideful smirk lines her lips, "Oh yes, several. That is why I know the move you just did will lead to your death."

"Says who?" I ask through my annoyance. Athena taught me that move.

"Me. By just slicing the first few layers of skin, your adversary will eventually bleed out. But not before they get the chance to ram their weapon through you because you let your guard down. Trust me, I've seen it with my own eyes several times."

"Then what do you purpose I do?" I ask.

Keres narrows her eyes, looking me up and down with her sneer. "Go grab the wood dowels from the wall."

"Why would I do that?" I furrow my brows, lifting the perfectly suitable sword already in my hand.

She rolls her eyes, "I am going to show you what you

DELANEY NICOLE

should do but I will not do it with real weapons. My brother may have been dumb enough to get in the ring with you, but I'm not. The wood dowels have been made to mock the weight and fluidity of swords."

"Why would you help me?" I ask, suddenly wary of her intentions even if she doesn't want to use real weapons. I also wonder why Thanatos and I hadn't used the dowels during our brawl since Persephone was insistent that we didn't kill each other.

She huffs, "Gods you are stubborn. If you don't want my help then fine, but I don't want your soul to come crying when you die on the battlefield because you wouldn't accept help."

"Okay, I'll grab them." I raise my hands in surrender, turning to grab the dowels. Truth be told, I wouldn't mind learning new battle tactics, and learning from my enemy only allows me to form better attack strategies for them.

I square my shoulders and center my weight, controlling my breathing so that I may use it to drive each of my strikes. Keres stands just as she was before I gave her the wooden dowel. "Are you not going to get in a ready stance?"

A mischievous smirk pulls on her lips. "Come at me as you would any other adversary. Oh, and don't hold back."

Annoyance floods me. Are all of the siblings filled with inflated egos? "Very well."

I lunge on my right leg, swinging my dowel wide in hopes of disarming Keres first rather than going straight for a kill shot. But before my dowel is able to connect with hers, she turns to her left, spinning around my body and ramming her dowel into my back. I sputter a breath as the wind is knocked out of my lungs.

"You'd be dead if this were a blade," Keres says matter-of-factly. "Rule number one, never make the first move. Rule number two, if you must make the first move, don't go wide as you did."

"Why can't I make the first move? I've never heard that, even from my father who is the god of war if you recall," I say, rolling my chest in a circle to soothe the ache in my mid-back. My body had just stopped aching enough to train after the tonic The Fates gave me. Now I'm afraid it's going to be just as sore.

Keres circles around me, dragging the dowel on the cold stone floor. "Making the first move lets your enemy know everything they need to know about you. If you swing wide or try to disarm them first, then you are not confident in your ability for an armed match. If you go straight for a kill shot, then you don't have the skill or endurance for a long spar. Besides, when men realize they're fighting a woman, they are more than eager to take the first swing to prove their dominance."

Why hasn't Athena told me any of this? What Keres says makes sense but I feel I should have learned it if it were so important. "How did you learn all of this?"

"Let's just say I've had enough experience on the battle-fields to learn how to protect myself from anything and everything." Keres's stare was distant as she spoke, as if playing on a memory in her mind. Her gaze sharpens before she turns back to face me. "Now, shall we go again?"

I allowed Keres to make the first move this time, yet just

DELANEY NICOLE

like before, she was able to strike me within the first few seconds of our match.

"What am I doing wrong?" I pant through the pain of the strike to my ribs.

"Why did you choose to start training for the armies?" Keres paces around me again. The sound of her dowel scraping the floor fills my ears in mockery.

"I don't see how that's any of your business," I say harshly. Thanatos is the only person I've given even an inkling as to why I train.

She stops in front of me, her eyes full of skepticism. "I am trying to help you. If what drives you to fight is not strong enough, your fighting won't be either. Now, what made you start training?"

I toy with the idea of telling her the truth. I may not trust her but she has given me valuable information to help my fighting and we've only sparred twice. I sigh, "If I tell you, will you tell me why you chose to train?"

I watch as the same inner turmoil that previously plagued me now casts itself upon Keres. Finally, she says, "I suppose we have a deal."

"Very well," I pause, passing the dowel I hold between each of my hands. "I started to train because I want to prove the whispers that I would never be good enough wrong. That I can be just as strong as them even though I am a demigoddess. That mortal blood is not a curse but a reminder that there are people that need me somewhere, even if I cannot see them."

I start to pace in front of Keres, "When I noticed the men in the training facility staring at me as nothing more than something to fuck, I made a vow to myself that one day, I would show them just how strong and lethal a woman can be."

Keres's gaze snapped towards mine when I finished my last sentence. She looks at me as though she's seen a ghost and I almost want to turn around to see if there is one behind me. "What?"

"Nothing." She shakes her head, snapping out of whatever emotion had held her. "I believe I should go."

"We just started," I counter. Though I was opposed to her help at the beginning, I feel she could be very helpful.

"Another time, perhaps." She places the wooden dowel on the wall in a rather hurried manner before making her way to the door. "Oh, and one more thing. I've only given you a fraction of my knowledge and strength about fighting. I suggest not doing anything that warrants my full strength."

And just like that she's gone and back to the Keres I'm familiar with. What did I say that was so bad? Am I truly that bad of company?

I attempt to do a few more sparring exercises but find myself falling short so I call it a day and hang all of the weapons back on the wall. I will come back tomorrow with a fresh start and focused mind. For now, I must get ready to deal with Thanatos.

I STARE at the angry purple bruise littering my ribs, Keres says she only showed me a fraction of her strength and yet I find myself in pain if I take too deep of a breath. Nonetheless, I finish dressing, careful not to pull the crimson bodice too tight against my wounds.

I jump as I open my door to find Thanatos already standing before it, his arm raised as though he were about to knock to announce himself.

"Oh, hi," I say, rather surprised to find him in front of my door and not Leon.

"I thought I could escort you tonight for your reading session."

I nod, reminding myself that my dagger is still on my thigh if he attempts anything. Though I find it hard convincing myself that he will in light of recent events. "Very well. Lead the way."

We walk in silence through the corridors. I force myself to study the art on the walls so that I do not steal glances of the man at my side. His mahogany scent is enough to tempt me. I turn my head, watching as his jaw clenches and unclenches. A vein sticks out of his throat as he swallows.

"Is that a new dress?" He asks, he turns his head towards me and I see his eyes dip past my face. He swallows again before clearing his throat and whipping his head to face forward again.

I feel my mouth run dry. I smooth my hands down my bodice, "Yes. Persephone must have snuck it into my wardrobe. I find I quite like the style she and your sister wear."

Thanatos stops in front of a large oak door, his hand grabs its handle before he says, "It suits you."

I feel a blush creep into my cheeks, but it stops when I realize we aren't in the library and rather outside. Had I been so focused on Thanatos I hadn't realized we weren't going to the library? "Why are we outside? Where are we?"

"The garden of the Underworld," Thanatos answers, stopping just ahead of me as he cracks open a tattered book.

"Where did you get that?" I ask.

He flips through the pages before looking at me rather amused, "My, my, you've seemed to have lost your touch Elena. I've been holding this book the entire time."

I scowl. "I haven't lost anything. Now answer my question?"

Thanatos turns the book in his hands, handing it to me on a random page. "Since your accident I thought you would like to learn more about the plants in the Underworld. If anything, so to not have a repeat near death experience. So, here we are. Nearly every plant that grows in the Underworld is here."

I look around the scenery before me. Grey stone pillars encapsulate the plants in a large circle. Flowers fill the circle to my right, what looks like fruit and other sustenance line the outer edge across from me, and more flowers and leafy plants sit to my left. In the center of the garden, a statue of Hades stands in the center of a small pond.

Something warms and expands in my chest. When I speak I fail to hide the breathy awe in my voice, "Why would you do this?"

He stares at me with an unreadable emotion before walking closer. My breath hitches when the only thing separating us is the tatterbook I hold against my stomach. "I know what it is like to feel hopeless. I know that accident stripped something from you."

DELANEY NICOLE

My lips part as I suck in a breath. He towers over me, peering into my soul as I do the same to him. I study the exact pink hue of his plush lips and my mouth runs dry. Warmth begins to curl low in my stomach.

"I—" I pause, forcing myself to look away. "We should get started."

Thanatos's jaw clenches and unclenches twice. "Very well. As you wish."

Thanatos kept his distance as I studied each plant in the Underworld's garden. I found several more poisonous plants and kept my distance from them this time. There were several beautiful flowers that weren't poisonous. But what interested me most was the use of fruit in the Underworld's garden.

"Is this true?" I call out for Thanatos to find him already walking in my direction.

"Is what true?" He asks with his hands behind his back, peering over my shoulder to look at the page I'm studying.

I point to the line I ask about, "That eating a pomegranate seed from the garden of the Underworld forces the patron to return to the Underworld for one month for every seed consumed?"

"Ah, you've finally gotten to the fruit chapter. But yes, that is true. There are several different uses for fruit here. A pear will draw out its consumer's deepest desires. Grapes are a symbol of luck. I could go on."

"I see," I say, finding myself rather glad Thanatos brought me here. He was right. My accident had taken something from me—my sense of security. Being able to learn all these things is slowly bringing that back. "May we come back tomorrow night? It's getting rather late now. I would like to return to my bedchamber."

"Of course." He nods. "Until then, let this be a reminder that you are still in control."

I suck in a breath when he reveals a beautiful bouquet of peonies and lavender from behind his back—peacemaking flowers.

CHAPTER 28

"Persephone, where did you get this gown? I've never seen anything like it. Even Aphrodite doesn't have something like this," I say, watching myself in the mirror while Persephone finishes getting me into my dress for the ball. It's beautiful. The gown is black with small silver embellishments. The small sleeves drape on my arms, creating the illusion that it is falling off of my shoulder. The bodice laces with a black ribbon and cinches enough to push my breasts higher on my chest and causes them to look fuller. The skirt is full, much fuller than any peplos or gown I've worn before.

Persephone pulls the front pieces of my hair back and holds them in place with clips that resemble black pieces of laurel leaves. The rest is left free flowing down my back.

"It's a gown from the era the palace was inspired by. Maybe a little later. I can't remember. Hades draws inspiration from so many different eras thanks to The Fates," Persephone says, tying the back of my dress rather tightly. I had debated strapping my dagger to my thigh beneath the many layers of this dress since there will be so many unfamiliar faces, but I decided I did not need it. "The mortals won't see dresses like this for at least another millennium."

"Don't worry, darling. She did the same with me," Keres's voice breaks into the room. She sits in the sitting area. Her gown is more revealing of her legs and chest in a deep midnight shade but she looks beautiful.

"I don't see the problem," Persephone says while finishing the silk ribbon of my bodice off with a bow.

"There is no problem with your enthusiasm. But Elena's used to clothing she can lift a sword in," Keres says.

"You know me well," I reply, running my hands down the side of my dress. "The gown is beautiful, Persephone, thank you."

"I must be going," Keres announces as she makes her way back to the door.

"You just got here," Persephone calls after her with furrowed brows.

"Yes, but if I don't check on my brothers, they will show up in their training clothes," Keres shouts from the hall.

"They always are an entertaining bunch," Persephone offers after Keres passes the threshold of my bedchamber..

Nerves are bubbling low inside me. "They seem to be."

Thanatos's words ring in my mind yet again this evening. With the days in passing, all I could think about was his advice. *The Underworld is home to those that have been outcast—the misfits. Go to the ball, darling.* It made me wonder if he was hinting toward something else.

"Persephone?"

"Yes?"

"Who will be in attendance tonight?" Our gazes connect in the mirror. When confusion peaks on the goddess's face, I continue, "Thanatos told me something that has me wondering who is going to be here."

"Those in the court and some that live elsewhere. I don't believe any of The Twelve will attend. Hades tends to avoid inviting them anymore for the comfort of others and the safety of the home he's built."

"The comfort of others?" I ask.

Persephone straightens. "There are others like Leon and Sebastian that have had something taken from them by my father. As you know, Zeus likes to take anything good or anything he can use as a weapon for himself. Hades would rather keep what he has here small and secretive. It's why he doesn't try to change how others view the Underworld."

"He keeps it secret to keep it safe," I finish. My admiration and respect for Hades grows. Since I've been here, Hades has done nothing but show the lengths he is willing to go to for his people.

Persephone nods. "So…you've been chatting with Callan."

"A small bit. Nothing serious."

"You two seem like you've been growing closer."

"He's helping me with my task. I hardly call that growing closer," I counter, then walk toward my bedside table to grab my mother's necklace while ignoring the flutter in my stomach.

"Seeing that daggers have not been thrown and swords have not been drawn recently, I beg to differ."

I giggle. "You'd like me to start throwing daggers at him again?"

"Of course not. I'm not a fan of unnecessary violence," Persephone says as she makes her way toward me. She has a full gown as well, only hers is the color of stars. It shimmers in the moonlight. It looks stunning. She looks stunning. "I'm saying it seems like things are changing."

I deny it to her, but deep down, I believe I'm trying to convince myself that as well.

"I've seen the way he looks at you. I've seen the way you steal glances of him."

My breath stills. That is impossible. I do not have feelings for Thanatos. The same way he does not have feelings for me. We hate each other. "I do not know what you speak of."

Persephone sighs on her way to the door. "Don't let it slip away because you're scared or because it's hard. You are a woman of action. Don't let this be the time you shy away. Pretty flowers by the way."

I want to roll my eyes at the bouquet Thanatos gave me in the garden that I now have sitting on my bedside table. In reality, I can't help but grin at them and the sincerity in his face when he gave them to me.

With each step I take toward the ballroom, Persephone's words ring louder in my head.

"I see the way he looks at you."

Step.

"I've seen the way you steal glances of him."

Step.

"Don't let this be the time you shy away."

"Elena?" Leon's voice pulls me from my trance.

DELANEY NICOLE

"Yes?" I meet his gaze. He wears dark breeches that are the same color as my gown and a tunic the shade of Persephone's dress. It is pulled together with an overcoat Persephone mentioned earlier is called a suit.

"Are you ready?" he asks with his hand braced on the door.

Taking a deep breath, I nod. The large doors swing open with a gust and bring music into the corridor. A symphony of classical music fills my ears. The scent of flowers and other sweets meet my nose. The light from a thousand candles floating in the air greets my eyes. The flowers I smell are purple lilacs which line the edges of the room and form centerpieces on the tables.

Couples dance in the middle of the white marble floor. Others stand against or around white stone pillars on the outskirts of the room. My breath shallows. I've never been to a party like this.

Someone gently touches the small of my back. "Don't tell me this is what scares you when you've gone up against Death himself," Leon whispers. "The others are near the wine."

Leon descends the stairs and gracefully makes his way through the dancing crowd. I follow him with my eyes until he meets Keres, Hypnos, and Thanatos, all drinking wine cheerfully. Leon looks up to me on the stairs, then mutters something to the three of them.

My breathing ceases when my eyes connect with Thanatos's. I begin my descent down the grand staircase.

Thanatos's eyes stay fixed on me and mine on him. My heart swells with something that makes me feel giddy.

"Elena!" Hypnos exclaims, drawing me from my fixed stare on his brother. "You clean up nicely, and you're more modest than my dear sister."

Keres whacks his arm. "You're an ass."

"Thank you, Hypnos," I say. He and Thanatos are in suits like Leon. "You clean up nicely as well." Looking to my side, I meet Thanatos's eyes. "Both of you do."

Thanatos gives a nod but fails to hide his smile behind his chalice. I am vaguely aware that other guests have set their attention upon us. "If you'll excuse me, there is somewhere I need to be."

A flutter of disappointment spreads through me. This is ridiculous. I shouldn't care if he leaves. I shouldn't care what he's doing or where he's going. I shouldn't care if he chooses to find another young lady to share conversation with.

Part of me does care, but I bury that thought.

"Well, if it isn't my children." A stunning woman emerges from the crowd. She is a vision in a sheer fabric dress adorned with stars. Keres is the spitting image of her with pale skin and dark, chestnut hair. She looks young, too young for The Children of the Night to be her children.

"Mother." Keres smiles. "How are you?"

"I'm doing well. Although it would be nice if the three of you would visit," she retorts.

"Mother, you're showing your age by complaining about us visiting," Hypnos mutters while angling his head to keep his remark quieter.

Her eyes grow wide for a moment. "Where is your brother?"

"He's off somewhere," Keres says, casting me a short

DELANEY NICOLE

glance before looking at her mother again. "We'll tell him to find you when he comes back."

Leon whispers to me, "If you can't tell, that is their mother, Nyx. She is the goddess of the night."

"So the nickname The Children of the Night is literal," I whisper over my shoulder as I lean into Leon.

"Essentially, but partially because they do their bidding in the night," he answers.

"What of their father?"

"Ah, Erebus. He's around here somewhere. He is the god of darkness," Leon says.

"Nyx is beautiful," I say, watching as the woman before me speaks to her children.

"Yes, well, she's not that much younger than I," he says, noting my surprise. Compared to most guests in the ballroom, I am no more than a babe.

"And who is this?" Nyx asks, eyeing me beside her children.

Keres steps forward. "Mother, this is Elena. She's staying here while she completes a task for The Twelve. She is a child of Ares."

"Ares?" Nyx's brows raise. "I expected to hear you were a child of Aphrodite before Ares."

"I've been told that many times. It's lovely to meet you," I say. I can't help but be flattered as Aphrodite is known for her beauty.

Nyx smiles. "I must be getting back to the party." She bids her children goodbye before returning to the crowd.

I scan the flock, looking for faces I recognize. Hades and

Persephone are nowhere to be found. I haven't seen Thanatos since he abruptly left the group.

"Leon," I say as I watch a particular pair on the dance floor.

"Yes?" he asks. He is the only one who stayed by my side after the others dispersed.

"Who is Hypnos dancing with?" Hypnos is dancing with a beautiful woman. She has dark skin, a little lighter than Leon's. Her hair is pulled back into a braid that wraps around the crown of her head.

"Peitho, she's the goddess of persuasion and seduction. They've been close acquaintances for a long time. I think they both enjoy each other's company but don't want to admit it to the other," Leon says.

I wonder what business the god of sleep has with the goddess of seduction.

A woman in a silver gown stops in front of us. "Leon, how are you this evening? The top half of her light brown hair is clipped out of her face. Her bright blue eyes directly contrast her slightly tanned skin.

"Eileithyia, how lovely to see you. I'm doing well, and you?" Leon smiles.

"Very well."

"Have you met Elena?" Leon introduces me to the beautiful woman in front of me.

"Elena?" Her voice sounds slightly stunned, but she quickly masks it. The goddess's blue eyes stare at me strangely. I try to mask my uneasiness with a nod, but it's as though she can sense my uneasiness. She shakes off whatever

DELANEY NICOLE

strange trance she was in and says, "What a beautiful name. It was nice to finally meet you. I must be going."

Leon and I share a confused look before he shrugs it off. It takes me longer, but eventually, I chalk her strange behavior up to be the product of too many glasses of Hades's wine and I look to the other side of the ballroom.

"Who is Keres speaking with?"

Leon searches the crowd for Keres.

"Ah, that is Nemesis. She is the goddess of retribution and revenge. But if you'll excuse me, I'm going to ask her to dance."

The end of the song brings a hush over the crowd. Everyone is looking at the terrace, so I focus my attention there.

The doors swing open, allowing Hades and Persephone to make their entrance. They cling lightly to each other's arms.

"It is with great honor," Hades begins with a booming voice, "that I welcome you to this year's solstice ball. I'd like to thank Selene for all the work she does."

A goddess with hair the shade of stars nods from the middle of the dance floor. She nods with an appreciative smile at Hades. This is the first time I have seen Selene. I had heard tales of her but had yet to see her.

"This year's ball comes with an exciting change." Hades's grin deepens as murmurs spread across the room. "This ball is also a celebration of my engagement. This may come as a shock to most of you because I'm such a charming devil." Chuckles pass among the guests. Persephone rolls her eyes with an amused grin.

"But when you love something," his arm tightens on Persephone, "you must fight for it until your very last breath. You may have to fight tooth and nail for them, but if they love you the way you love them, they will always come back and shed light on your life. To my fiancée, Lady Persephone, the future queen of the Underworld."

"Lady Persephone," the crowd repeats, raising their glasses high.

With the commencement over, the music begins again and couples flood the floor, dancing to the melody. Persephone is making her way over to where I stand. She occasionally thanks guests for their congratulations.

"That was the news you were so secretive about?" I say as she embraces me.

"We wanted to keep it a surprise. We hadn't told the others either," Persephone says, glowing with joy. I can't help but feel happy for her. Hades and Persephone are meant to be at each other's side.

"Queen of the Underworld?"

"It's a bit intimidating," Persephone admits.

I eye the goddess, watching as she slowly scans the room of people who will soon be her subjects. "You have nothing to worry about. I've seen the way you care for everything. You will be a wonderful queen."

"Do you really believe that?"

"Having been on the receiving end of one of your lectures, yes, I do," I say sincerely. "I'm happy for you."

We watch couples dance. The entire ball is magical. I decided to let all of my worries about my task fade for just one night. "Have you seen Thanatos?"

DELANEY NICOLE

Confusion marks her face. "Have you not seen him?"

"I saw him for a brief moment, then he mentioned something about needing to do something elsewhere."

"I have not seen him." Persephone shakes her head. "I'm sure he will come around."

I scan the room for his face. I'm not sure why I feel so engrossed by his presence, or lack thereof. To distract myself, I take a heavy pull of wine from my chalice.

"Lady Persephone, please, allow me to offer my congratulations on your engagement," a man says.

"Thank you, Lord Ambrose," Persephone replies. "Have you been introduced to my dear friend, Elena?"

My attention snaps back to the goddess at my side. What is she playing at?

The man's eyes sweep over my frame, and his smile spreads. "I have not had the pleasure. Elena, would you like to share a dance?"

My eyes fall on his extended hand and back to Persephone who has a mischievous smirk on her face. Placing a slight smile on my lips, I meet the handsome man's gaze. "I would be delighted."

He takes my hand and leads us to the dance floor. He is handsome, but he is missing something. His eyes are like oceans of pale blue water, but they lack the amber amusement I find myself searching for.

"Persephone said your name was Lord Ambrose?" I say as we take our position on the floor.

"My real name is Ambrosia, but I go by Ambrose for short. Lord is my title in Hades's court," he says and takes hold of my left hand with his right and my waist with his left.

210

The dance begins, and I follow his lead as we dance in a circle. My breath catches as my eyes fall on a familiar muscular form.

Thanatos stands lazily against a pillar, arms crossed in front of his chest. He wears an expression that resembles that of anger and amusement.

"I'll be damned," I murmur under my breath. So that's what Persephone was grinning about. It wasn't my dance with Lord Ambrose at all.

"Pardon?" Lord Ambrose asks, pausing in his talk about his accomplishments.

"Nothing," I say, hoping he'll move on. Luckily, he does.

With each turn, my head snaps in whatever direction Thanatos is in. My breathing increases rapidly as my dance with Lord Abrose continues. I can practically feel his attention on me.

By the end of the song, my chest is rising and falling at such a rapid rate that it looked like I'd just finished a training session. I'm not sure how Thanatos manages to have such an effect on me, but he does.

"Would you like another—"

"Mind if I cut in?"

CHAPTER 29

My gaze slowly slips from Lord Ambrose and carefully slides from the man's feet up his suit until I reach his face. I don't know whether it is shock, joy, or excitement that bubbles within me when my eyes connect with Thanatos's. His amber eyes are bright as his gaze slips between me and Lord Ambrose. Lord Ambrose offers a tight nod and steps back. Thanatos's arm extends for me to take it.

I mutter, "Don't let this be the time you shy away." I take Thanatos's hand, and he leads us toward the center of the floor. He grabs my waist and my hand. His face is tight as if he's annoyed.

"Is something wrong?" I ask. He does not have to dance with me if he does not wish to.

"It's nothing."

"Tell me."

"I should cut his hands from his body for touching you,"

he mutters. My heart quickens. The way his eyes stay trained on me makes me realize how much he had wished to be in Lord Ambrose's place.

"I don't think Persephone would enjoy violence at her engagement ball," I tease. Thanatos leads us in a box formation as the strings pick up in another song. "But to ease your frustrations, what do you say you make this second one so great I forget I ever danced with another man?"

"I will." His hands tighten on my waist, stealing the breath from my lungs. My body is tense, but the feel of his hands on me makes me relax. They're firm without being invasive.

"You're going to have to do better than that," I tease when I notice the lively dancing around us.

"Challenge accepted."

Thanatos spins me around the floor and lifts me in his arms, spinning me as he does so. It is him and me right now. A laugh escapes me. I feel set free in his arms. I feel accepted.

And when I see Thanatos looking at me like he's never seen me before, I feel my heart flutter. A smile creeps on his lips. I've seen him smile before. This, however, is different. This moment is bigger than the two of us.

"You're smiling."

"I have good reason to," he says.

"I like it when you smile, Callan."

He dipped me in his arms on the last beat of the song. Our noses touch as we stand to catch our breath. I grasp his cheeks, and his hands hold firm to my waist. His eyes bounce from my eyes to my lips, then back to my eyes.

"You called me Callan," he says, briefly squeezing my waist.

DELANEY NICOLE

"I did."

My heart is practically beating out of my chest. His breath cascades against my skin and heat sparks all over my body.

The sound of applause breaks whatever bubble we are in. I look around to see that everyone had stopped dancing. They are watching us.

"I need to go," I mutter before rushing from the ballroom as I try to regulate my breathing.

"Elena!" Thanatos calls after me.

I hurry my steps, trying my hardest to get back to my room before he catches me. I have to get away from him. If he catches me, the reality of the feelings I've tried so hard to keep buried will finally hit, and everything will be so much harder.

"Elena, where are you going?" A firm hand grabs my wrist, halting me.

"I need to go back to my room," I reply, avoiding his stare. I try removing my wrist from his hold but find it useless.

"Why? We were having a wonderful time."

"Going to the ball was a mistake," I murmur, and my face heats with embarrassment.

"Why was it a mistake? Because you're having a great time in a place you're supposed to hate? Or is it because you're having fun with someone you're supposed to despise?" Thanatos's tone sharpens, and he releases my wrist.

"That's not fair."

"No, what's not fair is that you're not admitting the truth to yourself. What's not fair is that you're so fixated on keeping those images of everyone in your head that when they prove they are different, you still choose to run away from them!"

"It's not like that," I say.

Everything has gone from warm and welcoming to icy and frigid, I can't stop the pang of guilt spreading through me because I know it is my fault. I'm the one that caused this.

"Then what's it like? Please, tell me."

"I—" I stop. A tear escapes my eye. I don't know why I'm crying. My body can't keep up with the emotions I feel.

"You know what I think it is?" Thanatos pauses. "I think you know exactly how you feel, but you're scared to admit it because when you do, it will change everything."

"You don't know me!" My voice raises. The truth of his words wound me.

"But I do! I know you more than you know yourself!" he practically yells.

"Why do you care? Why does what I do matter to you?" I ask, my voice straining not to break while another tear escapes me.

"Because you aggravate me!" he shouts.

We stand in silence, his chest heaves up and down as he fixates me with a fierce stare.

"You have found a way to ebb yourself into my mind constantly. I cannot go an hour without thinking of you. You haunt my sleep for gods sake. Do you think I want to be transfixed by your presence? Do you think I do not loathe myself for wanting every part of you that you will give me? This was never a part of the plan. My feelings were never a part of the plan."

"What?" I mutter through the heavy lump in my throat. I

worry that he is lying. If he is, it will break me. I am one break away from being broken beyond repair. Yet, the sincerity gleaming in his eyes makes me doubt my fear. "Why would you say such things?"

"Because what you don't see in yourself," he pauses, "I see. I saw it the moment my eyes met yours. You matter. You matter so much more than you think you do. Something changed in me when you arrived. Everything changed. My world is no longer a planet. My world is a person. It is you."

The air seizes in my lungs. My mouth runs dry, and my heartbeat quickens. I am at an utter loss for words.

Callan paces, waiting for me to say something, anything. But I cannot find words. Every word falls short.

He sighs, then stops. "I should go."

"Kiss me."

Thanatos's head snaps toward mine. I stay fixed upon his bright, amber gaze, "What?"

"Kiss me, Callan."

Before I can take another breath, his lips are crashing onto mine. His hands cup my cheeks in an attempt to keep my lips on his. His kiss is everything I have longed for. Every torment and every struggle I have gone through in the past is worth it for this single moment.

Every past and present anxiety slips into a void of nothingness. That is the power he has over me. He makes me feel as though I am the only person in the world that matters.

Our kiss is passionate. It is longing. It is eager. It is as though we are animals that have been starved until this very moment. The taste of his lips is enough to set fire to my world.

"Never let go of me," I mutter through my breaths while resting my forehead against his.

"Now that I have you," Callan lifts my chin, drawing my eyes to his, "I would never dream of letting go."

Crashing my lips back onto his, I don't care what the costs of this will be. Tonight, I want the chance to live carefree. I break our kiss and take his hand into mine and lead him through the corridors in a half-hurried walk.

We half-run until we reach my door. He pulls at my waist, meeting me in a sweet kiss. I practically melt in his arms.

He braces his forehead against mine. "Elena, I do not want you to think I said all of those things just to bed you like the others. I do not want you to think so little of me."

"You are nothing like them," I say, feeling my heart warm.

Callan scoops me into his arms and rushes us into my bedchamber as a giggle escapes me. Before the large door could even click shut, our lips meet. Everywhere he touches feels as though it is on fire.

Without breaking our lips, he sets me back on the ground. "Turn around," Callan orders.

His lips meet my neck. My head lolls back, offering him more access. He tugs at the ribbons on my back.

I meet Callan's lips, and the ribbons fall from my back. Warm, calloused hands push the dress from my arms down my waist to form a pool of fabric at my feet, which leaves me utterly exposed.

Callan steps back and rakes his eyes from the top of my head down to my feet before trailing them back up a second time. "Beautiful."

He closes the distance between us, kissing the line of my

DELANEY NICOLE

jaw and slowly travels down my neck. I struggle to remove his suit despite how eager I am to rid him of it. Callan's hands meet mine to aid me.

Heat rushes through my body at the sight of him. His chest is sculpted with hard muscles that stretch all the way down and form a perfect V before reaching his mouth-watering cock.

I don't get much time to ogle him before he reaches for my thighs and hoists me atop his waist. A whimper escapes me when his bare chest touches mine.

"Elena," Callan murmurs against my neck, placing me on the soft mattress.

"Yes?" My voice is a whisper.

"Are you sure this is a road you want to travel down? Because once we do, I don't think I'll ever find my way back."

Grabbing hold of him, I say, "Of course. If it means I can call you mine, I'll let you ruin me a thousand times."

"I won't ruin you like the others." He kisses me feverishly.

His kisses leave a trail down my body, and he lifts my leg over his shoulder until they trace every inch from my ankles to the ache between my legs. His tongue laps over where I felt that ache the most.

Apollo had never done this. I'd heard tales of it from Stella. But feeling this is entirely new to me. And, gods, it feels amazing, much better than in that silly dream.

I whimper when his lips connect to my clit in a harsh suck. My hand shoots to Callan's hair and pulls at his roots. A grunt leaves him, which causes vibrations to spread throughout me that feel ravishing. My back arches.

"Callan," I say.

His eyes rise for a moment before he dives back down. I watch him and feel myself clench when the hand that was holding my leg starts pumping his hard erection.

A finger slowly enters me while he continues his skillful work on my clit with his tongue. I moan when he adds another finger. A tightness is coiling in my belly, so much faster than I wanted.

"Let me hear those sweet noises," he purrs, then sucks harshly.

"Callan, I'm going to—"

My back arches off the bed, and I feel that tightness snap and release when his fingers curl upward. He continues his attack until I finally come down from my high.

Callan sits back on his knees and licks his fingers. I clench at the sight. He leans forward and presses his lips to mine. "Would you like the rest?"

"You leave, and I'll kill you in your sleep," I say, pulling him back in for a kiss.

"Tempting," he says, hovering over me.

He stops as I can feel him pressing against my opening. "You have no idea how many times I dreamed of this moment."

His thick cock slowly pushes into me, and I moan. He retreats before pushing further in. He goes deeper and deeper. Finally, Callan groans when his hips meet mine. He stills, eyeing me to ensure I am okay.

"Don't hold back," I tease and wrap my legs around his waist.

"Is that an order?" Amusement flashes across his eyes.

"Take it however you'd like."

He thrusts roughly. I wrap my arms around his shoulders and meet his lips with mine. Waves of pleasure spread through me.

Callan increases his speeds, pounding into me with such ferociousness, I can no longer meet his lips as sounds emanate from my own. His head dips, and he meets the spot just beneath my ear.

I shudder at the unexpected feeling of his tongue lapping over the shell of my ear. I clutch his hair, pulling his roots, making him groan.

His hand drifts between my thighs. A sharp moan leaves my mouth when his finger begins rubbing slow tantalizing circles over the nerves bundled there.

"Callan," I whine. Tight coils build low in my stomach for the second time tonight. I wanted nothing more than to kiss him, but the pleasure I feel from him is too immense.

Callan's thrusts are becoming sloppy. Groans leave his mouth more frequently. "These sounds falling from your lips will be the death of me."

"You're the only one that draws them out like this."

I toss my head into the pillow and my back arches as I finally give in to the pleasure I feel after he nails me with a particularly hard thrust. I shudder beneath and around Callan.

Callan clutches the sheets in his palms as he becomes wholly undone above me, groaning my name.

When he's finished, his eyes stay transfixed on mine as if searching for any remorse in our actions. But there is none—only admiration and happiness.

Callan falls to my side and pulls me flush against his chest. We lay in silence while his fingers trace my spine idly.

Things are different with Callan. With Apollo, feelings were lacking. With Callan, feelings are what drive us. Though I know what we have shared will likely lead to problems, I don't seem to care.

"Promise me something," I say, looking into his bright, honey eyes.

"Anything," he says.

My fingers trace his muscular chest now glistening with sweat. "Promise me you'll be by my side through all of the problems we're going to face because of this."

He kisses my forehead gently as his fingers comb through my hair. "Always."

I nestle into his chest and feel content for the first time.

A piece of parchment flies under the door abruptly.

Callan sits up. "Elena? What is it?"

I climb from the bed and wrap the sheet around my bare body. I scoop up the parchment and scan the scrawled ink. My stomach drops.

"I, um…" I pause, swallowing the bile that threatens to spill from my mouth as he approaches me. His hand graces the small of my back, and I meet his eyes that are growing more worried by the second. "I'm being called back to Olympus."

CHAPTER 30

hanatos

Elena's lilac-scented hair wakes me as I lay at her side. I pull her closer into my chest and watch as she sleeps peacefully in my arms. Her lips pout slightly, and her face is the most serene I have ever seen it. She is beautiful.

It is hard to think I once believed her to be my enemy. It seems strange that we have gone from wielding weapons against each other to sharing a bed.

Elena stirs, turning into my chest. I find myself questioning how I ended up here. I was sure after I professed my feelings that she would run. But she didn't. She showed me in her own way that she felt the same. I felt it in the burning passions that flowed between us.

Elena can't leave. Not now.

A CURSE OF HONOR

I place a kiss on her naked shoulder and get up from the linen-tousled bed, grinning at the pool of black fabric strewn on the floor. I groan internally at her barely-covered body. I want to be here when she wakes. However, I also know that she'd like answers. And I want to be the one that delivers them.

I hurry to the dining hall where I'm sure Hades will be. He would know something of it.

When I push open the doors, I see his broad frame at the long table before me. Persephone is nowhere to be found. "Callan, how lovely to see you this morning. It was a pity to see you leave the ball so early. I'm sure you had more rewarding opportunities."

My gaze sharpens on his mischievous smirk. "Not now, Hades. Do you know anything about the request for Elena's presence back in Olympus?"

Hades sits back in his chair lazily. I know that as a gesture signaling he knows something. "Why should I enlighten you with my knowledge regarding our dearest Elena's duties?"

The amusement lining Hades's arrogant expression annoys me. "Because you and I both know that she is not treated justly atop the Mount. Is it because your 'brother' wishes not to allow such common decency?"

"You care for her," Hades says, folding his hands over his stomach.

My jaw clenches. Of course, I do. I may have believed Elena an enemy in the beginning, but that was before I met the true side of her, the beautifully broken side, the side that makes me want to kill every person, god, or creature that has ever made her feel less than she was.

223

DELANEY NICOLE

"She does not deserve the neglect she experienced while living in Olympus. Now, Hades, please tell me what you know of The Twelve's request."

"As far as I know," Hades says, leaning his forearms against the table, "she is to return only for a day for them to assess her progress in her task. She is to leave in one day's time."

"So it is a temporary visit to Olympus?" A weight lifts from my shoulders, and I make to leave.

Hades nods. "Callan."

I turn to find Hades watching me with a sincere eye.

"I must remind you that her stay here is supposed to be a temporary one."

Ice fills my veins.

* * *

"Elena!" I shout down the hall. She and Leon are heading toward the library, and I haven't seen her since I left her this morning. When I had returned to her quarters, she was gone.

"Callan, how wonderful to see you after your sudden departure last night," Leon says with amused eyes. Elena wears an expression I can only read as annoyed. "May I ask, where did you go?"

"Yes, where did you go?" Elena inquires, folding her arms across her chest with a clipped tone. I am not daft enough to believe she is asking about the ball. She is wondering where I was this morning.

"My apologies, I had an urgent manner to attend to," I say. Elena scoffs and turns her head to the side in a shake.

A CURSE OF HONOR

Leon's skeptical gaze moves between us as if working a puzzle for the answer. "Has something happened?"

"Of course not," Elena says before I could even utter a reply. I stand back in disbelief. Does she genuinely wish for us to remain secret? Annoyance floods my body.

"As she said," I say. The lie tastes bitter on my tongue. But, reading her expression, I know she is testing how far I will take our little charade. So I take it a step further. "Besides, as if I could get over her excessive nagging long enough for anything to happen."

I also know that it would be no use lying to Leon or anyone in Hades's inner circle. They all know something is happening between us. They've been pestering me about the details for ages. Even Persephone said she saw it painted on my face when I rushed Elena back to the palace after the accident.

"As if I could get over his massive ego long enough for anything to happen."

Leon's eyes narrow before he turns on his heel. "I see."

Elena's face is lined with amusement and annoyance as she turns toward the library doors.

I let out a breath and follow her. I find her unshelving books in the same annoyed manner. I take a seat in the chair next to hers and watch. "Penny for your thoughts?"

She huffs. "I woke up this morning alone. I did not fall asleep alone. You can imagine my surprise when I found the other side of my bed cold."

"I had an urgent manner in need of my presence," I say, watching as she places the heavy books on the table with a thud.

DELANEY NICOLE

"Are you going to indulge me with the details or leave me in ignorance?"

"Are you truly that bothered that I was not there at your side when you woke?" I ask, hiding the pleasure it brings me, knowing my absence brought her distress.

She shakes her head in disbelief. "Forget I said anything."

I seize her wrist and pull her into my lap as she passes. The annoyance written all over her face brings me excitement. "Where do you think you're going?"

"Getting away from you." She scowls and tries to stand.

I pull her down on her waist, holding her where she sits. "And if I don't want you to go?"

Her eyes darken and it makes my cock twitch. "I guess you can try remembering how much my incessant nagging annoys you."

I lean just inches from her lips. "I seem to remember a comment about my ego... surely you don't have a huge issue with that. After all, it was not me shouting my name last night."

Her breathing is switching to pants. Her breasts rise quickly, only making me want to take the swells in my mouth. "Callan—"

I kiss her lips before she can finish. I need her as much as she needs me. I place her on the table and force her legs open so I am standing between them.

She pulls me closer, and I kiss her jaw before placing my lips on the spot beneath her ear. It draws the sweetest whimper from her lips. My hand slides up her thigh as her hands find my shoulder and hair. Every time she pulls at my roots, she drives me mad. This woman is like no other.

I bunch the bottom of Elena's dress at her hips. She reaches to remove the dagger from her thigh.

"Keep it," I say and grab her wrist before she can remove the blade. "There's something about you with a dagger that keeps me on edge."

Her eyes become hooded with lust before me.

"Don't tell me you've been turned on every time I've wielded a weapon against you," she teases in a seductive whisper.

I brush the shell of her ear and say, "I'm a man of many secrets."

I trace the length of her thigh, finding her bare beneath her gown. Blood rushes straight to my cock. "You're going to tell me you walked around this palace in just your gown?"

The right side of her mouth pulls upward. "I'm a woman of many secrets."

I trace my fingers over the wetness pooling between her thighs. I groan at how wet she already is.

Sliding my fingers over her wetness, I rub her clit with my thumb. I don't wait before sliding two fingers inside her tight warm pussy.

"Is all of this for me?"

Elena pants as I slowly bring my fingers in and out, pumping at a sluggish pace before I curl my fingers slightly upward. I quicken my thumb's circles slightly while watching her eyes close and her head lull back.

"Use your words, Elena," I say, slowing my fingers close to a stop.

"Yes." She gasps. "It's all for you. Don't stop."

I hurry my fingers, feeling more blood rush to my groin

with each sound she makes. It's almost becoming painful to not be inside her.

"Callan," she whines as she runs her fingers through my hair. "I need you."

"As you wish," I whisper, silently grateful for her plea. I remove myself from my breeches, not bothering to bring them down more than I need to. Relief floods through me as I bury myself inside Elena. It is almost painful to go so slow, but I don't want to hurt her by going too fast.

Elena surprises me by wrapping her legs around my waist and pulling me in until our hips meet. I can't help the groan that leaves my mouth.

"Don't hold back."

"Are you sure you're ready?"

She smirks, then whispers, "I know what I like."

"Is that so?" I say before lifting her from the table to sit back in the chair with her in my lap. "Show me."

She watches me with slightly widened eyes.

"Show me exactly how you like it," I say, pulling her hips down from their elevated position. Another sweet whimper leaves Elena as I stuff her with my cock.

Her mouth opens slightly and she wraps her arms around my neck. Elena rotates her hips, which draws a pleasurable groan from my lips.

I hold Elena's waist as she raises her hips slowly, then slides back down with another whimper. It won't take many more of her sweet sounds before I take control back. But there is something about Elena being in control that drives me wild. Moans fall from her mouth more frequently, hardly keeping quiet.

"You're supposed to be quiet in a library," I tease as I watch her slowly coming undone atop of me.

"Callan," she whines before her mouth falls open with another moan.

Whatever self-control I had leaves me. Tightly gripping her hips, I thrust. As if reading my mind, she leans toward my mouth. She latches her lips on my neck and sucks just under my ear before nipping at the lobe itself.

Her loud cries fill my ears and drive me further into the pleasurable madness only she brings me. I'm flying over the edge after she shudders on top of me, crying out my name as she did.

We cling to each other as we calm. I hold Elena tight to my chest and run my fingers through her soft hair. I hope she knows that I did not wake this morning with regret. I care for her.

"If you must know, I was not there when you awoke because I rushed to Hades to get the details of your request from The Twelve. Do not think I left your side when I awoke because I did not want to be there. I would go to whatever lengths I could to wake at your side every morning, as long as you'll have me."

Her eyes soften and she hugs my neck. "You sought out Hades to learn about my request to Olympus?"

"I needed to know if you were leaving me," I murmur as a pang shoots through my chest at Hades's warning.

"Never." She leans into my lips. Her mouth tastes of nectar and apricots. She is so addictive in every way possible. I'm not sure I'd ever be able to rid myself of her even if I wanted to.

DELANEY NICOLE

She pulls back, making me miss the touch of her lips against mine. "What details did Hades give you about my visit to Olympus?"

I smile, knowing I will be the one to ease her anxieties about her upcoming visit. "He said it was a one day visit to track your progress on your task."

"Just a day," she repeated, visibly relaxing in my arms.

"Just a day," I confirm, pulling her against my lips.

I don't know how I was able to go so long without doing this. She is a goddess in my eyes.

CHAPTER 31

lena

"I will be back before evening hits," I say and graze Callan's soft cheek. His hand rubs soothing circles on my back before moving up and down my arm.

"I still do not understand why your presence is being requested for a day visit." His fingers play with mine, drawing a smile to my lips.

"Would you rather I return there permanently?" I ask with a serious expression.

I turn on my heel and step away. Callan grips my waist and turns me until I am flush against his muscular chest. "I would keep us locked away in my bedchamber for eternity if I could. Do not mistake my understanding of your duties for lack of affection."

DELANEY NICOLE

Heat spreads throughout my body. My breath hitches in his hold.

"Hermes is waiting for you out front," Callan says with a devious smile. He knows what that smile does to me.

My eyes narrow as I step out of his hold. "You're an ass."

Callan feigns amusement. "You wound me."

"I will see you when I return," I say before turning on my heel.

Callan pulled me back into his hold. "Promise?"

Warmth fills my chest as I meet his eyes. I bring my hands to my neck, and unclasp my necklace. "Here." I gently place my mother's necklace in his open palm. "Now you know I'll come back."

He presses his lips against my own.

I smile as I pull back. "I really must be going. Hermes is waiting."

"Hurry back," Callan says as he strolls in the opposite direction.

Hermes is going to be annoyed at my being fifteen minutes late. I hope he does not ask what kept me. I absolutely cannot tell him the truth about Callan. Hermes is the biggest gossip among the gods. The last thing I need is for The Twelve to learn of my most recent pursuits.

I also need to figure out what I am going to do. I was sent to the Underworld to bring Persephone back to Olympus and retrieve Thanatos.

I need to see why The Twelve requested my presence. Then I will start to find a way to have the best of both worlds.

"Elena, how nice of you to finally join me," Hermes says, his words dripping with sarcasm.

"I thought it would be a crime not to bless you with my presence on this fine day," I say, matching his sarcastic tone with one of the same caliber.

"How has life in the Underworld been treating you?" Hermes lifts me into his arms. "It's been a few weeks."

I shrug nonchalantly. I debate upselling it by saying that I am miserable. But I don't think I can pull off a lie of such magnitude. "Not as bad as the some make it out to be, but it is no Olympus"

It is enough of the truth to get away with but vague enough not to need to go any deeper. And it was true. The Underworld is not Olympus. It is much different. The people are different.

"I know what you mean," he says.

We glide through the air as smoothly as a bird. I catch a glimpse of the garden as we fly over the palace. I smile at the memory of the flowers Callan gave me when we studied the plants. Looking back, I don't see how I missed his admiration.

* * *

I SHUT my eyes as we enter Olympus. The sunlight is brighter than the eternal night I've grown used to. Yet another thing I have grown to admire.

"I see sunlight has become a stranger in your time away from us." Hermes chuckles while slowly descending toward the palace of the gods.

DELANEY NICOLE

"A stranger that is expressing its anger at my disappearance," I say as I shield my eyes with my arm.

Hermes places me back on my feet. "You'll be back in the eternal night before you know it."

I had grown used to Hades's palace, but the acropolis is different. It seems bigger. Maybe it is the nervousness of what this meeting will entail and what lies I will tell them until I have a viable plan.

"Shall we?" Hermes offers his arm, standing near the entrance.

I nod and take a deep breath.

The sunlight striking the white pillars radiates more light throughout the expansive building and strikes me as peculiar. Perhaps, I've grown more comfortable in the Underworld than I thought.

Hermes gives the guards outside the throne room an indicative nod before they open the doors. I can already see from a distance that it will be the same company as the last time I was here.

"This is where I leave you. I will be out here waiting for you when you are finished," Hermes says.

"Thank you," I say, releasing his arm.

Each step I take toward Zeus, Hera, and Demeter makes my stomach twist further. My feet are lead. By the time I reach them, it feels as though my stomach will never be able to unwind.

"Elena." Hera nods in greeting.

"Your majesty." I bow on shaky legs.

"You may stand," Zeus says tightly. At my silence, he says, "Well, are you going to fill us in on your progress or do we need to hold your hand through an explanation."

"Forgive me." I say, trying to collect my thoughts. I don't want to lie fully. I'd have to go with the vague truth as I did with Hermes. "I have become acquaintances with them both. However, I am no closer to removing them than I was on the first day I arrived. There are obstacles."

Zeus's eyes narrow. His gaze finds Demeter's and I cast my gaze to her for the first time. She looks drastically different since the last time I was in this room. Her eyes aren't as bright and dark circles line the skin underneath . She carries herself differently. The need for her daughter has taken over her mind, not giving anything else a chance to shine through. "We thought something like this might happen, which is why we are adding something."

"Adding something?" My brows crease.

A small, sinister grin forms on his lips, "Think of it as an incentive. Or don't, I couldn't care less."

My palms grow clammy at my sides. "And what is this incentive you speak of?"

"A trial." The god casually leans back on his throne, resting his intertwined hands on his stomach.

"What?" Hera and I say in unison.

Zeus shrugs. "We have given you a chance to have everything you wanted. All you had to do was bring my daughter back along with the man my brother has been using to kill mortals, and you'd have it all. However, you have shown us you lack the proper motivation, so we will have a trial."

"I have done nothing wrong," I say.

Something glints in Hera's eyes as she meets my stare. I

DELANEY NICOLE

don't know what it was, but it differs from how Demeter and Zeus are looking at me.

"We have trusted you with delicate information regarding The Twelve Olympians. We have given you a specific task to aid the problem we have regarding that information. Should you fail to complete your task of bringing Persephone back —and Thanatos alongside her—in three days, you will face trial for treason."

"Treason? I'm supposed to have three more weeks," I sputter. I would have never dreamed that things would escalate so quickly.

"And now you have three days. We're done here," Zeus says, then signals for the guard to open the doors.

I meet Hera's soft stare before taking my leave. Whatever I had expected from this meeting fell short. I can't feel anything but the shock flowing through my veins.

Hermes looks alarmed when I return to him. "What is it?"

"I…" The weight of what I'd been told sets in. A lump so large I feel like I'm choking forms in my throat. "I have less than one week to complete my task, or I'm going to be tried for treason."

Hermes's eyes grow so wide, I can see the white around his irises, "I see."

"I don't know what I'm going to do," I croak. It feels as though I am living a nightmare. Perhaps I'm still in my bedchambers in the Underworld. Perhaps the goddess of nightmares paid me a visit, put up to it by Leon or Hypnos no doubt.

Hermes takes hold of my arm, hindering me from

walking any further without him. "I know we're not close, but in the short time I have known you, I've found only kindness and friendship. So, would you mind if I took you to lunch before returning you to the Underworld?"

"I'm not sure."

"You're going to need time to process this before you go back."

He's right. If I were to be taken to the Underworld now, they would know something was wrong. And I won't be able to evade the truth with them—from him.

"Okay."

* * *

As we touch down on the grassy expanse, I sweep my gaze over the lone home present. It is pale cream with a dark, mahogany roof. The fields surrounding it are bright green and occasionally hold bright patches of flowers that vary in shape, size, and kind.

"Hermes, where are we?" I ask from behind him. His strawberry-blond hair shines in the light of the sun.

"My home."

"You wanted to have lunch at your home?" I ask, slightly skeptical of his intentions.

"I figured you'd want to keep a low profile before you return to the Underworld tonight," he says.

Whatever intentions I thought he might have had are wiped entirely. Instead, thankfulness fills my mind.

"Thank you."

DELANEY NICOLE

I enter the tiny home behind Hermes. We walk straight into the living area and kitchen. The kitchen is more extensive with white cabinets and a bright glow from the windows, but the setup reminds me of the one the mortals had. His home feels brighter and not as homey as the mortals.

"So this is your home…"

"Not what you pictured?" Hermes chuckles as he shuffles around the kitchen prepping our meal.

"I envisioned something large." I sit at the table situated to overlook his garden. "And dripping in wealth."

He grins. "I prefer the quiet life to the flashy life the others live. I hear everything and know more than the others, so I enjoy the quietness this offers."

"It lets you be who you wish to be without the interference of others."

"Exactly." He places a plate and cup of wine before me.

"Thank you."

Hermes made a fresh salad with cherry tomatoes, chicken, and a tangy aioli drizzled on top.

"This is wonderful, Hermes," I say after my first bit. "Where did you learn to make this?" I ask, hurrying to take a second bite.

"When I'm not sent on errands, I have a lot of free time on my hands. I usually use that to try different recipes I pick up from the mortals."

"And do they always taste like this?" I ask, sipping on the wine Hermes provided.

"No, not all the time. But when they do, I usually write them down so I can remember them later," he supplies.

A CURSE OF HONOR

"Do you mind if I see it?"

"It's on the counter." Hermes leans back in his chair and rests his palms over his stomach.

I walk to the counter and pick up the stray piece of parchment. The handwriting is so familiar.

"What is it?"

"It was you." I look up, meeting Hermes's confused stare. "You wrote the letter telling me I was summoned. You were there. At Hades's ball. You saw— oh gods."

"I saw you with Thanatos," he finishes.

"Did you tell them?"

"No, I have not." Hermes is remaining calm despite my panic.

"I can think of plenty of people that would have."

"I am not one of those people." He motions for me to sit. "Yes, I know more than most. I know things that could make those people fall from grace. However, I have no intention of enlightening Zeus, or any of The Twelve, of the events I witnessed that night."

"What you saw was a dance," I say.

"What I saw was a connection between two sides of the same coin. I saw something I hadn't seen in many years," Hermes corrects.

"I..." I try to think of anything to deny him, but I know it is no use. "Then you see why my task is difficult."

Hermes nods slowly, then gazes to the wind-blown grass. "I don't think it's difficult."

"Hermes, I'm going to be sentenced to trial if I do not bring Persephone and Call— Thanatos here in three days."

He stays silent. It is almost as if he's ignoring me. "In the

239

end, you will do what is suitable for all. You've changed the way you do things. From what I've gathered, you've always done things to appease the wants and needs of others. What if you did something for yourself?"

Shock runs through me at what Hermes is implying. "Hermes, I cannot go against The Twelve."

He smirks. "Naturally. But I believe it is time to return you to the Underworld."

* * *

As we fly, ideas race through my mind about how I can complete my task, but I come up empty each time. I can't betray my friends. I can't betray Callan.

I'm a mess of worry and panic when Hermes places me upon the steps of the palace in the Underworld.

"You will do what is right for those that matter in the end."

"How can you be so sure?" I ask, feeling as though panic is crawling up my throat.

"Because that is all I can hope for."

After watching Hermes leave, I rush through the palace corridors, trying to get to my chambers as fast as I can.

"Elena?" Leon calls as I pass him.

I want to get back to my chambers to think. My steps come to an abrupt halt when I see Callan standing idly against the wall across from my door. Panic spreads further within me. I can't see him right now. It will only make everything worse.

I speed forward, hurrying for my door with watery eyes.

"Elena, you're back," he says, pushing off from the wall. His face contorts when he notices my eyes. "Elena? What is it? Has someone harmed you?"

Before he can utter another question or follow me into my chambers, I close the door, barricading myself from everyone.

"Elena?" Callan's muffled voice sounds from outside the door. I crouch against the door, trying hard to steady my breathing and ease the tightness in my chest as I hug my knees. His sweet voice fills the space around me again, "Elena, let me in. Please."

And because I'm a weak person, I turn the doorknob. I can't seem to want to stay away from him.

"Elena," he mutters, closing the door behind him. He takes me into his arms, and I lean into his chest, letting his warm mahogany smell fill my nose. I try to memorize it while tears stream down my cheeks because I don't know how much longer I'll be able to take comfort in it. How much longer will I get to hold him?

"Elena, what happened in Olympus?" His voice is soft and comforting like his hand rubbing my back.

"I— I can't do it," I say through the tears. My hands bunch in his shirt, pulling me closer in his arms.

His lips press into the top of my head. "Shhh, we'll figure it out. Everything will be okay."

We. That word breaks my heart in half because how can I continue with him at my side when I'm supposed to bring him to Zeus?

DELANEY NICOLE

I can't.

I can't bring him to a god that will use him for his gain. I'd never be able to live with myself. Tears began falling from my eyes and one thought stays persistent in my mind: what am I going to do?

CHAPTER 32

hanatos

UNEASE FILLS me as I lay Elena's sleeping form on the mattress in her bedchamber. I knew something was wrong with her the moment I saw her.

I lightly brush my lips over her temple before marching through the corridors. Bursting through the doors of Hades's study, I find not only Lady Persephone but my siblings and Sebastian as well. They all look at me with alarm.

"Callan?" Hades says, angling his head toward me with concern. I must look as worried as I am.

"Something is wrong with Elena."

"Has she been harmed?" Persephone jumps from her seat on Hades's desk. Alarm was evident on her face.

DELANEY NICOLE

"Where is the bastard that has harmed her?" Hypnos stood from his chair while reaching for his short sword.

"Sit down, brother," I insist. "No one has harmed Elena."

Everyone sags in relief. Hades asks, "Then what do you mean?"

"I believe something happened in Olympus. When she returned, she could no longer look me in the eye. When I finally entered her room, she wept in my arms until she fell asleep," I say, feeling a new wave of worry rush through me.

"Oh, dear," my sister mutters.

Hades rubs his chin in contemplation. "Callan, stay. The rest of you, go up to the dining hall. Dinner will be served shortly."

I wait as everyone departs the study and take a seat in the chair across from Hades.

He leans forward and says, "What is it you believe happened in Olympus?"

My mind races with many possibilities, mainly thoughts of that sad excuse of a god, Apollo. He emotionally abused her for gods know how long. The things I would do if I could only get my hands on him. "I do not know. All I know is that it was bad enough to make Elena hardly able to speak to me."

Hades lets out a sigh. "Then we will leave her be until she is ready to speak with us."

"And if she doesn't come around?" I ask, feeling anger make its way to the surface.

"Then that is her choice. We cannot force her to speak of what happened in Olympus if she does not wish to."

"So we are supposed to sit idly by and watch as she cries herself to sleep every night?" My voice turns bitter. He can't expect me to sit by while the woman I care for is dealing with something that troubles her significantly.

"No, you are supposed to give Elena her space because that is what she needs as the woman you love!" Hades snaps.

I swallow thickly. "I think you mistake my feelings for—"

"I mistake nothing," Hades barks. 'You have loved her for ages. You have found the other half of your soul in that woman. Pushing her for answers will only scare her away. So you will leave her be until she is ready to talk."

Hades is right. Elena needs time to deal with whatever happened in Olympus. When she is ready, I will be here.

Finally, I nod. "I will leave her be until she is ready."

"Elena is a strong woman. I'm sure she will persevere through whatever she is dealing with."

CHAPTER 33

lena

I FIND myself unable to leave my chambers. It's only been a day since I was threatened with trial, but I haven't let anyone visit, especially Callan, since I cried in his arms. It's too hard.

I need to find some way to get my task completed. But the thought of ripping Persephone from Hades and taking Callan to Zeus makes me ill. So, instead, I find solace in reading through the diary I found in the library.

Today, however, I plan to train. It was always the easiest way to clear my mind when I lived in Olympus. Hoping it will give me answers, I dress in training clothes before proceeding out to the corridor.

"Elena." Leon stands from the wall. Surprise lines his features in my presence. "I didn't expect to see you out."

"I'd like to train," I mutter, barely meeting his eye as I speak.

He nods, leading us down to the ring.

The ring is empty when I enter, thankfully. I stand in the center with a sword and shield, but nothing feels right. I need an opponent.

I walk toward the entrance and peek my head through the door to find Leon standing outside. "Leon, I was wondering if you'd like to train with me? I do better with an opponent."

"I suppose I can," he says jovially.

Leon grabs a sword and shield from the wall. He walks to the center of the ring, readying himself.

I slash my sword through the air and meet Leon's shield in a loud clamber. I put forth all the emotions I've been feeling in past days into this fight. It clears my mind. It is also why Athena claimed I was different than most. I lead with compassion and great emotion, something many in my field lack. Most soldiers simply enjoy the combat.

I duck, driving my shield up to protect myself from Leon's swing. I thrust my sword forward as I spring up from my crouched stance and narrowly miss Leon's arm.

"Woah, Elena. That was a close one," Leon says.

I begin to feel all of the stress from what lay ahead start to rise. I start swinging my sword in all directions, not caring if any hit as my eyes begin to sting and my throat constricts.

When a slash lands dangerously close to Leon's neck, he starts meeting each of my swings, pushing me back each time as our swords meet. I am so distracted by the terror of my future that I no longer try to stop him. My sword springs free of my hand and clambers loudly on the ground beside me.

My eyes trail from my sword to my empty hands, then up to Leon. The last sliver of light within me is vanquished by the dark storm that terrorizes me.

"Elena?" Leon asks cautiously.

My eyes sting. "I— I don't know what I'm going to do."

Without so much as another word, Leon opens his arms to me. Though I've been trying to distance myself from everyone as I figure out my plan, I need this.

His arms wrap firmly around me, allowing a safe space while I cry. It's ironic that I am in the arms of a man that, when I met him, knew I came ready to watch the Underworld burn.

"Elena," He says timidly, "what happened when you went back to Olympus?"

"I..." I stutter in a cry. "I'm going to be sent to trial for treason against The Twelve if I fail to complete my task in two days."

His hand stills against my back. Even people that live in the Underworld know what being tried for treason against The Twelve meant.

"Then I will help you complete your task. Callan will help you complete your task," he supplies, a new wave of determination filling his voice.

"No." I break free of his arms. "I can't. I won't."

"What could be so bad that you would rather be tried for treason?" he counters.

No matter how much I wish I could talk to someone about this, I can't tell him. I can't tell anyone. "I need to go."

A CURSE OF HONOR

Running through the corridors, I avoid everyone I pass until I reach my chambers. Once inside, I draw a warm bath, adding scented oils to soothe my aching muscles. I grab the diary and climb into the warm steam bath.

The diary acts as a short distraction. It calms me. And for some reason, I felt connected to it. As though I was meant to find it. I had read through the majority of parts about the woman's life with her husband. It seemed rather dull like it was missing something.

Dear Journal,

I felt it. That spark I've seen so many others have. The same spark that many think I have because of who I am. I felt it with him.

It was raining, so we ran back to his stables for shelter. We were too far from his main home. There was something about the way his eyes shined when they looked at me. Maybe it was the way his smile made my heart skip a beat. Either way, I was drawn to him.

Before I knew it, my lips were on his, and we were tussling around the ground of the empty stables. I don't think I've ever felt so alive, so... loved. Everywhere he touched felt as though it were on fire. We held a burning passion that I never thought possible.

I still find it hard to believe he feels the same. He's more than I thought he would be. If only things weren't so complicated.

It's almost as though I can feel her passion and love for the man flowing from her very writing. By the time I climb out of the bath, it has long since turned cold. I am exhausted both physically and mentally.

DELANEY NICOLE

I fall fast asleep before my head even hits the pillow.

* * *

I AWAKE to the sound of knocking on my door. Disoriented, I stumble toward the door. Upon opening it, I see Persephone's worried face. The goddess stands before me with a tray of steaming soup and bread.

"May I come in?" she asks, peeking over my shoulder into my empty room. I wish she hadn't come, but I miss speaking to her.

"Is that the soup you had the chef make when we first dined together?" I ask. My voice is timid, scarce even.

Persephone gently places the tray on the small table by the couch, ushering me over. "Yes, it is. I always enjoy it when I'm not feeling my greatest. Now, come sit."

I hum in satisfaction at the deliciousness of the soup. I've barely eaten since I returned. This feels like a godsend to my body. But that is overshadowed by unease. "Are you going to ask me what happened in Olympus like the others?"

Persephone pours herself a glass of wine. "I'm not. You'll tell me if you want to. But I did not come here for answers. I came to make sure you had eaten."

I sigh after another spoonful of soup. "I do not believe I am ready to."

Persephone's hand gently grasps my forearm. The touch is welcoming, caring. "That is absolutely okay. You never have to tell us anything you're not ready to."

"How do you do it?"

"Do what, darling?"

250

"How do you stay so positive all the time?"

A small smile pulls on Persephone's lips. "Because even though my life was much different than yours in Olympus, I still struggled a lot. Eventually, I learned positivity is not pretending as though everything is okay all of the time. It is knowing that, eventually, it will be."

Giving my hand one last squeeze, Persephone makes her way to the door. "Do me one favor?"

"Yes?" I ask, feeling tears brim my eyes.

"Don't shut us out," she says before exiting the room.

While finishing my soup and bread, I consider the friends I've made during my stay. They've shown me kindness that is unmatched by anything I've ever seen. Callan has offered me a connection more substantial than any other.

My hands wipe at my wet cheeks as tears fall from my eyes. "I do not wish to shut you out. But I cannot see how things will get better."

CHAPTER 34

*I*t has already been two days, yet all I have done is read the strange diary and languish in the idea that I will not find a way out of my trial. There would be no way I would forgive myself if I went through with my task.

Sitting in another warm bath, I take hold of the diary yet again.

Dear Journal,

Worry has webbed its way into my heart and mind alike. I am with child, but it is not my husband's. It is with the man that I have fallen for. And while I am overjoyed to be bringing his child into this world, my husband can never know. I fear what Hephaestus will do if he were to find out. It could mean harm to my child.

You should have seen the light in my love's eyes when I told him of the news. I don't believe I have ever seen him so happy. With that happiness came strategy. I suppose going to war frequently will make one quick on their feet.

A CURSE OF HONOR

I am to tell my husband the babe is his to avoid harm coming to me or the babe. My love has promised to visit throughout the pregnancy and hide from Hephaestus. Then, I will raise the child with my husband while allowing secret visits with their actual father, the man I truly love.

I sit up straighter in the tub. This is the first time one of the men has been named. The woman's husband is Hephaestus. That makes this Aphrodite's journal. And not just any journal, a journal noting a secret affair.

This is astonishing.

The babe she speaks of must be my brothers before she realized they were twins. It has to be. Aphrodite is only known to have stepped out on her marriage once.

I climb from the tub and dress in a silk gown. A tray of food is on my bed when I enter. Leon must have put it there when I was bathing. He's been trying to ensure I eat since Persephone visited. I, however, seem to lack an appetite.

"May we talk?"

I nearly jump out of my skin.

"Apologies," Callan says from the same chair he sat in the first night he approached me. The memory brings a lump to my throat.

I hold his stare, only for a moment before I look away. It hurts too much to see him. "What are you doing here?"

"I have come to talk to you."

"I do not wish to speak with you," I say tightly, placing the diary on my bedside table. The lie tastes bitter passing over my tongue.

"Well, I do," Callan says. From where he stands across the room, I miss the way his arms feel around me. "I tried to visit

253

DELANEY NICOLE

you the day after you returned, but Leon said you insisted I not be allowed in. I tried to give you time to do whatever navigating it was that you needed to do, but Elena, it's been days."

"I know how long it has been," I snap.

"So what? Are you going to push us all away? We care about you. You're going to push me away because of whatever happened on the Mount?" His tone sharpens as his anger rises.

"You have no idea what you're talking about."

"Enlighten me." He waits for me to say something. Anything. "Perhaps you've come to your senses. Maybe you realized it was silly to make friends with the people that so many fear. Gods that kill the innocents. Or, maybe, The Twelve whispered in your ear. They only care for you when you're doing what they ask of you. And the worst part is that you know that."

"That is not why I've kept myself away!" I yell. I turn to face him for the first time. He'd walked closer since I'd turned away. We stand a few feet from each other.

"Then what is it?" He shouts.

My eyes begin to sting, "I can't do this."

"Why are you running?"

"Because." My throat constricts. "I am facing trial for treason against The Twelve in a day and a half because I cannot do what was asked of me."

His face grows pale. "But a trial for treason... if you are found guilty—"

"I will be executed," I finish in a hoarse whisper. Tears threaten to spill on my cheeks.

"What is the task?" A new sense of urgency finds its way into his demeanor. "Whatever it is, I will do it for you."

"No."

"Elena, you will not be executed. I will not let you!"

"You will not be doing it," I say with finality.

Callan's hand rakes through his hair in stress, "Are you so desperate to leave that you'd rather be executed? I thought you enjoyed it here."

"I do. I've become part of a family here. It is why I must do this on my own," I say, feeling a new wave of panic strike me. I can't bear the thought of Callan believing I did not want him.

"What is the task?"

"No."

"What is the task, Elena?" he demands.

My head drops to my hands. It feels as if someone has placed a stone block on my chest. My hands grow shaky. I can't breathe.

"Elena." Callan's hand lifts at my chin, making me meet his eyes. But I can't look him in the eyes. Not like this.

"No." I push from his hold, finding it harder to breathe with his calm touch. He stands watching me with a devastated gaze, making this hurt that much more.

"Elena, you're okay," he mutters, trying to calm me from my frantic state.

"There is a reason," I mutter.

"I know," he says in a gentler tone.

"If I do not bring Persephone and you to Zeus by the end of tomorrow's dawn, I'm going to trial for treason against

DELANEY NICOLE

The Twelve." A tear falls down my cheek as my eyes finally meet his.

Callan's face crumples in understanding. His jaw hardens. It is as though he finally realizes why I isolated myself from them. I won't be the reason their family is torn apart. His head hangs between his arms as he braces his neck for several long moments. I prepare myself for his fury.

His head slowly rises and his arms drop. "If I'm not mistaken, you must get at least half of The Twelve to agree you are guilty for you to be charged, yes? You already have your father and Athena, maybe even that bastard Apollo. I'm sure Hermes will help. You'd only need two more."

I shake my head, my throat constricting. "I am only a demi goddess."

"So?"

I sigh, wiping my wet cheek. "In a trial for demi gods and goddesses, Zeus is the sole decision maker. The rest of The Twelve are just witnesses. He is the one that arranged my trial for failing him. And I will fail him. I cannot do that to Hades and Persephone, or you."

He catches me with the amber gaze I love too much for my own good. Yet I only see pain in them now. "Elena, I was only ever yours to have."

Another tear falls on my cheek. "That's the problem."

Silence passes between us. How I wish things could go back to the way they were after the ball when I was happy with him. When we were happy together.

"So this is it? You're going to leave. You expect me to sit around and wait for you to be unjustly executed?" I watch his face twist in anguish at the mention of my execution. As though it is as painful for him as it is for me to think of living in a world without him.

"If you love me, then you will let me be. You will let me go because this is what I wish," I say.

His eyes rake over my frame as I lean against one of the bedposts. "Elena, don't do this. I love you."

A crack forms deep in my chest before I speak. "And how do you know that love is not merely the repercussions of the bond we share?"

Anger crosses his eyes before another layer of hurt. "You do not believe that. Otherwise, you would have brought it up sooner."

Another crack forms in my chest when his face crumples at my silence. "I need you to leave."

"Elena, I am a man of my word. I will not break the promise I made to you," he says through a hardened jaw. I could have sworn I heard his voice waver.

"It is not breaking your word if I am asking you to," I say, twisting the invisible knife in my chest. "Callan, I need you to leave."

His jaw works, his eyes stay fixated on mine. They hold so much hurt and I caused it. A tear falls down his cheek as he strolls toward the door. "Goodbye, Elena."

The door closes, leaving me in darkness. The darkness that, for the first time, feels so unwelcoming it causes more pain. I fall to my knees, clutching my chest as I weep.

I am alone. I am all alone.

CHAPTER 35

Today is the day I will leave the Underworld for good. My trial is set for tomorrow's dawn. Should I be found guilty—as most demigods are—I will be executed with a sword, forged by Hepaestus, cursed to rip the soul of whomever it is wielded against.

Hermes took my belongings back to Olympus last night. The only thing that remains is me. Climbing from my bed, I slowly start getting ready. My stomach feels sick knowing that Hermes will be here soon.

I dress in a black peplos and tie my hair back in a loose braid. Finally, I take one last lap around the room. I reminisce on all the good, happy times I had here. The place I once despised had become a safe space.

With each step I take in the corridors, the more I realize how much of a home I've found in this palace. This family of misfits welcomed me with open arms, and I somehow joined them.

Just before reaching the palace doors, I stop and glance to my side. There, at the end of the corridor, is Callan. He stands in the same black chiton he wore on the first day I arrived. His face looks grave. It is not how I want to remember his beautiful face, so I give him the best smile I can without crying, then I continue forward. Leon waits at the palace door.

"It was a pleasure serving you, Elena." Leon bows at the hip.

"Don't get formal on me now, Leon." I chuckle but find it harder to hold back my tears. Goodbyes have never been hard for me. But, perhaps, it is because these feel final. I hug him. "I'm going to miss your snark."

"I don't know where I'll get my entertainment now," he snickers, releasing me from his hold.

"I'm sure you'll find someone," I say, looking outside to the group waiting for me. With them stands Hermes. "I suppose I must be going."

Leon gives one last nod as he holds the door open while I pass to begin my descent down the stone steps. Hypnos offers me a short, departing nod before I move on to Keres.

Keres grasps my hand, squeezing it once. "It is a shame you must leave just when I was getting used to you."

I offer a thin-lipped grin. Keres may have scared me most of my time here, but I have a feeling we would have gotten along if we only had more time.

Hades takes my hand next. "You were a good fit here. It is not going to be only Persephone and Thanatos that are going to miss your entertaining presence."

Callan must not have told him about my task. I give

DELANEY NICOLE

Hades my thanks for allowing me to stay in not only his kingdom but his home as well. I can never repay his kindness.

Persephone wraps me in a tight hug. "I do not wish for you to go."

"I wish I did not have to," I mutter, finding it completely useless to hold back my tears now.

"Then stay." Persephone holds me at arm's length.

I cut a glance at Hermes to my right. "I'm afraid it is not that simple anymore."

Persephone pulls me back in. "You better write to us when you're up there."

A tear cascades down my cheek. "I will. I promise."

Hermes slowly walks forward. "I'm afraid we must be going."

Persephone releases me from her grasp and allows Hermes to lift me into his arms. I give one last wave before Hermes leaps into the air. I watch as the people who really care for me grow smaller and smaller until they look like nothing more than specks of dust.

"You're crying," Hermes says.

I wipe my cheek dry and rest my chin upon his shoulder. "They do not know what lies ahead of me."

Silence falls for the remainder of the trip back to Olympus. I do not feel like talking, and Hermes, thankfully, notices that. Hermes lands outside my townhome's door.

"Do you think you could take me to my father's house? I'd rather be there for my last night." My eyes scan the small part of the city I can see from where I stand. It seems bleak, not as lively as it had before all of this.

He nods. "Of course."

My father's estate looks larger than I remember. Strange, seeing that I have just come back from staying in a palace.

"You know where to find me if you need me," Hermes says as he touches my arm gently.

"Thank you. Either way, you will see me. Whether it is on my time or before The Twelve as my life hangs in the balance." My gaze stays fixed upon the house.

"Way to keep things bright and happy," Hermes replies, turning solemn. "I do hope to see you before I must fulfill my impassive role in your trial."

I stand alone on the steps of the home I was raised in, the home where I knew love when my father was around, the home where my brothers tormented me upon their arrivals, and the home where I learned to pick myself back up when no one noticed I had been down.

Breathing deep, I walk inside. The house seems quiet, empty even. "Hello?"

"Elena?" My father's voice sounds from a distant room. His footsteps could be heard on the marbled flooring. "Elena, I didn't expect you."

"I—" He pulls me into a comforting hug. "I needed to be here."

His hands strokes my back, soothing me the way he always used to when I was a child. "You will always have a place here."

* * *

DELANEY NICOLE

I SPENT the next hour looking over my belongings in my childhood room. This room is more lavish than my father or I liked to live, but it is expected that The Twelve live in lavish estates.

And Ares always does what is expected of him.

Sitting on the soft couch, I grab Aphrodite's journal from my bedside table. I'm not sure how Aphrodite would feel if she knew I was reading one of her journals, but it brings me an odd sense of comfort. I'll take anything that gives me comfort over these next few days.

To my daughter whom I did not get to raise,

I will never get to hear you giggle for the first time or whimper in your sleep. You were torn from me too early.

I am sorry. I never wished for things to end up the way they have. How I wish I could have held your sweet little hand or taught you the beauty of true love.

To my dear daughter, I love you.

I stare at the pages before me, feeling a new wave of anguish. This time it's not for myself but for Aphrodite. The babe was not one of my brothers. Even worse, she lost it.

A knock sounds on the door. "Elena, would you like to join me for dinner tonight? We can eat on the terrace."

I look back at my father, standing at the door with hopeful eyes. The world's greatest soldier is looking at me with pleading eyes to join him for a meal.

After a moment's silence, I nod. "Yeah, okay."

A faint smile peaks through on his lips. "Dinner will be ready at dusk. For now, I must go to the Mount to prepare things for tomorrow."

A CURSE OF HONOR

* * *

THE WAVES CRASHING against the rocks beyond the estate's land are exactly like the inside of my mind these past few days. I am drowning in my thoughts. Whenever I come up for air, another wave crashes, taking me deeper into the whirlpool of darkness in my mind.

"Elena?" A voice calls from the door, a voice I haven't heard since before I left for the Underworld.

I glance at the door. "Athena, what are you doing here? Shouldn't you be atop the Mount with my father?"

"Come with me," she says and leaves before I can utter my rejection.

I catch up to Athena as she's walking out of the estate and onto its yard. I walked these fields many times in my youth. They always held a sparkle. But, now, they appear grim as though the light of innocence and youth was stolen in the night.

"So," I trudge forward, "are you going to tell me why you've dragged me from my bedchamber?"

Athena stops in front of the training ring in the field. "Sometimes going back to the beginning will lead you to a different end."

I shake my head as I eye the goddess before me. "I am no longer worthy. I am being tried for treason in less than a day against the very institution you lead."

"I get to decide who is and isn't worthy of training with me. And you, my dear, are more worthy now than anyone else in Olympus. Get your sword."

Reluctantly, I grab my sword and shield and meet Athena

DELANEY NICOLE

in the ring. I never pictured myself back in the ring with Athena.

The last time we trained together, everything was easy. I would wake up, tend to my balcony flowers, walk in the city, train, and visit Apollo. I had a fixed set of activities each day that kept me distracted and pushed me toward my goal.

Now, I stand before the woman I looked up to, the woman I aspired to be, as a failure. I always have been. The signs were always there, and yet I chose to ignore them.

Athena and my father probably only said I had potential because they didn't want to hurt my feelings. Or maybe my father couldn't handle having a failure for a child so he told Athena to train me in hopes that I'd somehow be great. How pathetic am I? I deserve my trial and execution for failing The Twelve.

"Hey," Athena's grasps my forearm, "it's just you and me."

When I swing my sword, metal clashes with metal. Athena knows all of the tricks. After all, Athena taught me most of them. This, however, means I know most of hers as well. This is a battle of strengths not tricks.

Sweat lines my skin. Hair starts sticking to my neck. My breathing is heavier, and my muscles are pulled taut.

I haven't been challenged like this since I battled Thanatos, the same day I saw his wings for the first time, the same day I made him laugh for the first time. Thinking of him brings a pang to my chest.

And, because of Zeus's twisted ways, I'll never get to see him again. I will likely never see anyone again.

In a surge of strength, I spin and swing my sword with such might that it knocks Athena's sword from her hand.

With a loud clamber of the metal sword, Athena grins with proud eyes. "That is why I chose you."

"Well," I pant, "it doesn't look like it will make much of a difference after tomorrow."

Athena assesses her hands. "You may be right. It may be foolish to hope for a different outcome. But if that is true, then I will gladly be a fool, at least for tomorrow."

"Athena," I pause.

She turns back towards me and her green eyes meet mine with sadness gleaming in them. "Yes?"

"Is there truly no way I will make it out tomorrow alive?"

Her face remains somber. "I'm afraid it is unlikely since Zeus is the only one to hand you your verdict."

"I was afraid you'd say that." My eyes begin to sting as another wave of hopelessness takes over me. I feel like I'm being suffocated. I look away as I will my tears to stay put until Athena is gone.

"One more thing before I depart." Athena waits for me to meet her eyes again. "Zeus may be the decision maker, but his confidence comes from the numbers behind him and the lack thereof behind you. Just think about that."

I stay in the center of the ring as Athena leaves. I lift my face to the sun and allow it to warm my body and soul.

My breathing settles. My eyes fall to the new calluses forming on my hands, covering the old smoothed-over ones. The wind rustles the hair that had fallen on my back and cools the back of my neck. Birds chirp in the distance.

With a tear slowly dribbling down my cheek, I whisper to myself, "I am not what they say I am. I am fierce. I lead with compassion. I am a warrior. I— I can do this."

CHAPTER 36

hanatos

I NEVER BELIEVED in love the way the poets write it. I never believed there were such things as a connection felt in the soul. But after meeting Elena, I know what they say is true. I feel it in my very bones.

Now, all I am left with is a gaping hole where my heart should be. Perhaps The Fates will grant me mercy when she is gone. Perhaps they will end my suffering.

"Callan," Hades says from behind me.

I turn and look at the god behind me with reddened eyes. I've hardly seen anyone since Elena departed. It was easier this way.

"She is gone." Hades's face softens. "You knew this day would come. You knew she would return to Olympus when her task was complete."

"Her task is not complete," I mutter, turning back on the soft bed made of purple linens. The very room where everything started and ended.

"I beg your pardon?"

"Elena never completed her task," I say again. I meet Hades's gaze as I walk around the large bed. "She was called back to Olympus because she failed to complete her task to The Twelve's satisfaction."

"What are you saying?" Hades's brows furrow.

Anger at Zeus bubbles within me. "I am saying that Elena is going to trial for treason against The Twelve for not completing her task."

Hades's eyes grow. "Treason? Why would she be tried for treason if she was merely reading over old military information? Unless— What was Elena's real task?"

I remain silent, knowing it will anger Hades if he knows the true nature of her presence in the Underworld.

"Callan, what was her task? I dismissed my worries of her after you assured me she wasn't here for nefarious activities. Now I command you to tell me what her task was." He says again in a calm calculated tone.

Letting out a defeated sigh, I relent, "Elena was sent here by Zeus to retrieve Persephone and myself." I watch as a fire builds in Hades's eyes. "Elena refused to complete the task because she knew what it would do to us. I was angry too when she told me. Hades, she is going to be executed tomorrow because she could not bear the thought of ripping Persephone from you and taking me to Zeus."

Hades's face softens. "Callan."

DELANEY NICOLE

"Hades, she is going to be murdered and I cannot do anything to stop it."

"Callan," Hades says in a soft tone. His face softens in sadness.

"I've lost her."

"You did not lose her."

"Hades, she pushed me away before she left," I counter, feeling another wave of pain at the memory of that night. The hopelessness in her eyes. "I watched as that fire in her eyes dimmed, and her will to live was extinguished. I watched her give up for the sake of my life and Persphone's life before my very eyes. After her accident, I thought I'd never feel worse agony. But I was wrong. Watching that light leave her eyes was the hardest thing I've ever had to watch."

"I do not know what to say," Hades mutters quietly. I have never seen Hades rendered speechless. "Elena is a strong woman and has been since the day I met her. It takes a great deal of strength to give up oneself for those you love. Elena didn't bat an eye before deciding to do so."

"That does not mean I wanted her to sacrifice herself in my place," I bark. "I'd choose to die a thousand times before I'd let her take her last breath even once."

Hades looks at me with an unfamiliar expression. "That is why I had the wards on the palace strengthened. You cannot leave. Things may come in, but they cannot get out unless I say so."

Anger flashes through me. I will not be forced into a corner. "Hades you cannot—"

"I can. I am the ruler of the Underworld. I rule as I see fit.

I don't need you doing anything rash, including flying to Olympus."

The thought crossed my mind nearly every time she did. "The Fates will not be pleased that you are keeping me from doing my job."

A knowing smirk draws on his face. "The Fates will understand when I tell them I did it to keep you away from capture by Zeus."

"Hades—" I sigh. "I cannot let her go."

"That's the beauty of love." He walks to the door. "It breaks you the same as it builds you. Love is both the aid and creator of madness."

CHAPTER 37

lena

When I walk out on the terrace and meet the chill night breeze in my lavender peplos, I look out over the ocean, searching for that same feeling I used to get when I was here before. It isn't there. Everything has lost its luster.

"You look like your mother standing out here, all alone," Ares says from against the door-frame.

"Then it must hurt for you to see me," I mutter.

He shakes his head. "Nonsense. When I see you, all I can think of is how proud she would be of you."

I swirl my wine in my chalice. I can only imagine how different things would be if I were raised by my mother. I likely wouldn't be waiting to be tried for treason. I'd probably have younger brothers and sisters who were mortals. I'd likely have settled down with a mortal man, not ever knowing the passion that could've been just beyond the mortal realm. But then again, I wouldn't know what it feels like to have it ripped from me either.

"Father?" I take a swig of wine as plates are placed in front of us.

"Yes?" he asks, spooning a heaping helping of vegetables in his mouth.

"Did you know Aphrodite lost a child?"

Ares goes stiff in his chair. "Yes, I believe I do. If I'm correct, it was the same night you were born."

I feel my eyes grow wide. "What?"

"Artemis was so busy trying to save both Aphrodite and the babe the night you were born that she was never able to make it to your mother's bedside." His jaw works. "Hephaestus was too busy welding to be at her side."

Something churns deep within me. I'm not sure what it means. "Do you remember what the babe was?"

My father tenses yet again. "I— I believe it was a son. I could be wrong. It's been quite a long time since then. Tell me, Elena, how did you find out about this child?"

I swallow the warm lump of roasted lamb before I say, "I was reading over some things in the library when I was in the Underworld. Thanatos knocked a journal off one of the shelves, and I read it. I figured out that it was Aphrodite's when she made references to Hephaestus."

My father slowly drops his fork and looks up at me with concerned eyes. "You worked with him? With one of The Children of the Night?"

I internally chastise myself for mentioning him. "Yes, I

did. Hades asked him to aid me in the completion of the task I told them I was there to complete."

"He didn't harm you?" Wonder hides behind his concern.

I shake my head. "He didn't. It's not how most think it is down there."

My father's eyes set upon me in an unknowing state. "I'm going to turn in for the night. I have an early morning."

Hopelessness spreads even further through me. Even my own father won't listen to what I have to say about the Underworld and the company I kept while there.

"Sometimes," Ares stops at the door, still facing away from me, "family is who we choose rather than who is given to us at birth. Most find that their chosen family will go to larger lengths to protect us."

"Father—"

"Goodnight, Elena." He rushes in, leaving me on the terrace alone.

* * *

I STAND OUTSIDE The Muses as the stars gleam in the sky. A place I always found security in. A place I had believed I met friends and companions in. I sit in my favorite spot to take in the landscape that I took for granted for so long.

"Wine?"

I look to find the woman who is offering me exactly what I need. "Melpomene, I can't believe you're here."

"Please, call me Mel," she says as she pours me a glass of wine and sits. "What is on your mind? I could practically see the trouble radiating from you."

I take a deep gulp of the sweet wine before I answer, "In about twelve hours, I'm going to be tried for treason... against The Twelve."

"I've heard about you," Mel says. "The favored female of Athena turned treasonous monster."

"Is that what they're saying about me?"

"I may have exaggerated a bit." Mel shrugs. "May I give you a piece of advice?"

"I suppose. It's not like there is much that can change my future."

"I've seen many failures. I see them before most mortals notice they are. Do you want to know why? Because they are not strong-willed enough to persevere when it gets hard. They don't seek the light and they give up."

I don't want my life to be considered some great tragedy.

"I've only been sitting with you for a few moments, but I am usually a good judge of character. You, darling, are different than the others. You have the power and strength to protect those you love. You'd go against the largest army if it meant the ones you hold most dear are able to live in peace." Mel stands from her seat. "You will always do what is right. It will work out in the end. You are not meant for failure or tragedy."

"You gathered all that in a few minutes?"

"Like I said, people talk and I'm a great judge of character."

It seems that everyone I speak with has the same answer. Everyone in Olympus is telling me things will work out as I go up against The Twelve. But it is not up to Athena, or

DELANEY NICOLE

Hermes, or my father. It is Zeus's decision tomorrow. It always is.

I leave as the crowds begin to pour in. I find myself disliking the night. It reminds me of what once was and what could have been.

"Elena?" A voice calls down the cobbled road. "Elena, is that you?"

I turn, awestruck by the woman in front of me. "Miss Alexandra."

"Oh my gods, Elena, I heard what happened," Miss Alexndra says as she pulls me into her arms while others pass. "I can't believe they have done this to you."

"Likewise," I mutter.

Her dark eyes soften. "Walk with me? I promise not to take long. It's on the way to your father's. I've missed your visits."

I realize I've missed the company of the woman I once considered a mother figure, and I nod. "It won't hurt."

A smile spreads on Alexandra's lips. "Wonderful."

We walk in silence until we find ourselves away from the others. "Is it true what they say, you didn't finish your task?"

My breath hitches. Word really has spread in my absence. "Yes, it is."

"That does not sound like the Elena I know," she says solemnly.

I huff. "I learned things in the Underworld that make me unworthy in the eyes of The Twelve. I suppose I never was one they were fond of."

"It pains me that you do not realize your worth here." Miss Alexandra brings her gaze upon me. "You are a beautiful woman with a kind nature. I have watched you run yourself ragged every day to prove your worthiness to people that will never understand. I never said anything because I knew you would brush it off, but, Elena, you are a powerful woman. I consider it an honor to have gotten the opportunity to raise you."

My eyes start to sting as she continues.

"You are bound for great things, but you're letting your need for acceptance tarnish that. The ones who truly care for you already see you as the strong woman you have longed to be."

$$* * *$$

THE HOUSE IS SEEMINGLY empty when I return. My father must be with The Twelve, preparing for the trial again. Wanting to fall atop my bed and slip into one last deep slumber, I walk to my room. I enter and my hand reaches for my arm. "Elena."

My heart practically jumps from my chest. I spin, readying my fist to strike. But I'm met with a pair of blue-green eyes, bright with hope. Their owner is someone I least expected to see tonight.

"Apollo, what are you doing here?"

"I wanted to see you before your trial. I can't believe Zeus would accuse you of treason. It's preposterous. You haven't done anything," he says.

"I have in Zeus's eyes. It is enough for a death sentence," I whisper while gathering some of the items on my bedside table to stow away.

DELANEY NICOLE

"What are you doing?"

"I'm putting stuff away to make it easier on my father when—" A lump forms in my throat. "When I'm gone."

"Elena." Apollo grips my arm and turns me until his forehead rests against mine. His eyes dart between mine and my lips.

"What are you doing?"

"I'm saying goodbye," he mutters, slowly connecting our lips. The touch of Apollo's lips on mine is soft. But it is wrong—all of it.

"Apollo," I call as his lips fall to my neck. He takes it as encouragement to continue despite me trying to push at his shoulders.

"Apollo, stop." I push him from me and fall into my bedside table from the force.

"What's your problem?" he barks.

"There's a few, but the main one is that this could very well be my last night alive, and all you're trying to do is fuck me," I snap. My actual main thought is Callan.

"Excuse me for wanting to be close to you." His hands fly up in surrender.

"Close to me?" I laugh. "You don't want to be close to me. You never cared for me. You used me when it was convenient for you."

"Where is this coming from?" he yells before his face calmly smooths. "Zeus is right, isn't he? You have been cavorting with everyone in the Underworld. That's why you failed to complete your task."

I scowl at him. "They have nothing to do with this."

"Oh?" A chuckle leaves Apollo's mouth. "Did you sleep with him?"

"Who?"

"Thanatos. Did you sleep with Thanatos?"

"That is none of your business." I scoff, feeling annoyed at whatever claim he thinks he has over me.

"I knew it." He laughs. "I knew you would go to the Underworld and welcome any man who paid you attention into your bed."

"If you're going to insinuate I am a whore, then you might as well say it," I bark, bracing my hands on the table behind me. "Because you can call me whatever names you find fitting, but it will never change the fact that he loves me."

"Loves you?" Apollo barks a laugh. "You believe that he loves you? Let me let you in on a little secret, princess. He let you think that so he could fuck you."

I scowl. "Not everyone views women as an object to be used."

"Maybe not." He shrugs. "But I don't see him here fighting for you."

Before I think of what to say back to the wretched god in front of me, my attention falls to the journal which has fallen on the floor. I pick it up, and a small parcel falls from its pages. I open the parcel to find my mother's necklace, the same necklace I gave Callan as a promise of my return to the Underworld, and there's a note.

"I am talking to you," Apollo says through gritted teeth.

"And I'm ignoring you."

My eyes scan the parchment.

You came home once. May this be a reminder of the

home you will always have and the family that will always fight for you.

Realization strikes me. The answer has been within me all along. I had refused to listen. I walk toward the door, forgetting Apollo's presence.

"Where are you going?" he snaps.

"I'm returning to my family."

Apollo's gaze stays fixated upon me. "Sooner or later, you will disappoint them the same way you have disappointed us. You will never win your case against The Twelve."

"Maybe." I look back at him. The same man I once thought I loved. "It's worth trying."

Hastily, I run through the door, taking long strides toward the cobbled road. I almost make it there before I hear my father's voice calling me from the stables.

I halt as he runs toward me. "Elena, what are you doing? Where are you going?"

I'm panting through my words. "I have to go."

"Go? Go where? Your trial is tomorrow morning, Elena," he warns. "It's best if you go inside."

"No!" I yell, coming out in a more emotional tone than I expected. "I cannot go back in there."

"Elena." He looks at me with an exhausted expression. "What has gotten into you?"

"You raised me to take pride in the way I lead. Athena praises me for leading with compassion rather than arrogance," I say. "Now my compassion has purpose. I will not let it slip."

"What are you..." His face smooths. "Elena, I will not allow you to go back to the Underworld."

"It is not about allowing. Return to the stables and act as though you never saw me leave."

Ares takes hold of my wrist, stopping me from walking forward. "You must stay here. I forbid you from going."

"You forbid me?" I laugh. "Father, I am a grown woman. I finally have something worth fighting for, and people who care for me."

His tone sharpens. "You have had an honor bestowed upon you that you are expected to uphold."

I release a disbelieving huff. Rage and despair fill me at my father's willingness to face my trial. "That honor is a curse if it keeps me from the ones I love."

Silence passes between us. My emotions rise to the surface.

"Please, Father, can't I have this one night?"

Awareness flashes across his eyes. "Does he love you?"

I nod. "The love he has shown me taught me to love myself."

His face softens, and his grip on my wrist relinquishes.

CHAPTER 38

My steps fall faster and faster on the cobbled road. Only getting back to the Underworld—to him—runs through my mind.

My muscles burn, but I sprint as I close in on Hermes's home. My knocks sound rabid on his door.

"Hermes!" I yell while pounding on the wooden door. The night air seems to warm the longer I stand out in the open. "Hermes, please!"

The door swings open, blowing air in my face. "What do you wa—Elena." His posture straightens. "What are you doing here? I didn't expect to see you."

My eyes flash bright with determination. "Hermes, I need you to take me to the Underworld, right now."

Pity flashes across his face. "Elena, your trial is tomorrow. I don't see how—"

"You once told me that I would find a way to do what is best for everyone and for me. I've found that way, so please, take me to the Underworld." I don't know what I'll do if Hermes refuses me.

He sighs. "Elena, I'm not sure if—"

"Hermes," I choke, "I am coming to you as a friend. Please, take me to them."

I can practically hear the blood pounding in my veins as I wait for Hermes's reply. My palms become clammy as my heart races. My future hangs in the balance of this decision.

I watch as something softens in his face, understanding maybe, and his shoulders relax. "Alright, I will take you there."

"Really?" A smile cracks through my lips. Relief floods me, and I pull him into my embrace. "I do not know how I will ever be able to repay you."

Hermes lifts me into his arms and says, "You do not need to repay me."

THE WIND WHIPS through my hair on our descent to the Underworld. My eyes are trained on finding the palace as soon as it comes into view. Knots form in my stomach the closer we get.

I want Callan to hear me out. We left things on an awful note, but I can't see my life without him. Should he refuse me, I will let the trial carry on as it is. I won't care about my fate.

"There's a fifth river," Hermes says plainly. He had to have seen it when he attended the ball or when he brought me back to Olympus.

"It was formed during my stay here. It was after—" I stop. I trust Hermes, but I do not know if I should divulge the information regarding the creation of the new river and field.

"After...?" Hermes inquires.

"It is this River Acheron. It is also known as the river of woe," I finish to avoid telling him the truth of its origin.

"And what of the fields?"

"They are the Fields of Mourning, for those wounded by love in their mortal lives."

"Do you know how they were created?" he asks, slowing as we approach the stone steps of the palace.

"I..." I pause as I try to decide if there is a point to withholding the truth now. "I went to the mortal realm with Thanatos. I touched a mortal woman who had just lost her husband. I somehow softened the trauma she was experiencing. Thanatos said I saved her from becoming a hollowed-out shell of a person."

Hermes's eyes widened as he placed me on the cold stone. "That would mean—"

"Hermes, you must promise you will tell no one. The Twelve cannot know." I grip his arm firmly.

He nods. "I understand."

I pull the strawberry-blond man into my arms. "Thank you—for everything."

He releases me from his hold. "Go, do what is right for you and everyone. Do not forget your trial in the morning."

I run toward the doors of the palace.

"Elena!" Hermes shouts, causing me to turn. "I'm proud of you."

A smile pulls at my lips, causing a certain warmth to fill my chest. I stride toward the door and convince the guards to let me in by threatening them with Hades's wrath should they not allow his dear old friend entrance.

The sound of my feet against the gray stone fill the corridors of the quiet palace. I run toward my old quarters, thinking there is some chance he is there.

"Elena?" A familiar voice calls from the opposing end of the hall. "Elena!"

I come to a stop breathing heavily. Confusion lines the face of the dark-skinned guard approaching me, which amuses me. "Elena, what are you doing here? Don't you have a trial in a few hours?"

"Yes, but I do not care about that now. Leon, I need..." I breathe. I know where he is. "I need to go."

"Where are you going?" Leon shouts.

"I'm righting a wrong."

The night air is chilly as I walk out on the balcony where we spent so much time together. It's the place Callan said he came to be alone. It feels right that he would be here. But when I walk out, I find no one.

He isn't here.

He is gone.

"No." I brace the edge. "Damn it." Tears spill over. I repeatedly hit the stone railing in my agony. The physical pain is finally starting to match the emotional. "Don't leave me too."

My knees begin to crumble as I lean against the railing.

Short steps approach, and a soft voice says, "Elena."

My heart jumps. "Callan."

I run and fling my arms around his broad figure. "I don't want to be alone," I cry. "I need you."

His grip tightens around me. "You're not alone. You never were."

I pull back to meet his amber gaze, "I—I'm so sorry. I wanted to reach my goals and get everything I had ever dreamed of. But then I met you, and everything got complicated. The dreams I once held changed. I realized that I only wanted to lead the armies because I thought it would mean they would accept me.

"But you showed me that it is okay to just be me. It does not matter where I came from or who others thought I was. I saw everything slipping, and refused to—"

"Kiss me." Callan's hands steady my shoulders.

I look up to him. "What?"

"Kiss me."

Our lips connect in a slow kiss. It isn't a kiss full of desire or hunger but a kiss of deep affection and love. I smooth my hands over his soft cheeks. I feel at home.

Callan pulls away, cupping my cheeks affectionately. "You were always enough. They weren't."

A warmth spreads in my chest. I admire him. He's shown me how special I am. I feel like I matter. I'm never expected to fit a mold with him.

I smile and rest my forehead against his. "I lied the other night when I told you our feelings were because of our bond. They are so much more than that."

"Elena, you do not need to tell me that. I knew it was a lie the moment it fell from your lips. This feeling cannot be brought on by a mystical bond.

"Besides, The Fates already said it is our lives that are bonded, not our hearts." His lips pull upward slightly, and I feel another weight lift off my chest. I can't help but bring my mouth to his at knowing what we share is genuine.

"You are the only person that has ever made me believe I am enough."

"There is a palace full of people here that feel the same." He rests his hands on my waist.

I can't help but believe him—every word. "That may be true, but it does not change the fact that those taking me to trial do not feel the same."

"Then we will go speak with Hades. We can form a plan. We won't let them take you."

"Did you honestly believe I came back without a plan?" I ask, raising my brows suggestively.

"Ah, I see. You came back to save yourself, not to get me back," he says with a sarcastic smile.

I giggle despite the looming thought that I may only have a few hours to live. "You've caught me."

Our lips meet in a short kiss.

Callan pulls away, grasping my hand in his. "Let's go find a way to get you out of this."

I grip tightly to Callan's hand as we make our way through the corridors. Everything feels right when I am with him. We fell for the darkness that swarmed the light.

"Elena?"

Persephone looks as though worry has worn her down in the hours since I returned to Olympus. She wears a black gown, a color I have never seen her wear.

I wrap my arm tightly around the future queen of the

DELANEY NICOLE

Underworld. The goddess returns the gesture, squeezing tightly. Persephone's hold provides a sister's comfort.

"I never thought I'd see you again and then Leon mentioned you returned in a hurry," Persephone says, releasing me from her grasp.

"I couldn't stay there. It felt wrong. I need to be here even if it is just for tonight," I say, looking back at Callan, who crept his hand to the small of my back.

"She thinks she may have figured out a way to win her trial," Callan says, meeting me with an endearing stare before moving his attention to Persephone.

"Have you been to Hades?"

"We were on our way," he says.

"Callan?" Keres's voice asks from the opposing end of the corridor. She stops in her tracks when she locks eyes with me. "Oh my gods, it's true."

In an instant, Keres runs to us. She stops in front of me and I see her hand raise as if she is going to strike me. Callan tenses against me and I know he is readying to stop his sister.

Only he doesn't need to. Keres's ebony eyes lock with mine and her hand drops. Before I know it, her arms are wrapped around me in a tight embrace. "Thank you for protecting him."

"Always," I say, wrapping my arms around her slender form.

Callan watches us with shock-filled eyes. Hypnos, who approached with Keres, shares the same reaction. Confusion fills me. "What is it?"

"We have never seen our sister care for anyone outside of

us. She's the bringer of violent death for gods sake." Hypnos chuckles in disbelief.

"I am not a monster that lacks compassion," Keres quips at her brother, releasing me.

"You may not lack compassion—which is debatable to some—but you can be a monster," Callan argues with a mischievous glint in his eyes.

"Alright, enough. I hate to ruin the fun, but I need to hurry if I plan on being alive by tomorrow's end," I add.

Callan flinches. It wasn't noticeable to most, but I felt it against my back. He is scared for me. Everyone had grown uneasy at my choice of words until Keres says, "We will come with you."

"You can't," I protest when everyone utters their agreement. "Zeus already wants Callan. If any of you come, he will use you for his gain."

Callan's hand rubs my back, sending shivers down my spine. "We are not letting you go alone. *I* am not letting you go alone."

Persephone is the only one to note my unease. "You can talk about this later. Elena needs to speak with Hades. If anyone can figure out a plan to help her, it's him. And by extension, we will help. But for now, she must speak with him—alone."

Unease lines Callan's features. I don't want to leave his side, but Persephone is right. Time is running out.

I cup his cheeks and bring his gaze to meet mine. "I'll be okay. You can wait outside. I promise to come back to you." My lips grace his in a short peck. "I am never leaving you again."

DELANEY NICOLE

"Unless The Twelve order your execution, then you will have no choice," Leon adds.

Everyone's attention falls on Leon standing behind the group.

"Way to make an entrance," Hypnos says facetiously and claps his hand on the guard's shoulder.

I clap my hands together. "With that fresh on my mind, I think it's time I find Hades."

"He is in the throne room," Persephone says.

I walk with Callan toward the throne room and leave the others in the corridor. My stomach slowly forms knots. I hope Hades agrees to what I have planned. If not, I will likely not survive the coming day.

Callan stops outside the door and squeezes my hand. "I'll be right here the entire time."

"I know." I smile softly. "You have always been here."

We share a silent moment before a guard opens the door. I step into the throne room with clammy hands.

"Elena," Hades's brows rise, "I see the rumors that you're back are true. May I ask what this is about?"

Hades's tone has a bite to it. He must have been told the truth of my absence. That will make what I am about to do all the more challenging.

I stop in front of his throne. "We need to talk."

"And why should I speak to you? It seems you've been keeping many secrets from me," Hades says, looking rather bored on his throne.

I stop just in front of his throne, my hands clasped at my waist. "Come now, Hades, don't tell me you didn't have your suspicions. The timing of my visit was too close to Persephone's arrival to not be phony."

His eyes narrow. "I am not a fool. I suspected you the whole time. Why do you think I had Callan sit in the library with you all those nights?"

I almost want to tease him but then I remember why I'm here. Clearing my throat, I say, "Well enough of the formalities, Hades. I think I've made it clear enough that I will not take either of them from you."

"So then why are you here?" He eyes me skeptically.

I start pacing, needing some sort of movement to escape the panic that creeps within me, waiting until I'm weak to strike me. "I have a plan that may aid all of us tomorrow. It may mean I get to live and it may stop Zeus from sending more soldiers to retrieve Persephone."

Hades's fingers trace the length of his dark beard. "And what might this plan be?"

"You, Persephone, and Callan will attend my trial with me tomorrow. Zeus's confidence will be shaken at least a little bit because of the crowd behind me. Then, I will offer him the chance for a truce. Persephone will spend half of the year in Olympus and the other half with you."

Fire lights in Hades's eyes. "If you think I am letting her go back around that monster of a god—"

"That monster will continue to send soldiers one by one until he launches a full-fledged attack on the Underworld to get Persephone back. Seeing how more than half of your court would like to never see The Twelve again, I don't think you want that," I interrupt him. "Need I remind you that Demeter is also killing hundreds of mortals a day and that number is only going to increase

DELANEY NICOLE

until mortals are extinct unless we let her see her daughter again?"

Hades glares at me silently. He eventually sighs and says, "Six months?"

"Six months." I nod.

"What is it that you want, Elena? I find it hard to believe you're doing all of this out of the goodness of your heart."

A small smile graces my lips before I relax. "That's where you're wrong, Hades. I would do this all over again in a heartbeat because you all welcomed me and showed me what it is to be a family—not a bloodline set to certain expectations."

He looks at me curiously. "I'm sensing a but in there somewhere."

The smallest of chuckles falls from my mouth. "But I'm afraid if tomorrow goes in our favor I will be banished from Olympus with nowhere to go."

Hades is silent for a long time and the same panic I kept at bay earlier gains more footing over my body by the second. Finally he says, "If tomorrow works in your favor, you may live here. I may not appreciate the reason you visited, but I cannot ignore that you are ready to sacrifice your life for us. Besides, I'm sure Zeus will eventually find another reason to attack the Underworld and I'm going to need someone to lead us."

A genuine smile graces my lips. "So we will try my plan?"

He nods. "We shall try."

CHAPTER 39

hanatos

I sit up in bed and watch Elena sleep peacefully at my side. I never thought I'd have this again. And there is still uncertainty of what our future holds.

I can't stomach the thought of losing her a second time. This time if I lose her, I will never see her again. It makes my heart race, and my hands clammy.

There has to be a way to ensure: one, no harm will come to Elena. And two, Persephone will not be ripped from Hades. Hades has to know a way to save them both.

Careful not to wake Elena, I leave for Hades's study. I need answers, and time is running out. I find Hades sitting in his grand chair, and Persephone perched on his desk. The others are nowhere in sight.

"Callan," Hades says.

"I hope I am not interrupting anything."

"Of course not. I am surprised to see you here. I would have thought you would be spending the rest of your evening with Elena," he says in an even tone.

I nod, still feeling anxiety fill my body like a disease. "That was the plan. But I cannot shake the worry for the morning."

My purpose for coming here returns to the forefront of my mind. "Hades, there must be a way to ensure the safety of Elena and Persephone."

"That is why Persephone is here."

"We cannot think of a way to get around my father. Elena's plan may work but we need the security of knowing my father cannot take us the moment we turn our backs." Persephone sounds sad.

"There has to be a way around him." I rack my brain for everything I know about The Twelve. "Persephone, if one is found guilty of treason they are executed, yes?"

Persephone nods and even though I knew the answer to that it feels like a stab through the heart to think Elena will experience that in just a few hours.

I turn, "Hades, you've granted bodies to souls before to serve you. What if you were able to do that for Elena? That way Zeus still thinks he's ended Elena's life but really she's safe to live here."

Persephone shakes her head before Hades even has time to answer. "That won't work. The sword used against those who have been convicted of treason has been cursed to rip their soul from them. Nothing ever remains of them."

Fuck. That bastard has a loophole for everything.

"Let's think about this," I say. "Zeus wants you and me. Elena has proposed a way to allow him to think he's got us."

"It is improbable that will change his verdict. Once my father makes up his mind, it is hard to change it."

"And if you think I would let Persephone anywhere near Zeus when we both know that was the reason Elena was sent here in the first place, you are mistaken." Hades has an edge creeping into his voice. "He would take her the moment she arrived, you as well."

"I can take care of myself," I mutter, feeling anger grow within me. I know where Hades is coming from. He is worried for Persephone. "And I know you don't think for a second that he won't keep sending soldiers down here until he gets what he wants." My eyes grow wide with realization.

"What is it?" Persephone asks, turning toward me.

"What if there were a way to ensure Persephone's return even with the terms worked out with Elena?"

"What are you saying?" Hades asks with furrowed brows. His hand skims Persephone's back as if for reassurance that she's still here with him.

"I need you to follow me," I say with determination, "to the gardens."

CHAPTER 40

lena

"I cannot believe you let them come. This was not a part of our plan," I say to Hades through my clenched jaw. I try to keep my voice down since we are surrounded by Olympian guards.

"You clearly do not know us well enough if you thought we would leave you alone during this trial," Hypnos interjects.

A gentle hand takes mine. "Elena, you are family. And in the Underworld, we fight for our family."

I smile as best I can at the spring goddess. In the weeks I've spent in the Underworld, Persephone has shown me kindness like no other. She showed me what it means to live in the Underworld as an outsider.

"She's right." Callan steps away from the wall outside the throne room on Mount Olympus. "We fight for those we love."

I feel a small flutter in my chest at Callan's words. No matter what we go through, he never fails to make me feel loved. I allow a smile to grace my lips as he takes hold of my hand.

"What is it?" Callan peers down at me.

I feel my smile grow. "We went from holding daggers to each other's throats to wanting to be in each other's embrace until the very last moment."

Everyone lets out a small chuckle before Hades says, "That's typically how it starts. But—in our case—Persephone was never well versed in the art of throwing daggers. However, she was sharp with her tongue.

"Keep it up, and I might have Elena teach me to throw daggers," Persephone jokes.

I'd teach her for sure, at least, if I can get through my trial. I'm nauseous at the thought of Callan having to watch my execution.

"Will you excuse us for a moment?" Callan says, pulling me off to the side while the others continue their conversations. His hands grasp mine comfortingly. "What's going on in that beautiful mind of yours?"

I sigh. "Callan, I'm so scared. I failed. When I started this task, Zeus never mentioned the stipulations of a trial. Just that if I succeeded I would lead the armies with Athena. Now, I must face The Twelve as they watch Zeus decide if I get to see tomorrow or not. And the worst part is, he would be completely justified in his decision because *I did* fail."

DELANEY NICOLE

"Do you remember why you wanted to lead the armies in the first place?"

"I..." I huff. "I thought if I did, it would prove that a demi-goddess is as strong as a full-blooded god. I wanted to prove that because my mother was mortal, I could lead better than those like my brothers. I wanted to make her proud. And... I wanted to protect those like her."

"Look at me," Callan ducks to meet my gaze, "your mother, from what you've told me, would be proud of you whether you opened a shop in the village or became one of the great soldiers. But I think she would be prouder to find that you've found people who love you for who you are rather than who they want you to be."

"Do you believe that?" I meet his amber gaze. He nods, holding my cheeks in his warm, soft hands. A small smile cracks on my lips.

"What?" He grins at my smile. Based on the look in his eyes, you would believe I had lit his world on fire.

"You have indirectly said that you love me twice today." My smile deepens as my hands come up to hold his wrists at my cheeks.

He smiles. "Well, there are many things I love about you: your smile, the way you laugh, your precious lips, and of course, when we fuc—"

"Way to ruin the moment," I say, hitting his arm playfully.

His eyes dance with bright amusement. "Oh, come on. You have to admit. We have some fun times together."

"That's not the point." I giggle, then stand on my toes to connect our lips. Our kiss is gentle but says all of the feelings we couldn't seem to find the words for. The emotions that no words could seem to match.

A blond figure emerges, catching my attention. My breath hitches as I realize who it is—Apollo.

"What is it?" Callan's glare meets Apollo's.

Apollo's stare flicks between us before he turns and walks into the throne room. The disgust that lined his face changes my worry into anger. He will try to use this against me.

"Hey, look at me." Callan pulls my focus back onto him. "It doesn't matter what he sees or what he says. What matters is that you go into that trial, and you fight with all the strength you've built up over the years. Hades can help you, but he can only get you so far. This has to be you. Think of your mother."

The white doors leading to the throne room open with a whoosh of wind. Hermes steps out, failing to mask his worry as he finds me. "They are ready for you."

I meet the eyes of everyone accompanying me—Hades, Persephone, Hypnos, Callan, Keres, Sebastian, and Leon— each of them give me a nod before following me toward the door.

On the last step, I'm yanked backward into a tight embrace. The scent of cinnamon lets me know it's Keres. "Don't die, okay?"

A puff of air leaves my mouth, and my eyes sting slightly. Of course, she chose the moment before I entered the throne room to tell me this. "I'll try. I promise."

Passing through the doors, I am determined. I am ready for this trial. The trial that will decide if I live or die. But I'll be damned if it is the latter.

DELANEY NICOLE

The large, white-marble columns and the fresco of the gods overlooking the mortals no longer hold the same luster they had six weeks ago. The yellow dianthus flowers don't seem as bright as they used to.

Every throne is full, and then some. At the forefront sits Zeus and Hera, per usual. To Zeus's right is Demeter in her typical green peplos; Ares is in a blood-red chiton; Artemis wears a silver peplos with her bow at her side; Apollo has on a white chiton and laurel leaves in his hair; and furthest from Zeus is Dionysus wearing a purple chiton and an ivy crown. Standing off to my father's side are my brothers, Phobus and Deimus.

To Hera's left sits Poseidon wearing a golden chiton, holding his trident; Athena is in her aegis with her shield at her side; Hephaestus wears an orange chiton with his double ax at his hip; Aphrodite is to his left, wearing a pale pink peplos with the top half of her hair clipped back in a golden clip; and lastly, Hermes sits at Aphrodite's left in a pale blue chiton and his infamous winged shoes.

Coming to a halt in front of Zeus, I don't bow. He doesn't deserve my respect. Hera makes no indication that she is offended. Zeus, however, lets out an annoyed huff. Zeus thrives on his praise. It has thrown him off. That might work in my favor later

"Elena, what a pleasure it is to have you in our presence today," Zeus purrs. "Let's begin."

A pin drop could sound as loud as a sword's clamber. Everyone's gaze is fixed on the king of gods and the small demi-goddess before him.

Zeus says, "Elena, daughter of Ares, is here today to stand trial against The Twelve for treason—"

"Brother, I believe you must clarify what actions she has done for her to be charged with treason," Hades interrupts, striding a few steps toward my side. The others are a few steps back. Keres is holding Callan at her side. Things will get worse if the relationship between us is revealed.

Zeus glares at the god of the Underworld for a short moment. "Yes, brother, I was getting to that before I was rudely interrupted. Elena was sent to the Underworld to retrieve my daughter, Persephone. She was also tasked with retrieving Thanatos, who is accused of killing many mortals—"

"You're wrong," I spit, unable to stop the words from falling out of my mouth. "Thanatos is not the reason mortals have been dying faster. There is sickness spreading due to the famine Demeter has caused. Thanatos delivers them peace in their suffering. You know he is not the reason. It is Demeter's lack of duty that is causing them to perish."

Zeus chuckles. "It appears things are worse than I thought. She not only failed to complete the task set in place for her to be given the honor of leading armies with Athena, but she is now defending those who have committed crimes against us."

"If I may say something, Zeus," Athena says, waiting for the god's permission to continue. He nods. "Though she did defend him, it appears, unless I'm seeing things, she has completed her task. She not only has Persephone in this room but all of The Children of the Night. Therefore, I see no reason to convict her of treason."

DELANEY NICOLE

Zeus's jaw works, which causes a bit of nerve to swell within me. I feel a warm presence against my back. It is Callan. He and everyone else walked forward to show their support.

Mischief flashes in Zeus's eyes. "That is a good point, Athena. And while I cannot ignore the fact that she has brought who she was asked to, and some," he grins, eyeing Sebastian and Leon, "it appears the root of her defending The Children of the Night stems from a much more profound relationship than friendship. Relations with the enemies of The Twelve will not be tolerated."

"So you're going to kill her for finally finding people who care about her?" Callan grinds out.

Worry flashes across Athena's and Ares's faces. Aphrodite looks concerned before snapping back to a solemn expression.

"Care about her? Please, only a fool would care for a demi-goddess that can't even complete a simple task. Apollo knew it and so should you," Zeus quips. I'd be lying if I said his harsh tongue didn't make me flinch.

I huff, feeling as though everything has just snapped into place. "You were never going to let me lead with Athena, were you?"

Zeus's harsh gaze fixes on my frame. "Don't be silly, girl."

I meet the arrogant king's gaze and hold on tightly to Callan's hand. "You told me what I wanted to hear because you knew I would work hard enough to complete the task for you. But you never had any intention of letting me lead the armies. That is why we are at this silly trial.

"You kept your plan secret from Athena and my father because you knew they would tell me. You sent me on this task because you thought I was your best bet at getting your daughter back, but instead of rewarding me, you decided you were going to kill me to get me out of the way. That is why you asked my father which of my brother's he favored before I was given my task."

"Watch your tongue," Zeus says while pointing an accusing finger. "It is one thing to have relations with the enemy, but another to accuse me, the king of gods, of planning your murder. I will not tolerate it. If there are no objections, I hereby find Elena guilt—"

"Stop."

Aphrodite stands from her chair. My father's eyes grow wide from across the room, almost as though he knows what the goddess is doing. Panic lines his face. It's odd seeing such strong emotion on my father's face. He's always been so good at schooling his emotions.

"What?" Zeus spits.

"I said, stop." Aphrodite meets his gaze. Her eyes meet mine and my father's before meeting Zeus's sharp glare again. "This case is different."

"How so?"

"Because she must have a majority rule for this trial."

"Aphrodite, I know you are the goddess of love, but now is not the time. She is a demi-goddess. She does not need the majority for me to charge her."

"Yes, she does," Aphrodite snaps, bringing her fierce eyes back to my form.

DELANEY NICOLE

"What are you saying, Aphrodite?" Hera asks, with a skeptical glance.

"Elena is my daughter."

Ice-cold shock runs through my veins. This can't be. My mother was mortal. My mother died while giving me life. There is no way I grew up without a mother if my birth mother was living just down the cobbled road.

Callan squeezes my hand, which pulls me from my shock to remind me he is at my side. Persephone takes hold of my other arm. She always knows what I need, sometimes before I know what I need.

"You're lying," Zeus says, shock lining his features. A slight panic appears in his eyes. Needing a vote might sway his control over my situation.

"I most certainly am not," Aphrodite says plainly.

"Aphrodite," my father says quietly as if questioning whether she should continue.

"It is time they know, Ares." She nods. Hephaestus looks angry in his seat. "A few years before Phobus and Deimus were born. Hephaestus was spending more time with his welding. I was lonely, but I had no intent on having an affair. Then, one night, I met Ares in The Muses, and we had a connection."

"It started with small meetings where we would do nothing more than talk. Eventually, it became more, and I felt loved for the first time in so long. Soon, I discovered I was with child. I knew it was not a child of Hephaestus. Ares knew too. We decided that we would tell Hephaestus it was his child."

A CURSE OF HONOR

I look at Hephaestus who appears furious and in sorrow. I'd never thought about how hard it must have been for him.

"Looking back, I know that it was wrong. We should have come clean. But when I was pregnant with Elena, I was scared of what Hephaestus would do to the child or me. So we lied."

"When it came time for Elena's birth, Hephaestus was away welding, and Artemis was aiding a mortal woman on the edge of death. It was just Ares and me at her birth. I made Ares promise to take her and raise her in his home because I knew if she stayed, Hephaestus would know Elena was not his.

"And so," Aphrodite sighs, "our affair and child were kept secret. The tale of Ares's affair with a mortal woman spread to cover Elena's origin, and I told everyone I had lost the babe. When we were later caught having relations around the time of Phobus's and Deimus's conceptions, we knew based on Hephaestus's reaction, that no one could find out about Elena—for her safety."

Aphrodite turns back to Zeus. "We must vote because she is a full-blooded goddess."

Silence fills the throne room. All the attention is on four people—my father, Aphrodite, Hephaestus, and me. Even Phobus and Deimus are gawking at their mother, well, our mother. Apollo straightens in his chair, his attention on me.

Shock, pain, and anger flow through me. I was the child I read about in Aphrodite's journal. I grew up believing my mother had died while trying to bring me into the world. I've been lied to my entire life. I have been hated my entire life because of a lineage that wasn't even real.

303

DELANEY NICOLE

"That's how she leads with compassion," Athena says with the wonder of the discovery. "She is a child of love and war."

Zeus eyes each of the gods and goddesses around the room, noting each of their shocked expressions. "We will take a short recess to digest this news and begin again shortly. The correct way."

CHAPTER 41

I pace outside the throne room. So many thoughts run through my head.

I am a full-blooded goddess.

I was hated and talked down to my entire life because everyone thought I was a demi-goddess who'd been given special privileges. My father knew, and yet continued to let it happen.

"Elena," Callan says gently, grasping my arm enough to stop me.

I stop. "I've had a mother all along. She never took steps to get to know me. She could have visited as a friend of my father's to see me. But she didn't."

His face softens, and he pulls me flush against his firm, warm chest. "It's okay."

"My father lied to me about who I was my entire life." I sniffle.

"Look at me." Callan holds my shoulders at an arm's

length. "Just because you now know that you're a full blooded goddess does not mean you aren't who you were last week, last month, or last year. Elena, you are still you. No matter what. No one can change that unless you let them. People only have the power to change you if you give them that power."

I slowly feel my eyes sting less and less. He's right. I am still me. I still need to convince at least seven of The Twelve that I am innocent of treason.

I wait until Callan walks back to his siblings before I make my way to Hades and Persephone. There is one strategy we haven't tried.

"Hades, I think the time has come to suggest our agreed upon plan," I whisper, hoping none of The Twelve overhear.

Hades sighs as Persephone gently rubs his arm, clearly agreeing with me. "As much as I hate to admit it, I think you may be right."

"You better lock that into your memory because he's never going to tell you that again." Persephone smiles.

Hades rolls his eyes but fails to mask his grin. "We'll meet you inside."

I watch everyone file back into the throne room, leaving only Callan and me standing near the door. I take a deep, steadying breath, and I walk toward Callan.

"Elena!"

I turn to see my father running toward me from the side entrance designated for The Twelve. I signal for Callan to proceed into the room while I wait for my father. "Yes?"

"I want you to know that this was never how we wanted you to find out about it. Your mother—"

"I do not want to speak of this," I say. My eyes begin to sting with the memory that it was not my father who pleaded for my life but the mother that never tried to know me. "Right now, I have to plead my case as to why I should be allowed to see tomorrow's sun."

My father's face softens in what looks like regret. "As you wish," he murmurs, gently touching my arm as he passes.

As I turn to enter the throne room, a soft voice calls, "Elena."

I meet Apollo's gaze and my stomach flips. "What do you need, Apollo?"

"I wanted to apologize," he says softly.

An incredulous chuckle falls from my lips. "Are you apologizing because you've found out I'm a goddess? Because now I'm somehow fit to be considered a partner for you?"

"That is not what I meant."

"Then what did you mean?" I ask, maintaining eye contact with the same bright green eyes I used to admire.

His voice sharpens slightly, "You never were easy to talk to."

"You never tried to talk to me! All you ever wanted to do was to rip each other's clothes off whenever *you* saw fit. I thought that's what love was back then. But now I know that it is not.

"But, gods, Apollo, you don't get it. You ruined me, and he showed me how to fix myself. I will not apologize for my actions. And if you are done, I would like to go back to the one person who freed me from the pain I felt before."

His head sinks. "If that is what you wish."

DELANEY NICOLE

Walking back in, I stop at Persephone's side. Hades stands on her other side. Callan falls into step on my other side.

"Now that the court is back in session," Zeus announces as the last of The Twelve take their seats, "we will conduct a trial where the majority rule determines our verdict. Should seven of us find you guilty, you will be charged. Should seven of us find you innocent, all charges will be dropped."

"Before we begin," I say. "I have proof that will not only prove me innocent but partially give you what you want as well."

Demeter shuffles in her seat to lean forward. "Continue, my dear."

I take a short breath, then look between Hades and Persephone. "Persephone will stay in Olympus six months out of the year."

Zeus laughs. "And what of the other six months?"

"She will be in the Underworld."

"And you expect us to agree to let Persephone, a child forged from the goddess of agriculture and myself, to dwell in the Underworld for half the year." Zeus chuckles again. "You are much dafter than I believed you to be."

I can see vexatious grins spread across my brothers' faces behind my father. They enjoy watching me fight for my life.

"Ah, but you cannot keep a queen from her kingdom," Hades says.

"A queen?" Zeus asks, failing to mask his shock and confusion fast enough.

"Yes, Father, I've been crowned the queen of the Underworld with my marriage to Hades," Persephone says, gripping Hades's hand in hers.

308

"You did this," Zeus spits, pointing in my direction.

"No, *your majesty*," I quip. "My idea was to convince you to allow Persephone to stay in the Underworld with the man who loves her for half the year. They took it upon themselves to move the wedding up."

"Is it true?" Demeter asks, looking at her daughter. "You're married?"

Persephone nods. Her gaze turns cold when she meets Zeus's. "You sent someone to the Underworld to take me from those who have shown me nothing but love and acceptance. She has given you an option that I have agreed to. You must accept it because I have eaten six pomegranate seeds."

Gasps fill the room. My alarmed gaze meets Callan who is surprisingly calm.

"I gave her the seeds after you fell asleep. I knew there was a possibility that Zeus would not agree," Callan whispers in my ear.

"You remembered?" I whisper.

"Of course, I did. I was with you that night in the garden," he says. I fight the grin pulling on my lips, remembering the night he took me to the garden and gave me the peace-making flowers.

"You stupid girl. You drove my daughter to imprison herself in the Underworld for half the year for eternity," Zeus snarls, cutting me a sharp glare.

Callan takes a step forward. I try my best to stop him, but there is no use. Keres grabs hold of my shoulder while reassuring me of this safety. Before our arrival, Keres ensured us she'd unleash the side no one got to see and live to tell the tale if they tried to make a move against any of us.

DELANEY NICOLE

"You sent Elena to bring Persephone back here and me along with her. She has given you a portion of what you want." He smirks. "I'm afraid I'm off the market."

"It's a twist of fate. You are trying to change the fate of my daughter's life," Zeus argues.

"I was hoping you'd say that brother." Hades signals for the guards to open the doors.

Through the open doors walks Lachesis, Clotho, and Atropos. "Hades called in a favor when everyone was getting over the shock of your parents," Persephone whispers in my ear.

"What are they doing here?" Zeus asks.

The three women stop in line with me and the others. Each of them eye Zeus with skeptical and challenging looks. Zeus answers to them whether he wants to admit it or not.

Hades says, "May I introduce Lachesis, Clotho, and Atropos. They are known as The Fates."

"I know who they are," Zeus snarls.

"Zeus." Lachesis nods with a mischievous grin.

"Why is there presence needed?" Zeus bites out. The Twelve watch Zeus's behavior closely. Watching their king slip slowly into madness.

"We are here to tell you what has been written in stone, what we have seen, and what we know to be true," says Clotho in a sing-song voice.

"And?"

Atropos, with her fiery red hair, steps forward. "You claim that your daughter becoming the queen of the Underworld is a twist of fate. That is a mistake. We've known your daughter's fate as the rightful Queen of the Underworld since she was set into existence."

"The woman you seek to convict," Lachesis steps forward, "is also fated for a different life than you plan for her to live."

Zeus stays silent, looking as though he is growing more and more annoyed with each word. Each member of The Twelve, save Zeus, looks more and more intrigued as each woman continues.

"You see," Clotho starts, "it has been written since the creation of mortals, the same time the Children of the Night originated, that death will have a companion. A companion that will provide healing in her partner's wake. A companion that holds empathy and compassion for mortals without being one themself. It was a matter of them crossing paths, which they have you to thank for that. However, when we say Death is meant to have a companion that brings healing, it does not mean they will share a connection. That happened on its own."

Hearing The Fates confirm what Callan already told me sends a surge of relief through me. I shoot a short glance toward Callan, and he presses his hand on the small of my back.

A small flicker of my power thrums within me as if reminding me that it is there even if it doesn't feel like it. I am meant for healing. I am meant to heal the hearts of the broken, to heal those wounded by love in death.

"And you believe this companion to be Elena?" Zeus asks, disbelief dripping from his tone.

"We know it to be Elena." Atropos holds his stare. "It was proven when she visited the mortal realm with Thanatos.

DELANEY NICOLE

While there, she healed a mortal woman after the loss of her husband with her touch."

"Then, last night, Hades had her visit the mortal realm again to prove it wasn't a stroke of luck. She healed another mortal after the loss of their loved one. This time it was a mother and father that lost their child. Famine has been killing the mortals, brought on by Demeter's lack of duty, Zeus not Thanatos. He delivers peace to those who have run out of time."

Before Zeus can utter a counter-argument, I step out of Callan's comforting touch. "I'd like to say something."

I make eye contact with each of The Twelve before I continue. "My entire life, I have been talked down to because it was believed that I was a demi-goddess. As a young girl, I couldn't understand why I was hated." I glare at my brothers. "But if I didn't go through all of that, I wouldn't have excelled in fighting. I wouldn't have had the same fuel for my fight. And I wouldn't have been considered one of the best fighters Athena has seen in ages. I wouldn't have been picked for the task that was given to me. I would have never met my fate nor the love and acceptance that has come with it."

My gaze narrows on Zeus. "A wise person once said, 'You can only get where you're going by starting where you are.' So if you want a battle, fine," my face twists into a deceitful grin, "but make no mistake, I will bring you a war."

"Is that a threat?" Zeus's nostrils flare. "Because I swear to you—"

"Zeus!" Hera snaps. "Enough. I've had enough of this. I'm sure the others have as well."

Hera flicks her gaze to everyone in the throne room

A CURSE OF HONOR

before speaking. "You asked the girl to bring Persephone back, and she has given you a fair offer. After all, you cannot keep a queen from her throne. You asked her to bring in the man you claimed was killing innocent mortals, and we found out that he was not the one killing them; it was a famine caused by Demeter.

"The Fates," she continues, "whom we all answer to, have provided enough evidence to prove that you are letting your pride and arrogance cloud your judgment. We have sat here long enough to decide our votes. All those in favor of Elena's innocence and to clear all charges made against her."

I latch onto Callan's arm firmly. He squeezes my hand. This is the moment we've dreaded. Even Keres and Hypnos find a way to grip my shoulder. My heart rate quickens to the point that I begin to think it will burst from my chest.

The Twelve eye one another, waiting for someone to move until my father stands.

"To the daughter that shouldn't have had to grow up without her mother." Aphrodite stands.

Artemis stands.

Hermes rises from his seat.

Athena stands at my father's side.

Apollo stands quietly, not uttering a word but giving me a caring stare. Shock and thankfulness fill me.

I look around at the rest who remain in their seats. I just need one more. One more, and I get to live. My hands grow clammy as I wait. I can hear the blood pumping in my ears. I wouldn't be able to bear it if I lost by only one vote.

Hera moves in her seat. "To finding those you not only

313

DELANEY NICOLE

love but who love you just the same, to living in happiness, *forever.*"

Tears prick my eyes. Callan hugs me tightly. A tear falls down my cheek when the others—Hephaestus, Dionysus, Poseidon, and even Demeter—stand from their chairs. The only one that remains sitting is Zeus.

Hera looks at the other members of The Twelve standing from their chairs. "It appears you have won more than the majority. Elena, you have been found innocent of treason against The Twelve Olympians and are hereby cleared of all charges."

Happy and relieved tears fall from my eyes. Everyone from the group behind me wraps me in their arms.

I get to live with them, with my family. Even Zeus's angry look can't bring me down.

"We did it," I say, wrapping my arms around Callan's neck as he pulls me in tighter.

"You did it. We just stood there and looked pretty." Callan chuckles, amusement flashing across his eyes.

I pull Callan onto my lips. This kiss feels promising. It promises a future that will last an eternity.

Resting my forehead against his, a bright smile lines my lips. "Let's go home."

EPILOGUE

hanatos

My feet touch the ground, and the sound of a weeping woman fills the air. I ushered the soul of her husband quite some time ago. But time does not take away the sting of his absence.

"I should have known I'd find you here."

I smile at Elena sitting in the corner of the tiny home we visited together the first time I brought her to the mortal realm. She comes here quite often. Truth be told, I feel a connection to this place just as she does. It was a stepping stone for us.

I meet her bright blue gaze. "I owe her a lot."

Elena now possesses her own glamour. The Fates were

DELANEY NICOLE

right. She brings healing in my wake but only when the mortal is ready to accept it.

I wrap my arms around her petite frame. "I'm sure if she knew what you've done for her, Anastasia would feel the same toward you."

Elena nestles her ear against my chest, watching as Anastasia's tears slow, and she regains her composure. "Perhaps. I'm glad I was able to help her. She doesn't cry every time I visit."

"I know many that are similar."

"Now," Elena leans back, catching my eyes, "are you going to tell me why you've come to spy on me?"

I smile. "I've missed you, and I thought if you were here, you'd allow me to bring you back to the Underworld. Persephone is supposed to be returning tonight."

She grins, making my heart skip a beat. "Why didn't you say so? I've missed her. I want to ask her if she's talked to either of my parents." It had taken some time, but Elena was able to smooth things over with her parents, both of them.

I follow her out of the quaint home. "It's nice to know you like to see her more than me, your companion."

Elena walks backwards before coming to a stop in front of me. "That's a lie, and you know it. Now, I'd like to go home before she gets there."

Elena once told me she cherishes our flights through the wind in my arms. She said it feels as though it is just us in the world. Little did she know, I felt the same.

I land us on the balcony overlooking the Fields of morning. It is the spot we come to when we want to clear our heads or be alone. It is a symbol of our beginning.

A CURSE OF HONOR

"I've been thinking," Elena says, grabbing hold of my wrists, which have found a home on her stomach.

"Oh?"

She nods. "About the whole nickname versus formal name thing you and your siblings have."

"And?" I grin, knowing she can't see it.

"You once asked me if I ever wanted to find a formal name like yours. I dismissed it at the time, but I think I've found one: Eleos."

"Eleos?"

Elena angles her head to look back at me towering over her. "I was speaking with The Fates after doing some reading in the book of prophecies, and I thought it fit."

"What does it mean?"

Her hands idly rub mine while she gazes to the fields. "It means mercy, pity, and compassion."

I can't think of a name that suits her more. It *is* her. Her compassion brings healing and light after death and darkness. She brings grief and mourning to heal. She leads people out of their darkest times. She is selfless.

From the moment I saw her in Hades's throne room, I knew she would be the one. She would be the one that drives me crazy and makes me want more every time I see her.

"It's perfect." I kiss the top of her head.

Elena's bright, smiling face meets mine.

Genuine admiration and love fills me. "You are what brings light to my life. I knew I was in trouble when you glared at me in the throne room and more so when you threw that dagger at my head." I lean down to meet her soft lips. "I love you forever and always, *Eleos*."

DELANEY NICOLE

"And I love you, Callan."

Printed in the USA
CPSIA information can be obtained
at www.ICGtesting.com
LVHW090008101224
798709LV00006B/60